ONE OF US
IS LYING

D0167744

BOOKS BY SHALINI BOLAND

The Secret Mother
The Child Next Door
The Millionaire's Wife
The Silent Sister
The Perfect Family
The Best Friend
The Girl from the Sea
The Marriage Betrayal
The Other Daughter

ONE OF US IS LYING

SHALINI BOLAND

Bookouture

Published by Bookouture in 2020

An imprint of Storyfire Ltd.
Carmelite House
50 Victoria Embankment
London EC4Y 0DZ

www.bookouture.com

ISBN: 978-1-78681-936-9
eBook ISBN: 978-1-78681-935-2

PROLOGUE

She slammed the car door and strode across the gravel drive, wincing as the security light momentarily blinded her. She was vaguely aware of an impending headache, not helped by the fact that someone nearby was playing inhumanly loud music. She should go and tell them to turn it down. Maybe later, because, right now, she just couldn't dredge up enough energy. It had been another long, difficult day. A day of whispers and sidelong glances – some pitying, some filled with such loathing that it made her catch her breath. Like *she* was guilty too.

She didn't know how she was supposed to go on like this. How long she could put up with everything. And what about the kids… what was she going to do about them? They'd gone to stay with her mother for a few weeks, supposedly to give them all some breathing space while it got sorted out. But how would it ever get 'sorted out'? *How?* She bit back an angry sob, jammed the key into the front-door lock and gave it a vicious twist, scraping her knuckles on the door frame in the process.

The churning feeling in the pit of her stomach seemed to have become a permanent fixture – a kind of low-level background hum – and as she stepped over the threshold and into the bright hallway, her guts clenched even tighter. Why was she even here? Why was *he* still here?

'I'm home!' She walked through to the kitchen and dumped her bag on the counter. Reached for a couple of headache tablets and poured herself a tumbler of water, waiting for her husband to shuffle, round-shouldered, into the kitchen, to greet her with that hangdog expression he'd recently taken to wearing. The one that gave rise to both sympathy and fury. She downed the tablets and gulped at the water, discomfited by the liquid's cold snaking descent into her empty, grinding stomach.

'I'm back!' Cocking her ear, she waited for his reply. He better not have spent the whole day sleeping. That would really be the final straw after she'd been running around doing everything. Again.

She had a strong urge to hurl the glass of water through the dark kitchen window. Pictured the flying shards of glass. Imagined the gloriously shocking crash, followed by her husband running in, eyes wide, mouth open. But she managed to restrain herself. Instead, she placed the glass carefully on the counter while moving her jaw from side to side, attempting to loosen it. To relax her bowstring-taut muscles. She might as well take a few deep calming breaths while she was at it. Inhaling, she rolled her knotted shoulders back and forth. Tried to shake off the tension and growing despair.

Abandoning the kitchen, she popped her head into the dark lounge, finding it empty. She'd try their bedroom next. Taking the stairs two at a time, she called his name and noted a bitter inflection in her voice that she'd never used before. He'd always been the love of her life. But now... *now*.

Their bedroom was deserted, the bed unmade, the curtains closed. The kids' rooms also lay empty, as did the bathroom. Maybe he'd finally stirred himself into action and gone out. But who did she think she was kidding? It had been days, weeks. Jogging back down the stairs, a knot of worry began to tighten in her chest. She returned to the kitchen, dug her phone out of her bag and called his mobile. It went straight to voicemail. She left a terse message:

'Hey, it's me. I'm home. Where are you?'

It looked as though he really might have gone out. She'd check the garage, see if his car was still there.

Back out on the driveway, she smelt jasmine and caught the distant shouts of teenagers enjoying the warm summer evening. Closer to home, she could still hear that loud music, heavy and thrashy. Not *her* sort of music. She hoped whoever it was wouldn't have it on all night.

She bent to open the garage door, and found it already unlocked. She also realised with a shock that their garage seemed to be the source of the music. Was her husband in here? It wasn't *his* taste in music either. Could they have an intruder? Should she call the police?

Without thinking, she yanked up the garage door, ready for a confrontation. His car sat there, the engine grumbling while the music pounded hard and violent. For a brief second, she wondered what the neighbours would think. And then she realised that loud music annoying the neighbours was the least of her worries.

'Hello?' she cried, peering into the gloomy interior. But no one could possibly hear her puny voice over the incessant wail of guitars. *For goodness sake.*

She huffed over to the driver's side and tapped on the window. It was dark, but she could make out her husband's profile. What was he doing? He was just sitting there, facing straight ahead without even acknowledging her. He must be in a bad mood. Annoyed with her about something or other. Well that was rich, after everything.

She knocked angrily on the window once again. Still no response. The least he could do was get out and talk to her. She reached for the car handle and yanked open the door, and as she did so, everything seemed to slow down…

The music came at her like an avenging army. She suddenly couldn't breathe. She was choking, coughing, wheezing. Her eyes watering. What was that smell? *Fumes!* And through her discomfort, her husband didn't even turn to her. Didn't speak. Instead, he tipped forward like a sack of potatoes, his head landing on the steering wheel, hitting the car horn. At the same time, an empty pill bottle rolled off his lap, bouncing onto the concrete floor by her feet.

Then, just like that – as her eyes streamed and her lungs squeezed – she realised he was never going to get out and talk to her. Not ever again. Because her screw-up of a husband was stone-cold dead. And through the shock and the horror, a new kind of anger began to grow.

CHAPTER ONE

Wednesday

TIA

'Your Leo's a real bundle of energy.' Pip shields her eyes and stares out across the heat-hazed playground as my three-year-old son races around on his scooter with a couple of the other preschoolers, his brown springy curls streaming out from beneath his sun hat.

'He never stops.' I glance from Leo to Pip's son Milo, who's holding her hand and pressing himself into her legs. I smile down at her fair-haired child, wondering how two boys the same age can be so different. Glancing back at Leo, I'm all prepared for a possible wipeout and tears, my bag already stocked with antiseptic wipes and plasters. But for now Leo's grin is wide, and his energy is at maximum.

Pip sighs and runs a hand through her short dark hair. 'I wish Milo would join in more. He's always glued to my side.'

'He loves his mummy.' I give her a smile before glancing down at my watch. 'They're late out today.'

'I hope they're not much longer,' Emily huffs. 'Maisie's got a dental check-up at four. We're going to be late. You guys looking forward to Saturday?'

Pip and I nod and grin. The Ashridge Regatta is the town's social event of the year – a traditional family day where the adults relax, and the kids always have a blast.

'Are either of you racing this year?' Emily asks with a toss of her glossy hair.

'Not this time.' I shake my head regretfully, remembering the glory days where I used to win the ladies' race on a regular basis. 'Ed's having a go at the pursuit race this year.' My lovely husband isn't a natural sailor, but what he lacks in technique, he makes up for with a bucketload of enthusiasm.

'At last. Here they come.' Emily points to the broad, dark-haired figure of their teacher, Mr Jeffries, followed by an orderly two-by-two crocodile of five-year-olds. I'm in awe of how he gets them to come out of their classroom so neatly, especially as he's newly qualified. I can barely manage two kids. How he does it with thirty is a mystery.

'Leo!' I wave my son over from the far end of the playground, where he's in a huddle with some of the other preschool kids, but he's pretending not to hear me. Sighing and shaking my head, I scan the line of children. I can see Pip's daughter Sasha and Emily's daughter Maisie, but I can't seem to locate Rosie. The three of them are normally inseparable. I call over to my son once again. 'Leo!' This time I manage to fix him with a come-here-right-now stare. His shoulders dip and he scoots over, spraying gravel as he comes to a stop. 'Stay here. We're going in a minute.'

'Where's Rosie?' he asks in his little croaky voice that's so cute I can never stay cross at him for long.

'Mrs Perry!' Mr Jeffries catches my eye and waves me over.

'I'll keep an eye on Leo,' Pip offers, then lowers her voice, 'while you have some extra-curricular time with the sexy Mr J.' She winks.

'Er, I don't think so. He looks about sixteen.' I shake my head and shoot her a grin before walking across the playground to see Rosie's teacher, wondering where my daughter could be. He's definitely good-looking – he has that whole dark-haired, brooding Heathcliff vibe going on – but way, way too young. And anyway, I'm a happily married woman.

'Hi, Mrs Perry.' Mr Jeffries gives me a friendly nod. 'I won't be a minute.'

I wait while he hands off all the children to their parents, starting to feel a little uneasy about what he might have to tell me. Is Rosie ill? In trouble? Hurt? The playground is emptying. Pip waits under the oak tree with her two and Leo. I shrug my shoulders to let her know I have no idea what's going on. She waves away my concern. 'It's fine,' she calls out. 'I'll wait!'

'Thanks,' I mouth back.

'Thank you for waiting, Mrs Perry,' Mr Jeffries says in his calm, quiet way.

'That's okay. Where's Rosie? Is she all right?'

'She's back in the classroom with our teaching assistant, Mrs Miller. Don't worry, she's not hurt or ill. Just a bit upset.'

'Upset?' We walk over to the classroom together and it's a relief to reach the shade of the building.

'Yes, she's been in tears on and off since lunchtime.'

'Tears? Why?'

'She won't tell me what's wrong.'

'That doesn't sound like Rosie.' My daughter is usually a happy-go-lucky chatterbox who never keeps anything to herself.

'That's what I thought.' He pushes open the heavy glass door that leads into the bright, airy classroom. 'I didn't want to bring her out with the rest of the children. Thought it best if you collected her from the classroom and maybe try to get to the bottom of what's going on.'

'Okay, thanks.'

Inside, Rosie is sitting cross-legged on a cushion in the reading corner while Mrs Miller sits next to her, reading a story about a puppy. But my daughter's thumb is plugged into her mouth and she doesn't seem to be reacting to the story at all. Rosie hasn't sucked her thumb for years.

And then, the strangest thing happens – when Rosie sees me, instead of smiling and coming over, her eyes widen, and she looks… panicked?

'Hi, Rosie.' I walk over and kneel in front of her, my heart beginning to knock uncomfortably in my chest. Usually, she gives me an enthusiastic welcome, throwing her arms around me and then talking non-stop about her day. But, right now, she's staring down at the carpet, a tear sliding down her face. 'Hey, baby, what's wrong?'

Rosie scowls and I notice her fists clench by her side. I wipe away the tear from her cheek, but she doesn't even seem to notice.

'She's been like this all afternoon,' Mr Jeffries says in a low voice, crouching by my side.

Mrs Miller confirms this with a nod, closing the storybook and placing it back on the shelf.

'Rosie, do you want to tell Mummy why you're sad?' I ask.

There's no reaction other than a couple of furious blinks.

'Did someone upset you? Did they say something unkind?' She's never acted like this before. I mean, she's had a few sulks and tantrums, like any other child, but never this sad silence. I look from Mrs Miller to Mr Jeffries. I get to my feet and move off to the side. Mr Jeffries and Mrs Miller come and join me. 'What on earth's happened?' I whisper.

Mr Jeffries shakes his head. 'She won't say. Mrs Miller, did she speak to you while I was outside?'

'Nothing. Poor little mite looks like she's in shock or something.'

My heart pounds harder as my protective instincts start to kick in. 'And she's been like this since lunchtime?'

Mrs Miller thinks for a moment. 'Well, that's when I first saw she wasn't her usual self.'

'So, did something happen? Did one of the other children say something to her? Did any of the lunch staff see or say anything?' I hear the sharpness in my voice, the accusatory tone.

Mr Jeffries doesn't seem offended. 'I asked the teachers on playground duty, but none of them noticed anything out of the ordinary.'

I shake my head and grit my teeth, trying to calm down. I'm not the most laid-back where my kids are concerned, and I've always found it hard letting go. Rosie's first day of school broke my heart; it was the first step in her becoming independent; her first proper move away from me, spending all day with people who aren't her family. But for all my reluctance to be away from her, she's never been a clingy child, neither of my two are. When we're out socially, all I see is the back of their heads as they race off to be with their friends. She loves school, loves her friends. It's so odd to see her this way.

I stand decisively. 'I'll take her home. Maybe she'll open up to me on the walk back. Come on, Rosie, let's go.'

She doesn't move.

'Rosie, come on, babe, we need to go. Leo's waiting outside.'

At this, she looks up, her brown eyes huge and glistening. She adores her little brother. Treats him like her baby.

'He's wondering why you're not coming out to see him. Come on.'

She gets up and smooths her skirt. I hold out my hand, worried for a moment that she'll refuse to take it. Thankfully, she slips her hand into mine, but it feels light and distant, as if she doesn't want it to be there. Nothing like her usual squeezy grip.

Mrs Miller hands me Rosie's school bag. We say goodbye and leave the classroom. My daughter feels like a little stranger. My hands are clammy and my stomach flutters. Why is she acting so ill at ease around me?

Back outside in the still heat of the afternoon, the playground is now eerily quiet. I collect Leo from Pip, say goodbye to my friend without elaborating, and the three of us head for home. I decide to take the longer route around the lake to let Leo burn off some energy on his scooter, and to give Rosie a chance to open up.

We walk in silence for a while, just the pad of our footsteps and the whirr and scrape of Leo's scooter wheels on the pavement, until we reach the cut-through that leads to the lakeside path. It's usually thronged with parents and kids on their way home from school, but we're late today so the way is empty.

The lane opens up onto a vast swathe of blue sky and lake – a beautiful vista that still has the power to make me catch my breath despite having lived in Ashridge Falls all my life. The waterfall that gives the town its name is set further up the hillside in Ashridge Forest, but the lake itself is situated on the eastern edge of Ashridge – the *posh* side of town – with multi-million-pound houses ranged around the shoreline. The lake is so vast, you can't even see the other side. You could almost imagine you were by the ocean.

Half a mile west of here, the town centre is made up of a couple of main roads with all the shops and eateries a town could ever need. For more serious shopping expeditions, I head into the city, which is an hour out of town, but Ashridge can give any city a run for its money, with several cool boutiques of its own.

A sudden breeze skips across the water, throwing up silver ripples that wink and flash like fish scales. And then a movement catches my eye. 'Look!' I point up at the sky above the lake. 'Rosie, Leo, look over there! Geese!' They're honking over the lake, several of them coming into land with inelegant splashes. Usually Rosie would laugh and point at them. Today, she barely even looks up. By contrast, Leo scoots ahead along the path, trying to copy their cries. Normally his antics would make us both giggle, but Rosie is withdrawn and I'm too worried about her to be amused right now.

'Hey, Rosie Posie, shall we make some cakes when we get home? We need to make some good ones for the regatta on Saturday. I thought we could ice some sailboats onto them.' I pause to let her reply, but she simply takes a deep breath and lets it out again. 'Daddy's racing, so we'll need to cheer him on. Maybe you and Leo could make him a good-luck card?'

She bites her lip. I want to reach down and scoop her up into my arms for a hug. But she's never been one for prolonged cuddles and I think the hug would be more for me than for her. This is ridiculous; I'm going to get to the bottom of this.

'Rosie, was someone mean to you at school today?'

She shrugs. That's progress – at least she's responding.

'Was it someone in your class? Or one of the older children? You know you can tell me. Even if they said you mustn't tell, you can always tell Mummy and Daddy anything – you know that, don't you?' Something else occurs to me. 'Or was it a teacher? Did a grown-up say something to you? Did they tell you off?'

She shakes her head, and I relax a little.

'Was it one of the older children?'

She shrugs.

I think we're getting closer to the truth now. It's probably just some little bully. I'm determined to find out exactly who said what. And if she's being picked on, the school damn well better do something about it.

'Rosie, what did they say?'

Tears begin to stream down her cheeks, and she gives a few noisy gulps. I call ahead to Leo to stay where he is while I crouch down and give my little girl a hug. 'It's okay, it's okay. What happened, darling?' I smooth a few loose curls away from her face and fix her with a gentle gaze.

'Mummy…' Her voice wobbles.

'Yes? What is it? What happened?'

'Mummy, why did you *kill* someone?'

For a moment I think I've heard incorrectly. 'Why did I…? *What* did you say?'

My daughter's voice steadies. 'Why did you kill somebody? Were they not very nice? You're not supposed to hurt people, but you killed him.' Her eyes meet mine and she seems almost afraid.

'I… Rosie, who told you that?'

'A boy at school. And another boy too. They said you killed him. They called you a *murdiner*.'

'They said *what*?!' I snap.

Rosie flinches at my tone and I'm instantly contrite. 'Sorry, darling, I'm not cross with you. I'm cross with those silly boys for telling lies.'

'But they said it was true. They said—'

'Listen to me, Rosie. Sometimes people make things up. They tell lies. So when they do that, we should ignore them.'

'But everyone else said it too. They said, "Your mum killed someone so she's a murdiner and she has to go to prison." You're not going to prison, are you, Mummy?' Her eyes fill with tears again.

'Hey, hey, it's okay. No one's going to prison, and no one's a murderer. Those boys are just making up silly stories and I'm going to speak to their teacher and tell them to stop talking rubbish, okay?'

Rosie's lip wobbles, but she nods her head.

'So can I get a cuddle now?' I tap her nose with my forefinger, and she smiles shyly before launching herself into my arms so hard we bump heads. We laugh, but I don't feel as happy as I'm pretending to be. Despite the warmth of the afternoon, my skin feels clammy and my stomach is still fluttering. What the hell were those boys talking about? Why would they have told Rosie those things about me? And where did they hear it from? Bad memories echo through my bones, pulling at my sinews and pulsing along my veins, but I damp them down. This can't be anything to do with *that*. Can it?

CHAPTER TWO

FIONA

I look up from the conference table at my twenty-two-year-old assistant, hovering in the doorway. 'Molly, can you bring us a tea and two black coffees, no sugar?'

Molly sighs, nods and walks back into the showroom, her sleek blonde ponytail swinging as she goes. I'm well aware that she's already becoming disillusioned with the job. I employed her just over two years ago and I'm sure she hoped her role might be a little more creative. I own Salinger's, an interior design business in the centre of town and, while we're usually pretty busy, Molly is the one who gets all the mundane tasks. I did warn her at the start that the job wasn't as glamorous as it might sound, but she had that hopeful glow of optimism back then, which has since worn down to a patchy veneer now verging on rudeness.

I can't worry about Molly right now. Instead, I try to focus all my attention on my clients, Belinda and Harry Carmichael, a super-rich couple in their early forties that I've been working with for several weeks. They've just bought the old mill house which sits up near the waterfall. It's a property with lots of history and plenty of interesting features, so I was excited when they approached me to help them with it. They spend most of their time in the city, but they plan to come up to Ashridge Falls for weekends and holidays once the house is finished.

'What do you think of these initial ideas?' I ask, confident that I've fulfilled the brief perfectly.

'Fiona, I really like what you've come up with.' My heart sinks. Belinda is speaking with zero conviction and a smile that doesn't reach her eyes. She's got one of those ultra-short fringes that reminds me of when my mum used to cut my hair with the nail scissors, and I'd end up in tears. Only Belinda's hair is like that on purpose. 'It's just…' She drums her acrylic nails on the table top. 'It's just that I want more of a wow factor, you know?'

We're currently talking through the mood board I've designed for their home office-slash-library. I've been trying to steer them towards the Nordic look we first discussed, which will sit beautifully with the traditional building – lots of sheepskin rugs, woven fabrics and blonde wood. But they're now talking about possibly ripping out a lot of the original features and going for a sleeker, even more minimalist design. To be honest, I'm not sure why they bought the house in the first place if they're so intent on tearing it apart. But I don't want to lose their business. They're from out of town and extremely well connected. If I get this right, it could potentially mean a whole raft of new clients.

'Tell you what…' I slide the boards towards me, stacking them up like a deck of cards and trying not to think about how many days' work it's taken me to put them together. Work that they've barely even glanced at. 'How about we forget this look for the moment and I create something more luxe and architectural instead?' I flash my eyes and grin. 'Something that will really knock your socks off.'

'*Yes*, that sounds ideal.' Harry turns to his wife. 'What do you think, Bel?'

Belinda's expression instantly lifts. 'Luxe and architectural! I knew we could count on you, Fiona. We just don't want anything that's going to date. And while we really love the Nordic look, it seems to be everywhere these days.' She picks up her phone. 'I've also seen some amazing photos on Pinterest of this Moroccan-type vibe which could be fantastic in the den. As a contrast to all the minimalism, you know?'

'Sounds gorgeous!' I sigh inwardly and wonder how many times they're going to change their minds. I'm willing to lay money on it that Belinda will want me to design the whole place like a middle-eastern bazaar before declaring that it's all too much and we should go back to the modern look once again. In fact, I'll keep hold of this last lot of work in case they come back full circle.

Through the interior floor-to-ceiling windows I spot Molly talking to a couple who are standing awkwardly in the reception area. They don't look like any of my regular clients. They're actually quite official-looking – wearing ugly grey suits and serious expressions. Molly glances over at me, her eyes wide and somewhat panicked. She jerks her head in the couple's direction and I realise she wants me to come out and see to them. However, the Carmichaels aren't the kind of people you can ditch in order to talk to someone else. I shake my head at Molly and try to indicate that I need her to deal with them.

Molly rolls her eyes and turns back to the couple with a forced smile, but they don't look very happy at what she's saying. Molly gestures to the sofa and, after a moment's hesitation, they sit. I tip an imaginary teacup in Molly's direction to indicate that she needs to get on with making our teas and coffees.

Twenty minutes later, I've managed to instil fresh excitement into Belinda and Harry at the thought of how incredible and original and timeless their new holiday home is going to be.

'I can't wait until it's habitable,' Belinda says with a sigh. 'These things always take so long.'

Only because you change your mind so many times. 'How's your stay at the Ripple?' They're booked into the beautiful five-star hotel on the other side of the lake.

'It's lovely, but it's not like having your own place. One thing I will say, the spa's incredible. Have you been?'

I nod. 'I could quite easily live in that spa.'

'It's bliss, isn't it.'

Harry makes a harrumphing noise.

'Oh, ignore him.' Belinda gives his arm a playful slap. 'He's grumpy because of the distance.'

'I'm "grumpy", as you put it, because it's such an unnecessary trek from the hotel to the mill house every day. I don't know why we can't stay in town.'

'Because there aren't any decent hotels. It's a lovely town, but it's a bit rustic. No offence, Fiona.'

'None taken. But you really should check out the Scott Arms.'

'What, the *pub*?' Belinda's nose wrinkles.

I try not to smile at her distaste. 'They have rooms and a couple of apartments. The food is incredible. My friend Tia's husband, Edward Perry, is the chef there. In fact, I think they offer monthly rentals too.'

'Hear that, Bel? Let's go and take a look. To be honest, I'm not that impressed with the food at the Ripple. It's a bit bland.'

They finally take their leave with plenty of hugs and kisses, as though we're lifelong friends. I try not to think about how much more time it's going to take me to pull together their new concept. But, as long as the Carmichaels are willing to pay, then I'm happy to oblige. Plus, I guess it will be quite fun to see what I can come up with.

The walk-ins are still sitting in reception, perched on the edge of the sofa as though it's against the law to get comfortable. Molly is glaring at me as though I'm the worst boss in the world for leaving them with her. If this couple want to hire me for a project, they're going to have quite a long wait. I'm booked up for the rest of the summer and through most of autumn.

I feel a little hot and flustered after my meeting with the Carmichaels, but I don't have time to freshen up in the loo before meeting these potential new clients. Instead, I make do with running my fingers through my chestnut hair and pinching my cheeks to inject some colour before approaching them with a smile.

'So sorry to keep you waiting. I'm Fiona Salinger, how can I help?' They both stand.

'Hello,' the curly haired woman says without a smile. 'My name is Cathleen Docherty, and this is my colleague John Garland.'

Colleague? Must be a business project. 'Nice to meet you.' I hold out my hand. Cathleen's handshake is soft, her hand cold. She's about my height and gives me direct eye contact, which is a little unnerving. John's handshake is firmer, his hand a little sweaty. He's tall with mid-brown hair that's greying at the temples. Neither of the two seem particularly friendly or enthusiastic. Usually I like to guess at people's tastes in decor, but I honestly wouldn't have a clue about either of these two. They seem very unlikely clients.

'We're here from HMRC – Her Majesty's Revenue and Customs.' Cathleen opens her bag and extracts some papers, holding them out for me to take.

I need a moment to process her words. *HMRC?* Why are *they* here?

Cathleen continues talking. 'We've sent you several letters and voice messages over the past few weeks, but you failed to reply to the letters or return our calls. Here are copies of those letters.'

'I... er...' My chest tightens and I feel heat flood into my face. I vaguely remember receiving some letters from the tax office, but I set them aside to deal with at a later date. Somehow I forgot, not realising that they might be serious. That they might result in two tax inspectors showing up on my doorstep. I take the thin sheaf of papers from the woman's hand, giving the contents a brief glance, but the words swim on the page.

'Can you confirm that you received our correspondence?' she asks. They're both staring at me and, from the corner of my eye, I can also see Molly gazing over curiously.

'Er, would you like to come into my office?' I'd rather get them away from the reception area in case any of my clients happen to walk in and overhear our conversation. I don't want people knowing my business. Although Molly's bound to have heard all that, and I doubt she'll keep it to herself.

The tax inspectors follow me through the showroom and into my office, where I offer each of them a seat and try to collect my thoughts. I sit at my beloved marble desk and lay the letters in front of me, wondering what the hell is going to happen now. Am I in trouble? Do I owe the taxman money? I stare down at the letters once more, trying yet again to absorb what's written. I spot the words *tax audit*. I don't remember ever reading anything like this. If I had, I wouldn't have ignored it. But, then again, did I even open the original letters? I stare over at my in-tray on the shelf, it's piled high with unopened mail that I keep meaning to get around to dealing with. I'm such an idiot.

'So, as you can see by the dates on the letters,' Cathleen says, 'we gave you plenty of notice regarding your tax audit, which we'll be starting today.'

'A tax audit? Today?' A chill runs down my spine and my mind begins to race. I try to keep the panic out of my voice. If only I'd opened those letters, I would have had some advance warning. I could have... I don't know... been more prepared. I clear my throat. 'Am I in trouble? Did I do something wrong?'

'We hope not,' John says without smiling.

'So why do I need to have an audit?' I think about my books and receipts. Try to think whether there might be anything bad for these inspectors to find. Anything incriminating. But my brain doesn't want to work properly.

'We'll need access to all your business records. Your receipts, client information et cetera.' Cathleen looks around, eying up the shelves and filing cabinets. 'Is this where you keep everything?'

I nod, feeling like some kind of criminal, which is ridiculous. I work hard, I pay my taxes.

'Okay, so we'll set up in here, if that's okay?'

'Set up? I don't understand.'

'It's an audit, an investigation,' John says. 'We're going to look at everything and make sure it's all in order.'

'You're going to go through all my stuff?'

Cathleen grinds her teeth. 'If you'd read the letters we sent you'd know exactly what the procedure is.'

'I...'

'Why don't you take the paperwork out there and read through it.' John's tone is a little gentler. 'Then you can ask any questions when you're done.'

'But can't you at least tell me why you're here? Did I do something wrong?'

'Just read through the paperwork,' he repeats.

The enormity of what they're saying is beginning to sink in. I try to slow my breathing, wipe my sweating palms down the side of my dress. This investigation is going to mess up everything. And I'm not just talking about my business.

Cathleen makes a rising motion with her hand, coaxing me up out of my chair and back out into the showroom. I grip the sheaf of letters between my sweaty fingers and head over to the conference table as the door to my office closes behind me with a firm click. I've been ejected from my own office.

I start to read the letters, skimming through to see if I can find out why they've targeted my business, but there's nothing here to give me any idea as to why they're here. I snatch up my phone and do a quick Google search for possible reasons for tax audits. The results list several reasons why an investigation might have been triggered, including: mistakes on tax returns, omission of income, no accountant and unjustified expense claims. But it's the last one that has me really worried:

A tip-off.

Could someone have contacted the tax office about my business? Why would they do that? And, more importantly, *who could it be?*

CHAPTER THREE

Thursday

KELLY

'Have a good day, guys.' I rest one hand on the front-door frame as I watch my sons head off up the road to school. It's only a five-minute walk away with no busy roads to cross, so now that Ryan's eleven, I said they could both go without me, as long as Ryan keeps an eye on Sonny. I love that they're getting more independent, but it's a shame I don't get to catch up with Tia at the school gates any more. I miss our daily chats.

Right now, it's quiet as the grave out there, most of the other houses still with their curtains drawn, their occupants still asleep. My two are going in to school extra early today, as I've volunteered them to help out with preparations for Saturday's regatta. Ryan didn't thank me for the early-morning wake-up call, but it's good for them to help out.

Dark-haired like his father, Ryan lopes with long strides while his eight-year-old brother bounces along beside him, chatting incessantly. They're complete opposites – Sonny has fair hair and a cheerful nature, like me I suppose, while Ryan is quiet and introspective. Right now, he'll be gritting his teeth and telling Sonny to stop talking, to stop being so 'annoying', but Sonny will keep on anyway, unfazed by his older brother's irritation.

My late husband Michael would have loved to see how grown-up they're becoming. How beautiful they are. I imagine how proud he would have been.

I swallow the lump in my throat and blink a couple of times. This won't do. I can't dwell in a world of what-ifs; I need to bring myself back to reality. To occupy myself. The trouble is, it's my day off and it's stretching out before me like an endless ocean. Even more so because of the early start. I wish I was working more hours. Maybe Derek will give me some extra shifts. I say 'work', but it's mainly just volunteering at a local charity shop. I help out a few times a week, along with organising various fundraising events for the community.

Michael used to work in insurance. After he died fifteen months ago, he left us extremely well provided for. So much so that I'll never have to work again, if I choose not to. Only, I'm not sure if that was a blessing or a curse, because not having to work means far too much time on my hands. Time to think. To mourn. To sink into misery. Which is why I now throw myself into volunteering. My whole adult life, I've always done bits here and there for charity, feeling like it's my duty to help others less fortunate than myself. But these days it's almost as though helping others is actually helping *me*. Or, if not helping, at least it's a distraction. A useful way to fill my days.

I like to feel as if I'm doing good. I always have. It's probably my Catholic upbringing – the constant cloud of guilt. The feeling that I don't deserve what I have. That I'll probably go straight to hell for feeling any sense of happiness or enjoyment.

Maybe that's why, when my husband died, along with the crushing sense of devastation, I also felt the tiniest sense of relief. The thought that, now this terrible, awful thing has happened, maybe that will be it. That's my misery quota right there. After all, I never deserved so much happiness in the first place, so it's only fair that some of it should be taken away, right?

I never voice these thoughts or think of them in any coherent way. They stay a jumbled mess in my mind, swilling around like an oil slick on an ocean. Never properly absorbed; just changing shape a little each day.

I close the front door and head into the kitchen, where I start pulling various baking ingredients out of the larder. I'm going to make a cake for Saturday's regatta. My friends all envy my huge walk-in larder lined with its rows and rows of painted wooden shelves. The kitchen is original 1940s and I love it that way. None of that modern minimalism for me. I like warm, homely clutter. My best friend Fiona is an interior designer. She says she loves my quirky lakeside home, but I can tell she's dying to get her hands on it. To transform it into the 'right' kind of vintage look. To drag it into the twenty-first century and make it Instagram or Pinterest-worthy. I certainly have the budget to do it, just not the desire. I'm not big on social media – too many happy perfect families showing carefully edited versions of their lives.

I set everything out on the blue Formica table, pull a scrunchie from my pocket and twist my unruly blonde curls into a messy bun. It's far too quiet so I switch on the radio before settling down to make my famous Victoria sponge. I realise straightaway that I'll have to make two of them, because there's no way the boys will be able to see that cake and not want a slice as soon as they get home from school. I up the ingredients accordingly and tip them into my mixing bowl, smiling at the thought of their faces when they see what's waiting when they get home. I also have some fresh strawberries in the fridge that I can slice and use to decorate the cakes.

I'm busy stirring the mixture and listening to a tune from my school days when I'm startled by a sharp tap on the kitchen window. My first thought is that it must be a bird or a tree branch, because why or how would anyone be at the back of the house? But as I look up, my heart jumps at the sight of a thin, fair-haired girl with a tear-streaked face and a haunted look in her eyes. She locks eyes with me, and I feel a moment of alarm, followed swiftly by concern. I turn off the radio and wipe my hands on my apron.

I know I probably shouldn't, but I go straight to the back door and open it, pushing away all those judgy voices telling me that I should never open the door to strangers, that it could be a scam, that I don't know who this person is or what she wants. Michael used to go nuts with me for being too trusting and for always seeing the good in people. But I also think that's what he loved about me. He was the sensible, practical one in our relationship, whereas I'm the free spirit. The one who goes with the flow, who opens up her heart easily to everyone. No matter what happens, I never want to lose that part of me.

'Hello?' I step outside onto the wide flagstones, skirting over the wildflowers that have pushed their way up through the cracks.

The girl jumps at my voice and takes a step backwards. She looks older than I originally thought – maybe mid-twenties.

'Are you hurt?' I ask gently, looking her up and down. She's tall and thin, her translucent skin so pale I can see the thread of blue veins beneath. Wearing a pair of cut-off denim shorts and a pale-yellow vest top, her silvery blonde hair skims just past her shoulders and her pale eyes are the colour of Ashridge Lake. I can't see any visible sign that she's injured.

She bites her lip and shakes her head quickly, casting glances all around her. I wonder how she got into my garden. The side gate is usually locked, but I don't like to ask. I don't want to accuse her of anything in case she takes fright and runs off. She's obviously upset and in need of some kind of assistance.

'Are you okay?'

She doesn't reply. Perhaps she doesn't understand English?

I smile to let her know I'm friendly. 'Can I call someone for you?' I mime holding a phone to my ear.

'No, please don't call anyone!' Her voice is low and somewhat husky, no trace of a foreign accent. She's as jumpy as a baby rabbit. 'Please… I…' She lowers her voice. 'I'm… it's stupid, it sounds so dramatic, but I'm in trouble. I need—'

'*Trouble?*'

'Not exactly trouble, just…'

I give her what I hope is an encouraging look, but I can't say I'm not a little shaken by what she's just said. 'Yes…?'

'The thing is, I saw you in the paper – you did that fundraiser for victims of domestic abuse, and, well, I know that raising money for charity is different to helping someone in person. But… I really do need some help.' She exhales and her shoulders droop, as though she's already defeated. As though she already expects me to say no and send her packing. But she obviously doesn't know me that well. She doesn't realise that she's come to exactly the right person. I would never turn away a young woman in need, especially someone who might be in danger from a violent or abusive partner.

'If you need help… if you're in trouble, then we should probably call the police.'

She flinches backwards. 'No, please. Don't call them. They won't do any good.'

'How do you know?'

'I just do, okay!'

'Has someone been hurting you? Because if they have then the best thing would be to talk to—'

'I'm sorry, I shouldn't have come here.' She turns and starts to walk quickly back along the side of the house.

I feel bad for scaring her off. If she's running from someone abusive, I don't want to make things worse. There's something about her that tugs on my maternal heartstrings. 'Hey, come back. I promise I won't call the police if you don't want me to.'

But she keeps going. I watch her fiddle frantically with the gate latch. The sensible part of my brain tells me it's probably best if she leaves. After all, I don't know who she is or what she's running from. I don't know anything about her. My life is complicated enough without adding a stranger into the mix. But, without thinking, I tell her to wait. I tell her that she can trust me. 'Look, I won't call the police, but you're welcome to come in for a bit, if you like?'

Her hand freezes on the gate latch. She still has her back to me, but she's stopped moving.

'Just stay and catch your breath for a few minutes. You could obviously do with a bit of time to regroup.'

At this, she turns, fresh tears coursing down her cheeks.

'Hey, it's okay,' I soothe. 'Come on. It's hot out here. You're obviously upset and in a bit of a state. You can have a quick drink and then leave, if that's what you want.'

She doesn't reply. But she also doesn't make another move to go. The air is still and quiet. A car door slams in the distance.

'Would that be okay?' she asks, so quietly I can barely hear her. 'To have a drink? I'm pretty thirsty.'

'Yeah, of course.'

She swallows and wipes her face. 'It wouldn't be for long… I just need to get off the road. I need to stop him from…' But she shakes her head and tails off.

'Come on.' I gesture to the back door. 'Come on, come inside.'

She follows me onto the patio and through the back door into the kitchen. After the sharp morning brightness outside, it feels really dark in here, almost oppressive, and I have to blink a few times to adjust my vision. I gesture to the table for her to take a seat. She does so, pushing her hair out of her eyes and folding her arms across her chest. 'Thanks. I'm sorry about all this.' Her lip trembles.

'No need to apologise.'

'But I really am sorry. I shouldn't have come into your garden. I've basically just barged onto your private property. This isn't who I am.' Her eyes dart around, taking everything in – the cake ingredients on the table in front of her, the shabby but well-loved kitchen with its chipped counter tops and retro cabinets. She sniffs. 'I couldn't think what else to do, where to go. I read about your charity work and then I saw you standing in your doorway earlier, waving your kids off. You looked so nice. So kind. I thought… I don't know what I thought.' Her voice is wobbly, yet she's well-spoken, polite.

'Honestly, it's okay. We all need some help from time to time. So… is there anything I can actually do to help?' I don't remember seeing her in the road earlier. Maybe she was hiding behind one of the trees. 'Would you like that drink?'

'A glass of water would be good. It's already pretty hot out there.'

'I've got lemonade or orange juice if you'd prefer.' I make my way over to our big cream-coloured fridge.

'Water's fine.'

I grab a glass, drop in a couple of ice cubes and pour some chilled water before taking it over and sitting opposite her. 'Here you go.'

'Thanks.'

I watch her as she drinks. Her arms almost don't look strong enough to lift the glass, but lift it she does, taking big satisfying gulps until it's empty. She wipes her mouth with the back of her hand and sets the empty glass on the table.

'Want some more?'

She shakes her head. 'No thanks.'

'Hungry?'

She shakes her head again, but I notice some hesitation. I'll make sure to give her some food before she goes.

'What's your name?'

She takes a breath. 'Sophie.' She looks up and our eyes lock for a moment. I see the pleading expression and my motherly instincts ramp up some more.

'Hi, Sophie. I'm Kelly. Kelly Taylor.' I know I can't be more than six or seven years older than the girl, but she seems so much younger than me. What if it was one of my friends or one of my kids who found themselves in trouble? In danger? Wouldn't I hope that someone would look out for them?

I wonder what's happened to Sophie to make her so scared. She must be running from a bad relationship. I suppress a shudder at the thought. I need to get her to open up. To tell me just what kind of trouble she's in. I wouldn't be a good person if I simply let her leave without at least trying to help.

'Is there anyone you need to get in touch with? Parents? A partner? A friend? You can use my phone if you like.'

Her face clouds over and she shakes her head.

'Are you sure? Is there really no one? You're obviously in some kind of… difficulty.' I want to suggest calling the police again, or maybe the women's refuge. But I don't want to risk her bolting again. If she left now I know I'd worry about her.

'There's no one.' Her face darkens.

'Look, Sophie, I'm not going to call anyone if you don't want me to. But if there's anything I can do to help then why don't you just ask. If I can't do it, I'll say no. But you may as well ask me. What have you got to lose?' I know I'm opening myself up to trouble here, but I don't want to be one of those do-gooders who talk the talk and enjoy the power trip of organising fundraisers, but when someone genuinely needs help, they turn their back. I want to be better than that.

Sophie looks as though she's having some internal struggle. Working out whether or not she can trust me. Finally, her shoulders sag. 'You're so nice.'

'I have my moments.' I give her a quick smile.

'Okay, well, I feel really awful asking. I know it's really cheeky, but, well, I've been walking all night and I'm so tired. I just need somewhere to… not to stay, just maybe to hide out for a while.'

'Hide out?' I'm a little shocked, and a tiny bit nervous. 'Who are you hiding from? You said you were trying to get away from someone.'

She bows her head and twists her fingers. 'I'm sorry, I should probably go. Sorry again for any inconvenience. Thanks for being kind.' She obviously doesn't want to answer any of my questions.

'Don't be daft. You don't have to leave right now. You can stay a while longer. Keep me company while I make these cakes if you like.'

'I can't. I'm obviously getting in your way. You're in the middle of stuff. It's fine. I'm fine now. Much better. Thanks for the drink.' She gets to her feet and walks towards the door.

If she leaves now and something bad happens to her, I'll never forgive myself. 'Sophie, I mean it. Come back. You can give me a hand, if it makes you feel a bit better about staying. I could really use the help.'

'You're just being kind. You don't really need any help.'

'Honestly, you'd be doing me a favour if you helped me out with these cakes.'

'I'm not really any good at baking.'

'That's okay, it's easy, just a bit of stirring. I'll shout out instructions.' I give her a grin to try to put her at ease and she rewards me with a lukewarm smile in return.

Maybe I've been a bit foolish letting a strange person into my house, but I always prefer to trust people. To give them the benefit of the doubt. And this girl is definitely scared. She's running from something or someone and she needs some kindness.

As Sophie washes her hands in preparation to help me make my cakes, I take a good look at her face to see if I might recognise her at all. But there's nothing familiar about her features. She can't be from around here. I've lived in Ashridge Falls all my life, so I know almost everyone, if not personally then at least by sight. And anyway, she can't be from around here, because bad things like this don't happen in our town.

At least not any more.

CHAPTER FOUR

Her footsteps echo down the empty corridor. Past all the empty class-rooms. Past the artwork on the walls. Past the posters advertising this weekend's regatta. It's all exactly the same as before, but all so different. Everything is different now. She barely pays any of it attention. All she knows is she has to get out of here. She has to escape the cloying disinfected halls of this place.

Pushing open the heavy fire doors, she steps out into the playground, taking great heaving gulps of fresh air. But the fresh air and blue skies don't help. She has the feeling that nothing will help. Not ever.

It's silent out here. All her friends have gone home already. Why didn't she go with them? What made her go back inside? She knows what. She knows why. She could have waited until tomorrow to get that history book, but she thought she knew what she was doing. She thought she was in control. So cool and grown-up. But she's not. She's stupid. So, so stupid.

Tears fall hot on her cheeks and her skin burns with shame. With humiliation. What did she do wrong? How did this happen? She's supposed to come back here next term to start at the sixth form. She was looking forward to the next two years. To getting her A levels and then going off to college. But now… how will she ever be able to face everybody? How will she ever be able to come back to school ever again?

CHAPTER FIVE

Thursday

TIA

'You okay, Tia? I heard you talking in your sleep last night.' Ed pulls a T-shirt over his head, while I sit up and try to focus properly.

'Mmm, yeah.' I'm so wrung-out I can't even form a coherent sentence. Flashes of dreams come to me – Rosie crying in the dark, Mr Jeffries shouting at me… and a dead man floating on the lake. I shudder and try to shake away the disturbing images. Last night was one of the worst night's sleep I've had for years.

'Tee?'

'Still half asleep.' I stretch noisily and smile up at my husband as he leans down for a kiss, a hank of blonde hair falling across one eye. 'I had such weird dreams. And it was so hot and sticky. I need a shower.'

'Sorry you had a crap night. Looks like it's going to be another scorcher today. Pity me at work later. I'm hoping everyone orders salads. The thought of firing up the ovens…' Ed's a chef at the Scott Arms, a popular local four-star hotel. He works long hours, but he loves what he does. And when he's home, he's the best, most attentive husband and father I could wish for.

Our bedroom door opens and Rosie shuffles in, wearing a blue-and-white stripy nightdress and holding Shorty, her cuddly giraffe.

'Morning Rosie Posie.' Ed picks her up and blows a raspberry on her cheek, but instead of giggling, she frowns and pushes him away. 'What's up, pickle?'

She puts a hand on her stomach. 'I've got a sore tummy.'

He puts her back down. 'Maybe you're just hungry. Want some cereal? Or I could make blueberry pancakes if you like?'

Rosie shakes her head as Leo charges into the room wearing just his pants and dives onto the bed, yelling and making explosion noises.

'Shh, Leo, your sister's not feeling well.'

'Call the ambulance, nee naw, nee naw!'

Ed catches my eye, picks up our noisy son and pretends to fly him out of the room like an aeroplane. 'Come on, terror, let's leave your mum and sister in peace for a few minutes.'

As Leo's boisterous cries grow fainter, I pat the edge of the bed for Rosie to come and sit next to me. Her curls frame her sad little face as she gently kicks the bedframe with the back of her bare feet and worries Shorty's ear.

'Shall we go and have some of those pancakes?' I ask.

Rosie shakes her head, wearing the same closed-down expression as yesterday.

My chest tightens. 'What's wrong, baby?'

'Bad tummy.'

'Do you think maybe it's a nervous tummy?'

She shakes her head. 'I better stay in bed today.'

'Shall I tell you what I think?' I take her hand and give it a squeeze. 'I think your tummy is feeling a bit wobbly after yesterday. Those silly boys made up stories and it made you feel a bit strange. Is that what's happened?'

Rosie scowls.

'And the best thing for a nervous tummy is to take a deep breath and be brave. I'll come into school with you and talk to your teacher, okay?'

'I want to stay here with you and Daddy. It's *not* a nervous tummy, it's a *bad* tummy.'

My heart breaks a little. There's nothing I'd like more than for us all to stay home today, but that won't do Rosie any favours. She has to face those little troublemakers and let them see she's not intimidated. Easier said than done when you're a five-year-old child.

And now she's started crying. I need to think of a distraction.

'Hey, tell you what, why don't we invite Maisie and Sasha for tea after school today?'

I see her consider my suggestion, her scowl melting a little.

'They could help us make the sailboat cakes.'

'Can we go to the park too?'

'Yes. But we better get dressed quickly, or we'll be late, and I won't get the chance to ask their mummies if they can come.'

'Okay.' She hops off the bed and runs out of the bedroom.

I take a breath. Thank goodness for that. Now I just have to give *myself* a talking to and stop stressing about what those boys said. It's probably nothing sinister; just kids messing about.

The next hour goes by smoothly – well, as smoothly as it can when you're trying to wrangle two young children into their clothes and get them to eat a sensible breakfast. We finally get to school without a hitch and Rosie goes into her class okay, brimming with excitement about asking her friends to come over after school. I drop Leo around the corner at his preschool and now I'm back at Rosie's school to meet with Mrs Lovatt, the deputy head, to discuss what Rosie told me yesterday. I would have preferred to talk to Mr Jeffries, but he's not free to see me until after school, so Mrs Lovatt will have to do.

'Mrs Perry?' A woman in her forties, who I'm guessing is Mrs Lovatt, has popped her head out of her office door.

I nod and get to my feet.

'Would you like to come in?'

I follow her into her sparsely furnished office with a desk and three chairs. She's new to the area and only started working at Ashridge Academy last term. Slim, with short, fair hair that's flecked with grey, she looks to be a decade or so older than me – maybe forty-ish. We both sit and I waste no time explaining what happened yesterday. About how my daughter was extremely upset by some of the older boys making up nasty lies.

'What did these boys say?' She doesn't seem overly concerned or apologetic and this irritates me. I mean, I know it's not her fault and maybe it seems trivial to her, but she didn't see how upset Rosie was yesterday. And how much the lies shocked me.

'They told her...' I pause. 'They told her that I'd killed someone.'

Her eyes widen and she looks directly at me. I can see this isn't quite what she was expecting. 'And have you?'

I give an outraged laugh. 'Not to my knowledge. No.'

'Look, obviously that's not a nice thing for them to say, but quite honestly it sounds like it's simply boys being boys, playing detective, that kind of thing, you know how they can be.'

I take a deep breath and tell myself to keep calm. I really don't want to lose my temper with this woman, but it's annoying me how much she's making light of the situation. I try to keep my voice level. 'They weren't "playing detective", they were picking on my daughter and telling her that her mum is a murderer. Now, that might sound like harmless fun to you, but to me it's quite a serious issue and I don't want it happening again.'

She purses her lips and clears her throat. 'Of course not. Do you know the names of these boys?'

'No. Rosie didn't say. I think they were older though. In the year above.'

'Maybe we should call Rosie in and ask her.'

'What, *now*?'

'Yes. Hear what she has to say about it.'

'To be honest, I'd rather not dredge it all up with her again. It took a lot to calm her down this morning. She didn't even want to come in to school, and that's never happened before.' I realise I'm drumming my fingers on the desk quite loudly. I stop and put my hands in my lap.

'The thing is,' Mrs Lovatt continues, 'without knowing actual names, it's going to be quite tricky to do anything. I can't reprimand anyone if I don't know who did it.'

I take a breath and try not to snap. 'Maybe you could say something in assembly to everyone about not making things up and spreading lies. And about not picking on others.'

'We already do have quite a few *Be Nice to Others* assemblies. It's a strong part of the school's ethos.' She glances over at the clock on the wall and I realise she wants me gone.

'Well, it doesn't seem to be working at the moment. Perhaps you need to word it more strongly.'

'Hmm, well, we'll certainly see what we can do.'

What the hell does that mean?

She gives me a nod and gets to her feet. This must be her tactic for getting rid of unwanted visitors. But I'm not taking the hint. I stay seated and fold my arms across my chest. 'So you'll say something to the older boys?'

'We will.'

'And can you tell Mr Jeffries what's happened? And keep an eye on Rosie today at lunchtime and playtime? Make sure those boys aren't hassling her?'

'I'm sure Mr Jeffries has everything in hand.'

'But you'll tell him.'

'I will. Please don't worry, Mrs Perry. Now if you'll excuse me, I'm afraid I have another meeting to get to.'

I stand up, not feeling at all comforted by our chat. Maybe I'm an overprotective parent, but I don't want a repeat of yesterday with Rosie coming home upset. I also don't want to be the subject of nasty rumours. 'Okay, thanks for your time.' I grit my teeth, realising I need to stay on her good side. Rosie's going to be at Ashridge Academy for years; I can't afford to annoy the teaching staff. But leaving Mrs Lovatt's office and walking back out into the sunshine, I can't help feeling that I've made things worse.

CHAPTER SIX

KELLY

'This is so kind of you. I can't believe you're doing this for me.' Sophie takes the other end of the duvet and holds it out as I ease on a fresh cover. The attic bedroom is warm and stuffy, but I've thrown open the Velux windows and brought up a portable fan. There's a slight breeze coming off the lake which should make it a little more bearable up here.

'Thinking about it, you'll probably only need the sheet. It's far too warm for a quilt. But at least you've got one in case it cools down overnight.' I've offered to let Sophie stay in our attic room for a day or two. She was so grateful. I'm sure I've made the right decision. Once I've settled her into the room and she knows she has nothing to fear from me, then I'll broach the subject of contacting the women's shelter. She'll be better off going somewhere where they're equipped to deal with people in her situation – not that I actually know what her situation is. But at least they'll know the correct procedures and safety measures, whereas I'm just offering a temporary solution. I'll make her see that the right move is to seek proper help.

We didn't talk that much over the cake baking earlier, but when I mentioned that I was a widow, her eyes filled with tears. She said that she was grieving too. That her dad had died a while ago and that he was the only person in the world who had ever understood her. I gave her a hug, and, for a brief moment, it felt like we had a real connection.

'This room's really nice.' Sophie picks up one of my patchwork cushions from the wicker rocking chair and hugs it to her body. 'Thanks for letting me stay. You're so lucky living here.'

She's right. Despite everything I've been through, I know how fortunate I am. 'That's okay. Thanks for your help with the cakes. You'll have to help us eat some later.'

'Won't your kids think it's weird that I'm staying here?'

'Don't worry. They'll be fine.' Ryan and Sonny are used to me taking in waifs and strays. I'm always the one who offers to look after other people's kids or has people crashing in the spare room when they're stuck for a place to stay. I guess some people might say I'm a soft touch. But I honestly don't mind. I love getting to know new people. I would have done way more over the years, but Michael was quite a private person. He never enjoyed it when people stayed over. In fact, the only time we ever fell out was when I wanted to have a couple of foreign exchange students to stay one summer. I thought it would be good for the kids to learn about other cultures, but Michael put his foot down. Said he didn't want to come home from work each night to a houseful of strangers.

Sophie and I do up the buttons on the duvet. She starts at one end and I start at the other, meeting in the middle. I think about what the boys will say about Sophie staying. Sonny will be fine. He's a proper little socialite – a people person like me. It's Ryan I'm nervous about. The truth is I'm more than slightly worried how he's going to react. He's been pretty moody since Michael died – which is to be expected – but I thought he would have started to heal a little by now. I don't like to admit it, but, if anything, he's getting worse. Maybe Sophie's appearance will make him act a little nicer, jolt him out of his glumness and put him on his best behaviour. I can only hope.

My phone starts trilling. I draw it out of the pocket in my dress and see that it's school calling. 'Sorry, I'm going to have to take this.'

'Yeah, of course.' Sophie goes back to looking nervous again.

I walk out of the room and stand on the attic landing. 'Hello?'

'Mrs Taylor?'

'Yes.'

'It's Tina Lovatt here, deputy head at Ashridge Academy.'

My breath catches. This can't be good. 'Everything okay?'

'Can you come into school?'

'Er, what, *now?*'

'Yes please.'

'Are Ryan and Sonny okay?'

'They're fine. But Ryan has been involved in an incident.'

'An incident? What do you mean? What kind of—'

'I think it's best if you just come in.'

'Um, yeah, okay. Give me ten minutes.'

My heart has started beating out of control. What on earth could have happened? She said he was fine, so he's obviously not hurt. Could he have been in a fight? Maybe he's upset. And what am I going to do about Sophie? Can I really trust her enough to leave her on her own in the house? We don't keep anything valuable here, like jewellery or money. There are a couple of laptops, but that's about it. I know I offered to let her stay over, but I thought I'd be at home the whole time as I'm not due at work until tomorrow. I don't want to ask her to leave. Not after I've just said she can stay. But I can't let Sophie's situation sidetrack me from my family; I need to focus on what's going on with Ryan.

I slip my phone back into my pocket and return to the bedroom, where Sophie's looking at me with wide eyes. 'Everything all right?'

'Yeah… no… not really. Something's going on with my eldest and I have to go into school for a quick meeting.'

'Oh. Right.' Her face closes down and I'm sure she's waiting for me to throw her out.

'But, look, you're welcome to stay here while I'm out. I shouldn't be too long.'

Her face relaxes. 'Are you sure that's okay?'

'Absolutely.'

'Wow, thanks. I'll just stay up here. I won't go into the rest of the house.'

'That's fine. You can go downstairs and watch TV or help yourself to any food if you're hungry.'

'You're so nice. But it's probably safer if I stay up here out of view. Just in case...' She tails off. I'm sure she was about to open up to me, but, much as I'd like to, I can't stay and talk to her right now.

'Okay, well, make yourself comfy up here. The loo's downstairs and, like I said, there's food in the kitchen. I'll lock the front door behind me, but you can always go out the back way if you decide you want to leave. Just... leave me a note if you do, so I know you're okay.'

She nods. I want to give her a hug, she still looks so nervous, but I refrain, giving her a warm smile instead.

'Um...' she starts to say something but tails off.

'What is it?'

'Could you... I mean, would you mind not telling anyone I'm here?'

'That could be a bit difficult with the kids. Especially my youngest – he's not known for keeping quiet about *anything*.'

'I understand. It's just, if anyone found out about me being here, it could get... tricky for me.'

'Of course. Look, let's talk about it later. Maybe I could say you're a friend come to visit?'

She nods, her face relaxing a little.

'Okay, I better go.'

Downstairs, I grab my bag and lock the front door behind me. School is only a few minutes' walk away, but I don't want to waste a second, so I jump into my sky-blue VW Beetle and drive there instead, feeling more than a little shaky at the wheel. Luckily, the road is empty at this hour. Up ahead, I spot my friend Tia walking along, head bowed, in a world of her own. She turns down a side road in the direction of her house and I think about honking my horn to get her attention. But I don't have time to stop and chat, so I keep going until I get to school, pulling up in one of the visitor parking spots less than a minute later.

Inside the building, the receptionist is in the front office talking to Mrs Lovatt. They both look up when I walk in and Mrs Lovatt comes out and invites me into her office. We sit opposite one another and I wait for her to explain, my mind flitting between Sophie back at home and Ryan.

'I'm afraid Ryan has been disruptive in class. He was also extremely rude to his teacher Miss Santani this morning.'

I blow air out of my mouth and shake my head, trying not to let myself become stressed. Ryan misses his dad and he's still holding on to so much anger. I wonder if I should be doing something more to help him, if I should have tried to get him to open up more about his feelings. I realise Mrs Lovatt is waiting for me to respond.

'What happened?' I ask, trying not to sound too panicked.

'He was whispering to another child when he should have been listening to his teacher. Then, when Miss Santani reprimanded him, he muttered something rude under his breath. She asked him to repeat what he'd said, but he refused, so she told him to go and sit outside the classroom. He got very worked up, picked up his chair and threw it to the ground in anger before storming out. Luckily no one was hurt.'

My heart plummets. Obviously it's unacceptable behaviour, but I ache for my troubled boy. 'Where is he now?'

'He's sitting in a spare classroom with Mr Nichols, the PE teacher.'

'I guess I should go and speak to him.'

'I think it's probably best if we leave him to calm down with Mr Nichols for now. He did seem sorry after his outburst, but obviously we had to let you know what had happened.'

I'm relieved that Ryan has calmed down, and I'm also grateful that, for once, someone else is dealing with the fallout instead of me. Does that make me a bad parent? I don't know. Maybe just an exhausted one. Mrs Lovatt's face remains impassive. She's new to the school and seems like a cold sort of person. There's no warmth to her expression. No sympathy or understanding in her eyes. Just a kind of bland exasperation, as though this whole situation is an annoying inconvenience.

And all the while, I have this increasing background worry in my head that I've let a total stranger into our house. That she's there right now doing goodness knows what. But then what kind of person would I be if turned away someone in such obvious distress? What if I'd sent her packing and she came to serious harm? I want to live in a world where people care, where people don't turn away from helping others. But right this minute my son needs me more than anyone else.

'So what happens now?' I ask.

'I've spoken to the head and she's said we'll let it go this time. You really need to speak to him when he comes home. Impress upon him that he can't let this happen again. That there will be consequences next time. Obviously this is not the sort of behaviour we expect from Ashridge children.'

'Of course.' I'm a little miffed that she's talking about Ashridge Academy like she knows the place inside out. She's only worked here a few months, for goodness sake. My kids have been coming here since they were four, and I went here as a child too. But I squash down the uncharitable thought. She's only doing her job, after all.

'The thing is,' she continues, 'Miss Santani says that Ryan's work has been well below average this year. He's not at all engaged and he's been much quieter than usual. The playground staff have noticed that he's started sitting on his own at lunch and break times.'

This news surprises me. Although he's never been overly sociable, he's always had friends. 'Do you think he's being bullied?' The thought makes my throat constrict.

She shakes her head. 'Not that I'm aware of.'

'Well, that's something.' But teachers don't always know everything that's going on. I make a mental note to try and find out if he's being picked on. It feels as though my eldest son is slipping away from me. He's only eleven. He needs me. *He needs his dad.*

'Has he had any violent outbursts at home?' she asks.

My hackles go up and I take a breath to try to stay calm. I have to tell myself that she's only trying to help. 'No, nothing like that. He's been quiet and maybe a little angry, but never violent.' I sigh. 'He's just not interested in anything. He loves sailing, but he doesn't even want to do that anymore. He's refused to enter this year's junior regatta, and that used to be the focal point of his life. He used to enter with his dad though, so…'

'I understand that Ryan's father died last year?'

I nod, not trusting myself to speak.

'Have you considered getting him some grief counselling?'

'I did think about it, but we were doing okay. I didn't think things had got that serious.'

'If things don't improve, it could be a good idea.'

'I guess.'

There's a brief, awkward pause.

The deputy head clears her throat. 'Well, let's hope that after today Ryan settles down.' From her tone of voice, it sounds as though our meeting is coming to an end. It feels wrong not to go straight to my son right now and see if he's okay, but I know from experience that when I ask him direct questions, I tend to make things worse. Ryan opens up in his own way, in his own time. At least, I hope he will. I hate having to walk on eggshells around him.

Mrs Lovatt is on her feet now, so I follow suit.

'Thanks for coming in, Mrs Taylor.' She thrusts out a hand and I reluctantly shake it.

'Are you sure I shouldn't see him now? I could just have a quick word...'

'Best not. It may disrupt things further,' she says. 'Mr Nichols will make sure he's calm before going back to class.'

I take a breath and debate whether or not to kick up a fuss. But, quite honestly, I don't have the energy to push her on it. And she's probably right. If I give him time to calm down, our chat later will probably end up going better. Plus, I need to get home and work out what I'm going to do about Sophie. That's if she's even still there.

I leave the school wondering if I should have pushed to see Ryan. I know Mrs Lovatt said that he'll be fine, but I can't bear to think of him sad and angry without friends. It takes all of my willpower not to march back into her office and demand to see him. But I guess it's only a few hours until home time. My mind boomerangs back to the Sophie predicament. Part of me hopes that she's gone when I return. At least that would solve that problem. I really shouldn't have agreed to help her, not while my own family is having troubles. But I suppose I've always found it easier to focus on other people's problems than on my own.

CHAPTER SEVEN

FIONA

I fall asleep literally minutes before the alarm on my phone burrows into my consciousness. The soft tinkling alarm is one of those where the volume gradually increases, supposedly to gently ease the person awake, but, let's face it, there is no good sound for a wake-up alarm. They're all brutal. Even more so, as the events of yesterday come crashing back to me.

I open my eyes to see my husband Nathan on the other side of the bedroom, already suited and booted, moments away from heading out to the city, where he works in finance as a trader. He was late back last night. I didn't – and still don't – have the words to tell him about the tax audit.

Nathan and I have always prided ourselves on being this super-successful couple. The type of people who have a handle on life. It might sound arrogant, pompous even. But it's not like that. It's about being in control of things. Nathan always talks about *staying ahead of the game*. If you're ahead, then a few knockbacks can't send you spiralling into the gutter. But, with Nathan, even the knockbacks are theoretical. They're something that happen to other people. Not to us. Not to Fiona and Nathan Salinger. Sometimes it's exhausting trying to be perfect.

'Hey, sleepyhead.' Nathan bends down to kiss me, his brown waves held back with wax, his Nautica cologne evoking all kinds of emotions.

'Morning.' I sit up, attempting to banish the anxiety in my gut. 'You're up early.'

'We can't all lie in bed all day.' He fiddles with his cufflinks. 'I'll try to get back earlier tonight, but I can't promise anything. Things are crazy at work right now.'

'Don't worry. It's pretty busy at the showroom too. I'll be working quite late.'

'It's a good thing we don't have kids,' he comments.

'Yeah. We barely have time for ourselves these days.'

'Tell me about it. I'm looking forward to Saturday though.'

'Saturday?'

His face darkens and I desperately try to remember what's happening on Saturday, but my mind has gone blank.

'The regatta,' he says coldly.

'Oh, yes, of course. Sorry, I'm still half asleep.'

Thankfully, his earlier good mood hasn't been dampened by my memory lapse. 'Okay, well, we'll take a picnic, yeah? Champagne and strawberries, the works.'

'Don't worry, I'll sort it out.'

He rubs his hands together. 'I'm planning on whipping Ed's butt.' Nathan and Ed are both entered in one of the races.

'Remember, Ed's only been sailing for a year or so. You might want to go easy.'

Nathan grins. 'Nah, he's getting pretty good. You should have seen him at the trials.'

I smile. 'Worrying about the competition?'

He sits on the bed and grabs me around the waist. 'Never!'

I laugh, my mind temporarily taken from my worries as he kisses me.

'Anyway, stop distracting me, Fi. I need to get going.' His hand slides beneath the covers.

'*Me?* You're the one getting all handsy.'

He laughs and gets to his feet. 'I'll have to save the "handsy" stuff for later.'

I lean back into the pillows and close my eyes. If only we could be like this all the time, without the stresses of work and… well, all the other stuff.

'See you later, Fi.'

'Have a good day.'

'Love you.' He blows me a kiss and leaves the bedroom. His feet clatter down the wooden staircase and his keys jangle as he picks them up off the hall shelf. The door slams. I close my eyes and listen to the crunch of his footsteps on the gravel drive. The sound of his car engine starting up. The hiss of tyres. And finally the sound of him driving away.

Exhaling, my heart rate slows. I have a day's reprieve. A day to work out what I'm going to do. What I'm going to say.

A quick glance at my phone tells me it's not quite 7 a.m. The tax inspectors said they'd be back this morning at nine. Apparently their investigation could take weeks. *Weeks!* I'll never be able to keep it quiet. Nathan is bound to find out. Scratch that – *everyone* will find out. I'll be the subject of speculation and gossip, and that could seriously hurt my business. I feel a stress headache coming on at the thought of it. Why is this happening to me?

I push the covers back and get out of bed, heading to the bathroom. Okay, I need to think about this. I need to find a way to speed up their investigation and get them out. Maybe I should just be breezy and helpful. Make them see I've nothing to hide. It'll be fine. I can charm them. Win them over. Become their friend. But as I picture Cathleen's blank face, the word *friendly* doesn't exactly spring to mind. I suppose I could concentrate my efforts on John, but what if those two are an item? I can't see it, but knowing my luck, Cathleen probably has a crush on him. If that's the case, then if I started flirting with him, she'll have it in for me. No, I need to keep this professional. I'll be open and friendly. Breezy it is.

I shower, dress and go downstairs. Our open-plan kitchen-diner leads onto a wooden deck overlooking the lake. It's a stunning view by anyone's standards. A view that should make me happy to be alive. Everything outside is green and blue and sparkling. There are already people out on the water, rowing, swimming, sailing, canoeing – enjoying life. White sails billowing and distant dots of colour clipping along. How can I live in such a beautiful and idyllic place and yet feel so much anxiety?

I open the fridge and pull out a few vegetables to toss into the blender, adding a third of a banana for sweetness and energy. I don't fancy it at all – I'd kill for some Nutella on toast, but I'm watching my weight, plus I need to keep my strength up and stay focused today. Aside from the fact that Nathan doesn't like us keeping junk food in the house – *far too tempting*. So I pour the disgusting snot-green smoothie into a glass and force it down before leaving for work.

I'll leave the car at home today. The walk will do me good and hopefully clear my head. I should still get to the showroom an hour or so before the tax officers, which will give me time to have a nose around and see what they were doing yesterday. Maybe it will give me some clues as to what they're looking for. Yet again, I wonder what prompted the investigation. Did they find something suspicious in my tax returns, or was it a random spot check? Or were my earlier thoughts correct? *Did someone report me?* If they did, who might it have been? I suppose the most obvious culprit would be a professional rival. Someone who wants my business to fail. I'm good at what I do, and I have a lot of loyal clients. But I don't know my competition well enough to know who might be capable of such a horrible thing.

Nathan isn't going to be happy. He's suggested a couple of times that I might want to use an accountant, but I reassured him that I'm more than capable of doing my own books. He seemed okay with it. Respected my decision. But maybe Nathan was right. A professional might have prevented this distress. There's also another reason why I haven't used an accountant, but I push that thought away. *It'll be fine*, I tell myself for the millionth time.

The streets are busier at this time of the morning, with commuters heading to work on foot and by bike and car, people walking their dogs, and parents on the school run, pushing prams and calling after kids on scooters. I pass Kelly's road and have a sudden yearning to call in on her unannounced. To sit in her tatty but welcoming kitchen and have a gossip about everyday things. To forget all about my current situation. To have a laugh like back when we were kids. Before life got in the way. I wish I could turn back the clock…

I realise that wishing and moping aren't going to get me anywhere, so I pick up my pace, square my shoulders and try to be positive. Nothing bad has actually happened yet. I might be stressing over nothing.

Normally, when I reach the main road and see the name *Salinger's* above my showroom windows, my heart lifts and I can't wait to start my day. However, this morning it inspires a renewed feeling of dread. A sinking stone in my stomach. *It'll be fine. It'll be fine.* I say the words over and over again in my head. Willing them to be true.

I cross the road and take the keys out of my handbag. At least I'll have a short while on my own before Molly and the tax inspectors arrive. I'm looking forward to firing up the coffee machine and sitting in my office.

As I reach the pavement, from the corner of my eye I notice two people get out of a silver Volkswagen Passat that's parked further up the road in one of the parking bays. It's a man and woman. They're dressed in grey suits, and my whole body tightens in frustration. It's Cathleen bloody Docherty and John Whatshisface from the tax office. I check my watch and see that the time is only ten past eight. They said they'd be back in at nine. *Nine.* It's not nine.

They're heading my way. I try to calm down. Maybe they're going to go for breakfast first. Act friendly, *breezy*. I can't let them see my annoyance.

'Morning!' I call out through a fake smile. I insert the key in the lock and open the door, stepping inside to disable the alarm, then turning back to them.

'Good morning,' John says.

Cathleen gives a perfunctory nod.

'You're nice and early.' My voice is chirpy, like a children's TV presenter.

'We like to beat the traffic,' John replies. 'We didn't think you'd be in until nine. But we may as well get started now you're here.'

'Sure, sure. Come in.' They follow me through to the showroom. 'I woke up early myself, so thought I may as well get to work. You'll want the office again, right?'

'Please.' John nods.

'Or…' I try to sound nonchalant. 'There's a great breakfast place down the road if you'd rather come back at nine. Their full English is legendary.'

'That's okay,' Cathleen says. 'We have a lot of work to get through, so we'd rather make a start.'

'Of course.' I'm suddenly embarrassed by my crass attempt to get rid of them for a while. They've probably seen it all before. I need to try to accept that they're going to be in my face for the foreseeable future. The sooner I get used to it, the easier it will be, right? I should have stayed at home for longer. I could have sat and stared at the lake. Tried to get into a better frame of mind. Now it's going to be an even longer day than usual. And I get the feeling that John and Cathleen aren't the type to knock off early. They'll be here for as long as I am.

'We'll head on into the office,' John says, following Cathleen, who's already through the office door.

I should have come back late last night to take a look when there was no chance of them being around. I should have checked that there's nothing lurking in the files and drawers to land me in trouble. Too late now. I'll do it tonight though. I'll come back later and see what they've been up to.

'Can I make either of you a drink?'

'One black coffee, one black tea, no sugar, thanks.'

'No problem.' I head over to the oak dresser in the showroom that I upcycled into a drinks station. The countertop is covered in tea stains and cake crumbs. Molly's supposed to keep it clean, but she's been getting very lax about everything lately. I'll have to have a word.

Before I put the kettle on, I nip down the road to Ida's Bakery to pick up some pastries. I'm determined to get on Cathleen and John's good side, and if that means bribing them with freshly baked flaky pastry and apple custard, then that's what I'll do. Ten minutes later I walk into the office bearing hot beverages and an assortment of pastries.

Cathleen is sitting in my ergonomic office chair at my desk, while John is crouched over the open filing cabinet, pulling out a folder. I risk a quick peek over his shoulder but frustratingly I can't read what's written on the label, so I cross the room to lay the tray down on the desk. Before I do so, Cathleen takes her mug of tea and sets it straight down on my marble-topped desk, ignoring the coaster. It takes every inch of willpower I possess not to say anything about it. She then takes John's mug and does the same. I can already see a ring of brown coffee seeping into the Carrara.

'No cakes for me, thanks,' she says, getting straight back to her note taking.

'What about John? Would he li—'

'No thank you.' Cathleen replies on his behalf, which I feel is a little out of order, so I turn to him and show him the tray.

'Oh, no. No thanks.' Neither of them has cracked a smile yet. So much for me winning them over.

As I leave the office, Cathleen adds, 'Can you please close the door behind you, and would you mind knocking if you need to come back in.'

'Uh, sure.' I close the door, walk back into the showroom and set the tray down on the drinks station, feeling almost on the verge of tears. The two of them are so abrupt. Not rude, exactly – it's as though they're only as polite as they need to be. I know it must be the nature of the job. They can't allow themselves to get friendly in case they find something untoward in the books. They can't afford to be personal. But this is my space. The place I come to be me. And now it doesn't feel like mine any more. I glance back through the Crittall windows. Cathleen and John appear to be deep in conversation and I wonder what they're talking about. I wonder if their tone with one another is any different to their tone with me. But I can't hear anything through the glass. Maybe I should learn to lip read. On second thoughts, they'd see the payment for the classes and grill me for that too.

So what happens if they *do* find something untoward? I don't think they will. But they might. What if the truth comes out? Nathan will go mad. Could I go to prison for something like that, or would it just be a fine? I open up Google on my phone and start typing into the search bar. But before pressing 'enter', I pause, then delete the words. What if HMRC somehow have access to my phone and can view my search history? They might think I'm guilty just because I looked something up.

I'm becoming paranoid. Driving myself crazy. I need to get out of here.

I can't face knocking on my own office door, so I don't bother to tell them that I'm going out. I won't be long anyway. Just a quick walk around the block to shake off this restless feeling.

I step out onto the pavement, taking a deep, steadying breath. The thing to do is to concentrate on my work rather than on this intrusion. There's nothing I can do about it anyway, so it's pointless stressing. I head up the road, towards the town hall, past the library and the supermarket, the *clip-clip* of my heels on the concrete going some way to alleviating my anxiousness. The town is still waking up. 'Open' signs being turned around, doors flung wide, A-boards set out, and tables and chairs arranged for the breakfast and coffee crowd. I navigate my way past all of it, nodding good morning to friends and neighbours as I go. As though nothing is wrong.

I've lived in Ashridge Falls all my life, but I'm not a beloved member of the community. I'm too stand-offish. Too self-contained. Sure, I'm liked, maybe even respected a little – I like to think so anyway – but not loved. Not like Kelly or Ed, or even Tia. That's fine though. It suits me. Although a part of me admits that it would be lovely to be more easy going. More friendly and approachable. I guess it just isn't in my nature, though maybe it used to be.

I stop in my tracks. Up ahead I see a familiar dark-haired figure talking animatedly to Tia's brother, Ash. Ash Dewan is a local police officer. A nice guy, strait-laced and responsible – the complete opposite of his sister, who was always a bit of a tearaway. Right now, Ash is standing by his car sharing a laugh with Paul Barton, the local dentist. And Paul Barton is definitely someone I do not want to see.

If I turn around and head back the way I came, he might still spot me and catch up. So instead, I keep my head low, cross over the road and duck into a residential side street. I amble past the stone-fronted fisherman's cottages, deciding to go for a longer walk than intended. Molly will arrive at work soon anyway, so she can deal with any customer queries that might come in.

I try to empty my mind, admiring the colourful window boxes and smartly painted front doors. Most of these houses are spruced-up holiday cottages. I've worked on a couple of them myself. They're tiny, but full of charm and character. It's nice and shady down here. Cool and quiet. I'll keep walking until I'm sure the coast is clear.

CHAPTER EIGHT

She stumbles along the lake towards home. Her head bowed; her mind numb. She needs to get home. To close the door and fall onto her bed. There are too many people here – picnickers, clusters of kids hanging around chatting, skimming stones. It's a sunny summer's day, so what did she expect? She should have walked home via the quiet back streets. But the thought of that is almost as frightening.

'Hey!'

Before she can stop herself, she looks up.

Her best friends are on the grassy bank by the old willow tree, waving and calling her over. She can't ignore them. But how can she put into words what's just happened? How can she explain it to them? She decides the best thing to do is to point to her watch, shrug apologetically and keep walking like she has to be somewhere else in a hurry.

She feels like she's acting a part. Like those girls are not really her best friends. This town isn't really the place where she lives. Today is just a scene out of a really horrible play.

'Hey, wait!'

She quickens her pace, but her friends aren't put off. They catch her up and ask what's wrong. They want to know where she's going in such a hurry. They've seen her face and can tell she's been crying. They coax her up onto the bank and demand answers. Pull her down onto the grass beneath the frondy willow tree, where it's cool and dark.

After a few moments' hesitation, she finally succumbs to their concern, letting the words spill out of her like poison from a wound.

Her friends' eyes widen. They gasp and cry and hug her and vow to help her do something about it.

She is exhausted. But she is also relieved that her friends are here with her. That they have taken over. She'll follow their lead and do what they say. She thinks it will be easier that way.

But she's deluded. Nothing about this will be easy.

CHAPTER NINE

Thursday

TIA

Back home, I'm still fuming about the deputy head's attitude towards what happened with Rosie. I huff into the house, itching to tell Ed about the meeting we had. If I'd thought about it, I would have asked him to come with me. Maybe Mrs Lovatt would have taken the situation more seriously if we'd both been there. I often have that problem – I may be thirty-one, but I still look about eighteen, so people tend to dismiss me as young and stupid. Which I most definitely am not.

'Ed!' I call up the stairs. 'Want a coffee?'

'Yeah, be down in a minute!'

Good. I could do with a good rant about Mrs Lovatt and her hoity-toity ways.

I turn at the sound of the mail thudding onto the porch doormat. It's come earlier than usual. These days it doesn't usually arrive until lunchtime. I pick up the stack and head into the kitchen-diner. I love this room – it's so light and airy with its wide wooden doors that lead out onto the kid-friendly garden. Ed and I designed the room together and he transformed it almost single-handedly, except for the electrics, and my paintbrush skills. Before we bought the house, it was a bit of a wreck. But it was the only place we could afford on this side of town, close to the lake and to the school so that I don't have to drive the kids in every day. Plus, my best friends Kelly and Fiona live nearby. Although Fiona and I aren't nearly as close these days. Not like way back, when the three of us were inseparable at school.

I flip absent-mindedly through the mail. There's the usual slew of flyers that I dump straight into the recycling bin, a bank statement for our joint account which actually doesn't look too horrendous this month, and a large cardboard envelope addressed to me. I can't remember ordering anything, and it's not my birthday. I lay it on the counter for a moment and put fresh water in the coffee machine. While it heats, I open the envelope, mildly curious as to what it could contain.

As I slide my fingers in between the stiff card, I notice that I need to get my nails redone – the colour's grown out already. I'll make an appointment later. It looks like there are photographs inside the envelope. Maybe it's this year's school photos, but I'm pretty sure I already had those back in September. Surely they wouldn't do two lots in one year. It's great to have pictures of Rosie but the cost is always astronomical. With me being a stay-at-home mum for the past few years, things have been a little bit tight. Ed earns a decent amount, we're not badly off, but extras like school photos always hit quite hard.

I slip the photo sheets out of the envelope, prepared to be suckered into buying the lot at the sight of my gorgeous daughter pulling a heart-melting smile, but these aren't school photos – they're too grainy and blurred. And they're not of Rosie either. I frown. The photo is of a man and a woman coming out of a club. They're leaning into one another, kissing. My frown deepens.

When I see who it is, I almost drop the photos in shock.

I slide off the top photo and stare at the one below. This time, the couple are inside a cab, kissing more passionately. The photo is taken from outside, but it's obvious who it is. My stomach churns, and sweat prickles on my forehead. Upset and confused, I look at the final photo with trepidation. The couple are in bed and it looks like they're having sex.

Each of the photos has a date stamp in the corner. They were taken last month, in June. And I can recall exactly which day that was. It looks like the man in the photo has dark hair, but in each of the pictures, his face is turned away from the camera. The only face I can make out clearly is my own. The woman in the photos is *me*. The only trouble is, I have no memory of kissing anyone that night, let alone climbing into bed with them! I would never cheat on Ed. Never.

Who sent the pictures? I snatch up the envelope once again and peer inside, giving myself a paper cut on my finger in the process, but there's no note – nothing. I turn over the glossy, slippery photos, but there's nothing written on the back either.

Who are they from? What do they want? What the hell is going on? Acid burns my throat and chills ripple across my skin. I honestly feel like I'm going to throw up. But right now there are footsteps coming down the stairs. *Shit.* It's Ed. He'll be in here any moment. What should I do?

Think, think. I was going to make coffee for us both and talk about something – what was I going to talk about? My brain has stopped working. I yank open one of the kitchen drawers and shove the photos and envelope beneath some tea towels, trying to get my breathing under control.

I manage to close the drawer just as Ed comes into the kitchen. Then, like some kind of cliché, I wipe my brow. I need to compose myself before I turn around. Taking a deep breath, I smudge away a stray tear, but I can't bring myself to turn and look at Ed just yet.

'Are we having a coffee?' he asks. 'I've got to leave for work in twenty minutes.'

'Yep, just making it.' I walk unsteadily over to the cupboard and pull out two cups.

'How did it go at school?'

School? And then it comes back to me – I spoke to the deputy head earlier about Rosie. About those boys saying that awful thing about me. Was that really only half an hour ago? It feels like a week. And it seems almost trivial compared with the revelation of the photos. But then, are the pictures even real? Maybe they've been photoshopped. *Yes,* that's probably it. I'll have to examine the photos more closely, but that has to be the answer. But who would do such a thing, and why?

Why do awful things always have to happen at the same time? First that terrible rumour at school, and now these photos. Could my week get any worse?

'Tia?' Ed comes around the counter.

I turn and manage to smile. 'Hey, yeah, it was a bit…' I shrug, realising my voice is higher than usual and I sound like a crazy person.

'Hey, you okay? Sit down, I'll finish making the coffee.'

'Are you sure? Thanks.' I take a seat at the kitchen table. My left leg seems to be shaking uncontrollably so I try to still it with my hand. All I can think about is those photographs in the kitchen drawer, the images imprinted on my brain. I cast my mind back to the night in question. Try to remember what happened. But it's all a bit of a blur.

The sound of a drawer opening makes my stomach lurch. I stand up suddenly. What if Ed opens *that* drawer and sees the photos? 'Ed, sit down! It's okay, I'll finish making it!'

He gives me an odd look and waves a teaspoon at me. 'It's fine, I'm done.'

I sit back down and attempt to breathe normally, convinced my husband must be able to hear my heart banging against my ribcage. I need to make normal conversation until I figure out what I'm going to do. 'So how did your shift go last night? Sorry I forgot to ask about it earlier. You had that big birthday booking.'

'Yeah, it was good. Everyone seemed to like the new menu.' Ed brings our drinks to the table and sits opposite me.

I need to respond. To carry on with our conversation as though nothing's wrong. But my mind is filled with those shocking images.

'How did it go with Rosie's teacher this morning.'

'I… uh.' *Focus, Tia.* My mind flits from the photos to my meeting this morning. 'I didn't get to speak to Mr Jeffries. He was with Rosie's class, so I had to talk to the new deputy head instead. She didn't seem to take it seriously at all.'

'Really? Why, what did she say?'

'Not a lot. Just some crap like *she'll see what she can do.* Trying to fob me off.'

'I hope you told her what's what.'

'I tried, but she made me feel like I was making a mountain out of a molehill. But then she didn't see how upset Rosie was yesterday. And also, how would she like it if kids were going around calling her a murderer? She'd probably put them all on detention!'

'Probably. Look, try not to get upset about it. Rosie went in happy this morning so hopefully it'll all blow over. You know what kids are like, they bounce back.'

I nod and blow on my coffee. 'I suppose.'

Ed carries on talking, but I can hardly concentrate on what he's saying, my mind drawn back to the seedy contents of the envelope. I remember that I'm supposed to invite Rosie's friends over after school, which means also asking Pip and Emily if they want to come too. But how will I be able to socialise with friends after receiving such a bombshell in the post?

I glance at my husband as he's sipping his coffee, gazing out through the double doors without a care in the world, oblivious to the turmoil in my head. Oblivious to those photos in the drawer. I marvel at the idea that two people who know each other so well can keep such secrets. Ed has no idea of the nightmare in my head right now. He thinks everything is hunky-dory.

What would his reaction be if I showed him the photos? Would our perfect marriage be over? My whole body grows heavy at the thought. Ed and I have a great relationship. We're rock solid. Neither of us would ever do anything to jeopardise that. Not ever.

Those pictures must be photoshopped. The alternative just doesn't bear thinking about. The date on them is the same night I went clubbing with Kelly and Fiona last month – and yes I might have had a bit too much to drink, but that's because I hardly ever go out any more and I was making the most of it.

I had a good time that night but got tired quite quickly. I jumped into a taxi and went home early. But if those photos are to be believed, I didn't go straight home at all. I met someone, kissed them outside the club, got into a taxi, went home with them, got undressed and got into bed with them. *Slept with them.* Trouble is, I don't remember doing any of that. And surely my friends would have said something if they'd seen me with a man. Unless one of them is behind it? But that's an *awful* thing to wonder. I'm obviously not thinking straight. They're my friends, for goodness sake!

I inhale deeply, but this time even deep breaths won't save me. I rush from the kitchen and into the downstairs loo where I heave my guts into the toilet, throwing up my breakfast and coffee until there's nothing left in my stomach but air.

'Tia! Tee, are you okay?'

I manage to pull the loo door closed behind me and lock it. I don't want Ed to see me like this. I don't want him asking what's wrong. And I don't want to lie to him. I've *never* lied to him. I don't trust myself not to tell him about the photos. And if I do that before I've figured out who's behind it, he might not believe me. And, right now, I'm feeling more than a bit shaky about the remote possibility that I might have slept with a stranger. Or worse, that he might have taken advantage of me.

CHAPTER TEN

KELLY

I stand in the school playground trying not to bite my nails or chew my hair. I haven't done the school pick-up for ages, now that the boys prefer walking in on their own. The normality of it all seems alien – the little cliques of mums standing in huddles, the preschoolers charging around with footballs or scooters. I take it all in, feeling a mixture of anxiety and nostalgia as car doors slam and the breeze rustles the trees.

I notice Leo racing up and down the playground on his scooter. That means Tia or Ed must be here. I glance around, finally spotting my friend standing alone by the fence, staring off into space, her unruly curls framing her heart-shaped face. She looks so young and lost. That's not like Tia – she's usually surrounded by other mums. She's one of those warm, friendly souls to whom everyone gravitates. Always laughing and making others feel great, so it surprises me to see her caught up so thoroughly in her own world.

I decide to leave her be, wanting to collar Ryan and Sonny as soon as I can so that I can firstly see how Ryan's doing after today's episode at school, and secondly tell them about Sophie.

When I returned from my earlier meeting with the deputy head, Sophie was still in the house, tucked away in the attic room, sitting in the rocking chair. There was no sign that she'd been into the rest of the house and she was still incredibly grateful to me.

I'd got home with the intention of persuading her to contact a shelter or the police, but when it came down to it, I just couldn't bring myself to turn her away. She's a woman who's been through something and she needs a break. I know how that feels.

Tia glances over and catches my eye, interrupting my thoughts. She doesn't smile straightaway. Instead she looks hesitant, almost irritated to see me. I give her a short wave, but I stay put. If she isn't in the mood to chat, then I won't force myself on her. And anyway, it suits me not to get drawn into a conversation right now. *Too late.* She's coming over, albeit reluctantly.

'Hey, lovely.' I give her a hug.

'Haven't seen you here for a while,' she says. Her face is drawn and pale, her eyes cloudy and ringed with shadows.

'You okay?'

'Yeah. You know how it is with young kids. Not enough sleep.'

'I remember it well. It does get better. Well, the sleep part anyway! The rest of it is as tricky as ever.'

We each force out a little laugh, but it's obvious neither of us is in a chatty mood. Which is ironic, because I have so much I could talk about with her. Too much. I know she'd be sympathetic about Ryan, but I'm not sure what she'd say about Sophie. I think she'd probably be horrified and try to talk me out of it.

A couple of Sonny's friends' mums, Anna and Mo, spot me. They wave enthusiastically and come over. Tia seems to shrink at the sight of them. 'You sure you're okay?' I ask her, wishing I could invite her round for a chat, but knowing I absolutely can't. Not right now.

'Yeah, I'm fine.' She almost snaps the words out, but I don't have time to dig deeper because Anna and Mo are giving me enthusiastic hugs.

'Kelly! Haven't seen you here for a while? How you doing?'

'Fine. You know Tia, don't you? Her daughter Rosie is in Reception.'

The two women glance at one another and then nod coolly in Tia's direction. I'm a little taken aback by their reaction, which is verging on rude. But they're all smiles again now. Maybe I imagined it.

Tia's face is red, as though she's about to cry. 'I'd better go,' she mumbles. 'Leo…' She tails off.

Before I get a chance to say goodbye, she stalks off, and I'm snarled up in my friends' conversation about school matters. They haven't mentioned Ryan's classroom meltdown, so I guess they haven't heard about it yet. Well, I'm not about to enlighten them. Maybe it will be forgotten about. But I know that's unlikely. Some child will mention it to a parent and then it will be all around the town in no time. To my relief, the bell rings and everyone's attention turns to the children streaming out of their classrooms.

It takes a while for my two to make their way out, and I wave at them to get their attention.

'Mum, what are you doing here?' Ryan lopes over, his face a thundercloud of resentment.

'Hi, Mum!' Sonny beams, almost crashing into me in his enthusiasm. 'We had swimming today and they let us have the inflatables. It was so funny. George Mulcahy had a sharp point on his swim-shorts toggle, and it burst the inflatable crocodile.'

I ruffle Sonny's hair and tell him that sounds hilarious.

'Why are you picking us up?' Ryan persists. 'Do we have to go somewhere? We haven't got to go shopping, have we?'

'No, nothing like that. Aren't I allowed to walk home with my boys every now and again?' I smile distractedly at some of the other parents. Normally, I'd stop and go over for a chat, but right now I really have to concentrate on the kids. To explain to them about Sophie.

'Oh yeah,' Sonny says, 'Dr Barton said to say hello.'

'Dr Barton? You mean the dentist?'

Sonny nods.

'When did you see *him*?'

'He came into assembly to talk about looking after our teeth.' Sonny bares his teeth at me to make his point.

'So boring,' Ryan mutters. 'He went on and on about it.'

Sonny pulls a small tube out of his pocket. 'We queued up at the end to get free samples of toothpaste and Dr Barton said, "Say hello to your beautiful mother," and then he went red like he was embarrassed.'

'Gross.' Ryan strides ahead, his shoulders hunched.

That's all I need. I really hope Paul Barton isn't interested in me. If he is, I'll have to gently set him straight. But right now I have more important things to sort out. Ryan still hasn't mentioned anything about his outburst at school, even though it must be weighing on his mind. I decide that now isn't the time for me to bring it up. Not with Sonny within earshot. I'll talk to Ryan about it later when it's just the two of us.

'Hey, you two, come and walk with me.'

Sonny falls back and takes hold of my hand. He may be eight, but he's not yet too embarrassed to be hugged and kissed by his mum, unlike some children his age who don't want to be seen anywhere near their parents, let alone have physical contact in front of their friends. Ryan slows to let me catch up, but I don't even try to take *his* hand, knowing exactly what reaction I'd get.

'So,' I begin, 'I wanted to let you know, we've got a visitor staying with us for a day or two.'

'A visitor?' Sonny's eyes widen.

'Her name is Sophie, and she's a friend from when I was younger.' I hate lying to my kids, but if Sophie really is hiding from an abusive relationship, then I can't let it get out that I'm giving shelter to a stranger, in case whoever she's running from susses out where she is.

'Why's she staying with us?' Ryan asks.

'Because she's my friend and she's having a little holiday in Ashridge Falls.'

'How do you know her?'

'Well, she's actually not feeling too well at the moment, so it's best not to bother her with lots of questions, okay?'

'You could make her some celery soup,' Sonny suggests. 'Like you do when we're not very well.'

'That's a very kind thought, Sonny. It might be a bit hot for soup though.'

Ryan huffs. 'Why have we got to have people staying? I like it when it's just us.'

I almost smile at his words – he sounds so like his father. But then I remember that Michael isn't here any more, and my almost-smile dies on my lips.

'You'll hardly know she's here. She's very quiet and she won't bother you if you don't bother her, okay? Sonny, can you zip your bag up? Your books are going to fall out if you're not careful.'

We wait for a moment while he sorts out his bag. Ryan doesn't say anything more. Just scuffs at the dusty kerb with the toe of his shoe. I have to restrain myself from telling him to stop it, that he'll ruin a perfectly good pair of shoes. I look away and resolve to give him a little bit of space when we get in.

'So while you two were at school, guess what I've been doing?'

'Working at the shop?' Sonny guesses.

'Better than that…'

Ryan feigns disinterest.

'I made my famous Victoria sponge cake for the regatta.'

'For the regatta?' Sonny frowns. 'But that's not till Saturday.'

'It's lucky I made two then, isn't it?'

'Yes!' He punches the air. 'So can we have some when we get in?'

'Maybe.' I wink.

We turn into our road and walk the remaining two hundred yards to our house.

'Oh, and, boys, there's one other thing I need to ask you.'

'What?'

'I'd like it if you didn't tell anyone else about Sophie staying. Because if you do, everyone will want to come and visit us.' I realise it's a very unconvincing reason, but I'm hoping that it will sway them both to keep schtum. Sonny always wants to please, so I'm sure he'll keep the secret. And Ryan might agree to do it if only to prevent the threat of more visitors descending.

'So it's a secret?' Sonny asks.

'Yes.'

'What, we can't tell anyone?' Ryan looks momentarily interested.

'No one at all,' I say. 'Do you think you can both manage that?'

'Okay.' Sonny nods vigorously while Ryan shrugs.

My phone buzzes as we reach the house. I check the screen and see that Tia's sent a text:

Got time for a chat?

She seemed quite down earlier. Maybe she wants to tell me what's wrong. I'd usually call her right back, but there's too much I need to sort out here. I'll call her later. I stuff my phone back in my bag and we go inside. Once the boys are settled in the kitchen with huge slabs of cake and tall glasses of iced lemonade, I race upstairs to see how Sophie's doing.

'Knock, knock,' I say outside the bedroom door.

'Come in.' Sophie's lying on the bed reading a magazine.

'Hi, just wondering if you want to come down and meet my kids?'

She looks a little taken aback.

'It's just… if you're staying here, it's probably best if you say hello. In case they bump into you on the landing or something.'

'Oh, okay, but what if they say something to their friends?'

'Don't worry, they've promised not to say anything to anyone. I've told them you're an old friend come to stay.'

'Are you sure they won't talk?' Her forehead creases in concern.

'It'll be fine, honestly.' Although I sound more confident than I feel.

'Okay.' Sophie gets to her feet. Wraps her arms around herself.

'I can lend you some pyjamas and fresh clothes later, if you like. And, I should've said before, you're welcome to take a shower.'

'That would be really nice. Thanks.' She follows me down the stairs and I walk back into the kitchen more breezily than I feel. Both boys have finished eating and are now fully focused on their phones. Heads down, tapping and scrolling.

'Hey boys, this is Sophie who I was telling you about.'

After a second or two, Sonny looks up and gives a shy smile. Ryan doesn't react.

'Ryan, put your phone down for a minute and say hi.'

'Hi,' he says without looking up.

I tut and open my mouth to reprimand him but Sophie's hand rests on my arm. 'It's fine,' she whispers. 'Leave him.'

I'm torn between telling him off and avoiding a scene. The latter wins out and I shrug an apology to our house guest.

'You don't look like one of Mum's friends,' Sonny says, staring.

'Why, what do they look like?' Sophie's more animated around Sonny than she's been around me.

'They're older,' he says, in that blunt way kids have.

'Charming!' I shake my head.

'Mum, can I have some more cake?' he asks, trying his luck.

'No, you'll ruin your dinner. Maybe later. Sophie, do you want a slice?'

'I'm fine. I'll go back up, if that's okay.' She eyes the window nervously.

I want to tell her that the kitchen window looks out onto the back garden. That she's hidden from view. That no one will be peering in. But then I remember that *she* ended up in my back garden and it wouldn't be too difficult for someone else to jump the fence or jimmy the gate lock. I give a brief shiver. 'Okay, sure. Let me know if you need anything.'

She nods and slips away silently, padding back up the stairs.

Now that Sophie's gone, I should probably have a word with Ryan about his behaviour at school today. I don't relish the thought, but I can't just ignore what happened, can I? I gaze over at the top of Ryan's head, remembering when he was younger with those beautiful dark curls rather than the short French crop he now prefers. Suddenly Ryan sighs, sets his phone down on the table and pushes it away. He glances up at me briefly, scowls and then catches his brother's eye. Something passes between them.

Sonny frowns and shakes his head.

I walk over and start clearing the table, psyching myself up to question my eldest son. But I need to speak to him on his own, not with Sonny earwigging. 'Sonny, have you got any homework?'

'No.'

'Are you sure?'

My phone buzzes again. I quickly check the screen. It's another text from Tia. I lay the phone on the table. She'll have to wait.

Ryan elbows Sonny.

'Get off!' Sonny pushes his brother.

'Sonny,' Ryan growls.

'Shut up. You say it.'

I stare from one to the other. 'Okay, what's going on?'

Sonny shakes his head, clamps his lips together and folds his arms across his chest.

'Ryan, why don't you tell me.'

My eldest son glares at me for a moment, gets to his feet and then storms out of the room, slamming the door behind him.

'Ryan!' I take a few steps after him. 'Ryan, come back!' Maybe I should go after him. No. Probably best not. I'll let him calm down for a few minutes.

Sonny interrupts my thoughts. 'Mum, why's he mad all the time?'

'Oh, sweetie, I don't know. I wish I did.' I use my most gentle voice. 'Sonny, whatever it was he wanted you to say, I'd really like you to tell me, okay?'

He scowls and then sighs. 'Okay. But it's weird.'

'What's weird?' I'm starting to feel more than a little freaked out.

'They're saying stuff about you at school.'

I swallow. 'Stuff? What stuff?'

Sonny flushes bright red before replying. 'Mum, did you kiss my teacher?'

CHAPTER ELEVEN

FIONA

Seated at the conference table with my sketch pad open, I'm trying to work on my new designs for the Carmichaels' mill house. However, my concentration isn't what it should be, as I'm hyper-aware of those two interlopers in my office. Even though I'm purposely facing the opposite direction, I keep imagining that they're looking over at me disapprovingly.

I'm trying to stay zen about the audit. Que sera sera and all that crap. But the thing that's worrying me most isn't what the inspectors might discover, it's how I'm going to tell Nathan what's been going on. I don't want him to see me so vulnerable. I've always prided myself on being self-sufficient, and he likes that about me. I hate the expression 'power couple' but I feel like that's what we are. Admitting weakness to Nathan doesn't come easy. It isn't how our relationship works. Or, at least, it isn't how the *perception* of our relationship works.

If I were to tell him that my business might be in trouble, would he be sympathetic and supportive, or would he blame me and get angry? There's no way of knowing, because we've never had any major hurdles like this to get over before. Our careers have always been pretty plain sailing. I guess it could go okay if I told him – maybe he'll give me some practical advice. Help me to get through it. That's how marriages are supposed to work, aren't they? You support one another through the good times and the bad.

Nathan and I met eight years ago at a local awards ceremony for young entrepreneurs, where he was presenting the prize and I won first place. On both counts, it was a big deal. Winning the award got me the publicity to really boost my client base, and meeting Nathan changed my life. I'd only been in one serious relationship before, but that one didn't work out. Nathan broke down a lot of my barriers and we ended up falling in love and getting married within a year.

That awards ceremony kind of set the scene for our lives. Success. Happiness. Perfection. Nothing less will do. I sigh. There's no way I can tell Nathan that my business is under investigation. Pushing my sketch pad away, I stare out through the window at the shops opposite, at the people walking past, going about their daily business. I wonder if they're happy. If their lives are straightforward and simple. Or if their minds are in turmoil and they're simply presenting a calm exterior. Sometimes I'm amazed at how everyone in the world isn't freaking out more.

'Fiona…'

I look up to see Molly walk in with an armful of next month's interiors magazines. She fans them out on the coffee table and then straightens up, smoothing down her skirt. I always like to have an up-to-date selection for clients to browse through while they're here.

'Thanks, Molly. Shall we have a cuppa?'

She nods and goes over to the coffee machine. She's always so immaculately turned out – her hair, clothes and make-up are all flawless. I often think Molly would be better suited to a career in fashion than interiors. I've tried to get her interested in the design process. I want her to wow me with fresh new ideas, but disappointingly she hasn't ever shown any real initiative. She does what's asked of her and that's it. She's a decent enough assistant I suppose, but I don't think her heart's in the business.

She stands at the coffee machine, her back to me, shoulders down. I'm not sure what's up with her at the moment. She's been distracted over the past couple of weeks. And while she's never exactly been the most enthusiastic employee in the world, lately her mind has been elsewhere. I think I'm going to have a word with her, check everything's okay.

Finally, she brings me a coffee and hovers awkwardly by my side.

'Aren't you having one?' I ask.

'No thanks.'

'Sit down for a bit, let's have a chat.'

Her cheeks flush and she pulls out a chair and plops down next to me. 'Are those the new mill house designs?' She nods at my sketch book.

'Yes, if you can call them that. I haven't got very far with them.'

'You will,' she says flatly. 'Your designs are always amazing.'

I'm surprised by how touched I am at her praise – even if it's said grudgingly. I honestly never thought she was that bothered by what I do. 'Thanks, Molly.' I give her a warm smile. 'You know, we could work on them together, if you like?' I'm usually quite precious about my designs, but I'm suddenly overcome by the need to be generous towards her. To be kind. I realise I haven't exactly been the most approachable boss. I haven't really given her any opportunities to shine.

'That's… that's nice of you. But I can't.'

'Oh.' I'm disappointed by her response. 'Sure you can. I'll help you with it.'

'I don't mean I *can't*. I mean, I'm sorry, Fiona, but I'm handing in my notice.'

'You're…'

'It's not that I don't like the job.' Her expression changes to one of barely concealed excitement. 'It's just… well… I'm pregnant, actually. Me and Josh are having a baby and we're moving back east to be nearer my parents.'

'Oh.' I realise I don't sound happy for her, so I make an attempt to recover myself. 'Well, that's fantastic news. Congratulations!' I reach forward and give her an awkward hug.

'Thanks, Fiona. I'll work out my notice of course.'

'Well, only if you feel up to it.'

She laughs. 'I'm pregnant, not sick.' Her hand goes to her stomach, which I realise is a little more rounded than usual. Funny I never noticed.

'I didn't realise you wanted to start a family.'

'It wasn't planned. But Josh is really happy about it and he's asked me to marry him.'

'Well, that's a double congratulations then!' I try to sound happier than I feel. It's awful to admit it, but aside from the inconvenience of losing my assistant, there's another feeling bubbling up inside my gut. Something visceral. Primal. It's not about Molly leaving, it's more to do with the fact that she's only twenty-two – ten years younger than me – and she's having a baby with her boyfriend. I realise that I'm jealous of Molly. Which is crazy, isn't it?

I've always known Nathan doesn't want kids, and I don't either. Before we got married, we both decided that we wanted to enjoy our careers without the guilt or distraction of having children. Nathan has always been extremely ambitious, and I've always loved my work, so it made sense to take the pressure off ourselves. To not conform to society's expectations. But lately, I've been having these thoughts that maybe it wouldn't be altogether terrible to have a family. I see my friends with their children, and I've always thought it looks chaotic and messy and painful and – to be frank – like bloody hard work. So why would I want to put myself through that? It makes no sense. These new maternal feelings are inconvenient. But I can't help them. And, looking back at the decision Nathan and I made, I can't help wondering whether it really was my decision to not have kids, or whether I just went along with him because I didn't want to rock the boat. But I must be crazy to be thinking about this right now, because how can I even contemplate having a family when everything else is such a mess?

'Are you okay, Fiona?' Molly's frowning at me.

'Yes, I'm fine. Just trying to take in your news. You must be so excited.'

'I am. Nervous about being a mum, but I also can't wait, if that even makes sense!' she laughs. It's the most animated I've ever seen her.

'You'll be great,' I say, taking a sip of my coffee.

'I hope so. I know I'm changing the subject a bit, but what are you going to do about those tax guys?' Molly jerks her head in the direction of my office. 'It looks like they're going through absolutely everything. I was talking to Josh about it last night and he said—'

'You told Josh about them?' I snap, suddenly furious that my employee has been gossiping about my affairs.

'Yeah.' She flushes. 'I didn't realise it was a secret. I mean, you can see them through the glass. They're not exactly hidden from view.'

'Yes,' I concede, 'but no one knows who they are. They could be anyone.'

'They're going through your files, Fiona. It's pretty obvious they're from the tax office.'

'Uh, no. They could be accountants, or lawyers or anyone. Look, that's beside the point. You shouldn't be gossiping about my private business to everyone.'

'Josh isn't everyone. He's my fiancé. And you never told me it was a secret.' She scowls. 'And it's a business matter, not a private one – I work here.'

I get to my feet and stretch my arms out in front of me, trying to dampen my anger. 'You're right, I'm sorry. I'm just a bit tense.

It's so disruptive having them here. Puts me on edge. And it's a real creativity killer, you know?'

She shrugs. 'What did Nathan say?'

'About what?'

She looks at me as though I'm losing the plot. 'About the tax guys.'

'Oh, well, not a lot.'

She raises an eyebrow. 'You didn't tell him?'

I sigh. 'Not yet. I haven't had a chance.'

'You should tell him. He might be able to help.'

I'm not enjoying this straight-talking Molly. I think I preferred it when she kept her opinions to herself.

She sniffs. 'I don't plan on keeping secrets from Josh. We've promised to tell each other everything.'

Well good for you. I try not to roll my eyes. Sometimes young love can be sickening. They think they've got it all figured out. But they just need to give it time. They'll see that love isn't always all it's cracked up to be.

'So, do you think you're gonna get in trouble?' She turns to look through my office window, being very unsubtle about the fact she's talking about them. Now she knows she's leaving she probably doesn't feel like she has to be a good employee any longer.

'No! Why would I get in trouble?'

'I dunno. They can get you on any little thing, can't they? My aunt got done for tax evasion and had to pay a massive fine. She also went to prison, but we weren't supposed to know about that part.'

Her talk of tax evasion and prison is seriously giving me the jitters. I look at Molly's face and realise she's loving the drama of it all. I want to tell her to shut up and get on with her work, but how would that look? I suddenly have an unwanted thought that sends my pulse racing – what if it's Molly who's responsible for the tax inspectors showing up? I know I can sometimes be a strict boss, but would that drive Molly to do something so awful? I don't know. All I do know is that she's enjoying this all a little too much.

She could have left an anonymous tip with HMRC. Maybe she feels that now she's leaving the area, she's got nothing to lose. She might have done it out of spite. People can be mean, bitter, all sorts. Over the years, I've had a couple of anonymous bad reviews online and I'm sure they wouldn't have been left by any of my clients, as I always ensure they're super happy with my work. No, I've always put the one-star reviews down to people who are angry and disappointed with their own lives. Either that, or they're jealous of my success.

I watch Molly as she talks about her relation's prison sentence, her blue eyes flashing, and her face flushed with the awfulness of it all. Could Molly really be behind my misfortune? Am I over-reacting, or have I actually hit upon the truth?

CHAPTER TWELVE

TIA

'Thanks so much for having us all over, Tia.' Pip gives me a hug. 'Sorry your kitchen looks like an explosion in a cake factory. Are you sure we can't give you a hand tidying up?'

'No, it'll take me two minutes to shove it all in the dishwasher.' I survey the devastation and think, *More like two hours.*

'If you're sure…' Pip slings her bag over her shoulder. 'Sasha, Milo, say thank you to Tia for a lovely afternoon.'

'Thank you,' they repeat dutifully.

Emily and her daughter Maisie are valiantly attempting to pick up some of the toys that are scattered all over the hall and down the stairs.

'Thanks, you guys, but honestly just leave it.' I grab hold of Leo, who's running past me into the lounge with another tub of Lego. 'Take that back upstairs!'

Why did I tell Rosie she could have her friends round after school today? I'm exhausted and I could barely concentrate on Pip and Emily's conversation. All I could think about were those photos of me with that man. About whether it even really is me. And if it is, then what the hell happened that night?

Normally I love having my friends over and doing homely stuff with all the children. I like being sociable, and baking makes me feel like a good parent, like Mother Earth. But this afternoon seemed to drag on forever. And I'm sure there was a weird atmosphere between me, Pip and Emily. I caught them giving one another funny looks more than once. Could they have heard about the rumour at school? Maybe Sasha and Maisie mentioned something. That's all I need – the parents speculating about whether or not I'm a murderer!

Finally, my visitors leave, and I settle the kids in front of the TV while I set about restoring some sort of order to the house. At least we now have several Tupperware boxes full of sailboat cupcakes for the regatta cake stall, which is another thing I can check off my list.

I've just got the dishwasher going and started wiping down the surfaces when Ed comes downstairs. He was hiding out in our bedroom while the chaos was going on. He did offer to help out with the kids, but I told him to take it easy and chill out in the bedroom, as he'll be leaving soon for his evening shift at the pub.

'Hey, Tee, want a hand?' He comes over and kisses me on the lips. I get another cold sweep of fear at the thought of what might happen if he sees those photos. How will I be able to justify them when I can't even remember what happened that night?

'No, that's okay. You've got work soon. Sit down and take it easy while you can.'

'Are you sure?' He leans his elbows on the newly cleaned countertop. 'That sounded like a full-on afternoon. How many kids were here?'

'Our two, plus two of Rosie's friends and little Milo.'

'Sounded like you had the whole school round.'

'Most of the noise and mess was caused by your son.'

'Love the use of the word "your".'

I grin, knowing full well that Leo gets his energy from *me*. According to my parents, I was also a handful at that age, while Ed was supposedly a mellow, easy-going child. 'How long have you got before you leave?'

Ed looks up at the kitchen clock. 'Half an hour max.'

'Got time for a sit down and a cuppa while the kids are occupied? I'll clean the rest up later.'

'Yeah, go on then. Just a quick one.' I make us both a drink while Ed gives the table a wipe over. He stops for a moment. 'I love the smell of baking. D'you reckon we could have one of those cupcakes with our tea? Or are they strictly for the regatta?'

'I think we could sneak a couple without Rosie finding out. She was acting like the cake police earlier, making sure that Leo didn't eat too many.' I bring two over to the table along with our drinks.

'These look amazing, Tee.' He examines the little cakes with their perfect blue-and-red sailing boats iced on the top.

'They're cool, aren't they? I used stencils.'

'These will go down really well on Saturday.'

'You think?'

'Definitely.'

Ed's phone buzzes in his pocket and he takes it out and stares at the screen, his forehead wrinkling.

'What's up?'

'Not sure. I just got a text. What are they talking about?' He passes me the phone.

As I take it from him and start reading the words on the screen, I get a sick, tingling feeling in my stomach. The words are stark:

Ask Tia about the photos.

My heart begins to pound, and my throat goes dry. There's no name attached to the text, and it just shows up as an unknown number. I have to make it look like I'm calm, even though my insides are churning. I can't give Ed any reason to think this is anything sinister.

'Hm.' I frown and hope my voice remains steady. 'Could be about the school photos. I asked Mrs Lovatt to let me know how

to order them, but I'm not sure why she would have texted *you?*'
I pass the phone back to him quickly so he can't see my trembling
fingers. 'She probably got your number off the parents contact list.'

'Doesn't make much sense though,' Ed persists. 'Why would
she be asking me to ask you about the photos when it was you
who asked the school?'

'No idea.' I shrug. 'It must be a mix-up. I wouldn't worry
about it.'

'You're right.' He shakes his head and shoves his phone back
into his pocket.

'The communication at school has always been useless,' I add.

'Didn't we already have school photos this year?' Ed asks.

Right this moment I'm cursing having such an involved
husband. Why can't he just shrug and move on? 'This was about
the sports day photos,' I say, marvelling at my new-found ability
to lie so easily.

Thankfully, Ed doesn't question the message any further. We
drink our tea and I listen to him talk about work, trying to latch
on to his words and act interested. Trying to pretend that my mind
isn't in turmoil about who could be sending me disturbing photos
and texting my husband. Are they trying to ruin my marriage? Is
that it? How did they even get Ed's mobile number? Maybe it's
someone we know. A friend, or someone he works with. Could it
perhaps be another woman? Someone who wants Ed for herself.
Maybe an ex-girlfriend?

Or perhaps it isn't personal at all. Maybe it's someone who
wants to blackmail me? Good luck with that. I have no money
to speak of. Ed and I live month to month. There are no savings,
other than about twenty quid in our emergency-fund jar, and we
have a mortgage with no equity in the house. But if they wanted
to blackmail me, surely they would tell me what they want. My
mind is leaping ahead to all kinds of conclusions. But I think
the most likely is that it's another woman trying to destroy my

marriage. If I find out who it is, I'll... Well, I don't know what I'll do. But I won't let them get away with it, that's for damn sure.

And then I remember that Ed used to go out with *Fiona*. It was about nine years ago; right before Ed and I got together. Fiona and Ed were pretty serious for a while, and I've always had the feeling that she wishes it hadn't ended. Not that she's ever said anything, but she's always far too friendly towards my husband, in a proprietorial, shared-history kind of way that gets my back up. Not that she and Nathan don't seem happy. She's always going on about how wonderful he is and how they're soulmates. Only it's never really rung true for me. It's like they're the image of how a perfect couple should be, yet something is missing.

Even though they're just thoughts, I hate feeling so bitchy. I like Fiona, of course I do. We've known one another since we were kids. But there's always going to be that distance between us because of Ed. Maybe she's jealous of me. But would she really go as far as to try to ruin my marriage with a few photos?

I think back to the night in question, when we were at that club. It was Fiona's birthday and Nathan was out of town on business, so she'd arranged a girls' night out. It wasn't really Kelly's scene at all, but she agreed to it because Fiona pretty much forced her to go. I'm sure I was only invited because Kelly asked if I could come too – probably for moral support, because she's not that comfortable around Fi's clients and work buddies. Although the three of us are supposedly all best friends, I have the feeling that if it weren't for Kelly, then Fiona and I wouldn't be friends at all.

In the end, I remember having a pretty good night at the club – lots of dancing and laughing. Although Kelly and I spent a good chunk of the evening trying to avoid Creepy Barton, the local dentist. He kept dancing up against us in this really cheesy way and offering to buy us drinks. I wonder if it could have been him in the photos. Please, God, no. The very thought of it makes me nauseous. But I get the feeling it wasn't *me* he was interested in that night, it was Kelly. He was as subtle as a brick when he asked her how she was coping on her own with the kids. He said if she ever needed to talk he was a good listener. Which is the biggest load of rubbish I've ever heard, because there's nothing Paul Barton likes more than the sound of his own voice.

Aside from Barton, Fiona was annoyingly judgemental that night, just because I decided to have a couple of drinks – okay, maybe more than a couple. She told me several times that I'd had enough, that I was making a show of myself, that I should calm down. I frown, remembering that we had a kind of mini argument. Yes, I remember it now – she said something about pitying Ed. Ugh, how dare she! Just because I know how to have fun. Fiona has never been able to let loose – she's wound up tighter than one of Leo's curls. But, then again, maybe she kind of had a point, because the end of the night is definitely a blur.

Seriously, could Fiona really have had something to do with the photos? She's been behaving oddly recently. Only last week, I saw her in town and waved, but she acted like she hadn't seen me and went into a shop. Ninety-nine per cent sure she did see me though.

I realise I've completely zoned out from Ed's conversation. I tune back in to his story about a local TV presenter who was in the pub last night. I nod and make the appropriate listening noises until he finishes talking.

'Why did Fiona end things with you?' I ask.

'Why did *what*?' Ed jerks his head up. 'What made you think about that?'

I shrug. 'It just popped into my head. I don't think you ever told me why it never worked out between you two.'

'I don't know. But it's all ancient history now. Do we really have to go into it?'

'No, course not. I'm curious, that's all.'

'It just didn't work out. She was too stand-offish and cold. Our relationship never really got going in the first place.'

'But *she* finished with *you*, right?'

'Way to make a guy feel good!' Ed flicks my arm playfully.

'Sorry!' I manage a short laugh. 'But she did, yeah?'

'She said she cared about me, but she'd met someone else. I was relieved, to be honest. I'd been wanting to break it off, but I didn't want to hurt her.'

I twirl a strand of hair around my finger. 'That must have been when she met Nathan.'

'Yeah, those two are perfect together. Both really ambitious and career-driven.'

'You're ambitious too!'

Ed leans forward to kiss me. 'I love my job, but I wouldn't say I'm ambitious. I'm more of a family man than a career man.'

I slide across to sit on his lap and wrap my arms around his broad back. 'I love you, Mr Perry.'

'Love you too, Mrs Perry.'

As we kiss and I run my fingers through his hair, I make the decision that I'll do whatever it takes to ensure that whoever it was who sent those photos will never come between me and my husband. My family means too much to me to let someone else's twisted agenda destroy my life.

'Right…' Ed pulls away from our kiss and smooths my hair away from my face. 'Much as I'd love to sit here all day snogging my hot wife, I have to go to work.'

I scowl and blow a raspberry. 'Spoilsport.'

'Someone has to be the grown-up.' He grins.

'Better you than me.' I jump up off his lap. 'Those children are being scarily quiet. Better go and see what's happening.'

'Stay here if you like. I'll go and check on them,' Ed says. 'I want to say goodnight before I leave.'

'Okay, thanks, babe. Have a good night.'

Ed goes next door and I hear him chatting to the children before he leaves for work. I sit back down at the kitchen table and take a sip of my tea, but it's already gone cold. Now that Ed's gone, the anxiety I'm feeling ramps up even more. Aside from being scary, this thing has the potential to completely ruin my life.

I can't go to the police, because that would risk Ed finding out. My brother Ash is a cop, but he has strong morals and might not believe I'm telling the truth. I've always been a bit of a rebel and I wouldn't blame him for thinking the worst of me. Even though I would never do anything like that. My family is sacred to me. No, I'll have to get to the bottom of this without his help. I did send Kelly a couple of texts earlier to meet up for a chat…

I think I'm going to risk confiding in her. She's always so caring and non-judgemental. She'll know what to do for the best. I should probably wait until later when the children are in bed, but I can't spend another moment with all these worries swilling around in my brain. I pick up my phone and call Kelly's number. Even if we can't talk properly now, I can ask if she'll come over for a chat, maybe even for dinner. She could bring the boys over. Ryan and Sonny are never any trouble. Annoyingly, her phone goes straight to voicemail. But that's fine, I'll get hold of her eventually, and when I do, she'll help me to come up with a plan. A way to get out of this mess.

But, even as I strengthen my resolve and try to act more positively, I can't help feeling that things are slipping and sliding out of my control. That if I don't do something soon, the life I've built will fall away, and I'll be left with nothing.

CHAPTER THIRTEEN

Friday

KELLY

Derek has left me a box of jewellery to display on the counter. The pieces are delicate and pretty – a golden dragonfly brooch, several twisted silver rings and various coloured bracelets and clip-on earrings. As I attempt to hook them onto the stand, I wonder about their previous owner. Did the person grow tired of the pieces or was it someone who died and had no one to leave them to? Did they originally buy the pieces for themselves? Or were they perhaps gifts from a loved one? I often do this with donations – wonder about each item's history, but it always makes me feel a little melancholy.

I could really have done with giving work a miss today. I texted a few other volunteers, but there was no one free to take over my shift and, whatever else I have going on in my life, I don't like to let my boss down. He relies on all his volunteers. Profits from the shop go towards local charities – the hospital, the lifeboat association, families in need and lots of other worthy causes. I wonder if perhaps Sophie could benefit from some of the proceeds. I'll have to discuss it with Derek.

Sophie is still at the house. I haven't had the chance to talk to her about getting some help, and I couldn't very well throw her out onto the street. With any luck, I should have some time this evening to sit down properly with her and have a serious discussion about how best to help. I'll pop back home during my lunch break too. Make sure she's okay.

The shop is quiet this morning. I've only had a couple of browsers in so far. My thoughts swing back to my children, and to the crazy rumour that I kissed Sonny's teacher, Mr Llewellyn. It's all nonsense of course. Just bored kids trying to cause trouble. Sonny told me that everyone at school is talking about it. *Poor Ryan.* If his friends were teasing him about his mum kissing a teacher, then no wonder he flipped out in the classroom. Especially as he misses his dad so much. I hope he realises there's no truth to it.

I did try to talk to Ryan last night, but all I got in return were monosyllabic answers. I asked him if this rumour was the reason he was rude to his teacher, but he just clammed up. At least he didn't kick up a fuss about going in to school this morning. I hate the fact that I can't seem to get through to my eldest son these days. He's shutting me out. I wish Michael were here. He would know how to jolt him out of it.

I have to admit, the rumour really shook me up too. Sent my thoughts racing back to that day at school all those years ago. I shiver, not wanting to think about that time. We've all managed to put it firmly behind us. This silly gossip is just an unfortunate coincidence.

The shop door swings open, rattling the bell and distracting me from my worries. I look up. It's Tia and Leo. I guiltily remember that Tia left a message for me to call her yesterday and I never got back to her. I was too preoccupied with everything and the message went out of my head.

Tia is one of those people who always manages to look effortlessly beautiful. She doesn't dress expensively like Fiona, yet all her clothes just seem to look perfect on her. If you didn't know her well you would say that today is no exception: her dark curls are wild, her print dress and sandals are cool, and her caramel skin is flawless. But Tia is one of my best friends, and I can tell that something isn't quite right. There's a tightness in her face and a few wrinkles in her dress. Her eyeliner is lopsided, and Leo (who normally looks like a child from a kids' clothing advert) is wearing mismatched sandals and it looks like his shorts are on back-to-front.

'Hi, Aunty Kelly, I got a lolly.' Leo waves an orange lolly at me before shoving it back in his mouth.

'That looks yummy.'

He nods vigorously.

'Hi, Kels,' Tia says wearily. 'How's it going?'

'Fine.' I give her a quick hug and briefly wonder whether I should confide in her about Sophie. But I promised I wouldn't say anything to anyone, and I like to think of myself as trustworthy. It's always the way that if you tell one person a secret, then they end up telling one other person and eventually the secret gets out. No. I'll stay silent. And anyway, if I told Tia the truth about everything that's going on in my life, we'd be here all week. Plus I don't want to burden her with my own problems; not when she seems so preoccupied and also a little down. 'How are you doing?'

'Oh, you know… It's… well…' She shakes her head and stares down at her feet.

'Tia, what's wrong?'

At that moment the door tinkles, and a group of women come into the shop, chatting and laughing. Tia gives a forced laugh. 'It's nothing. I'm fine. Probably hormones or something.'

I lower my voice. 'You and Ed okay?'

'Yeah, we're fine.' Her voice cracks. 'Leo, don't touch that, your fingers are sticky.'

Her cheeky son is under the table rummaging through a basket of toys.

'He's fine, don't worry about it. It's all second-hand stuff,' I say.

'Sorry, thank you. Actually, I was wondering if you had time for lunch?' She must sense my reluctance, because she puts her palms together and begs me with a puppy-dog look in her eyes.

I feel so bad for saying no, but I have to get back to check on Sophie. 'Tia, you know I'd love to, but there's some stuff I have to take care of at lunchtime. Could we maybe meet a bit later instead? What about this evening?'

'I really need to talk to you, Kels. Just a quick sandwich at Ida's? I wouldn't ask if it wasn't important.' Her eyes glisten as though she's about to cry.

Guilt tugs at my chest. My friend needs me. 'Yes, of course, okay.'

She exhales. 'Thank you!'

Maybe I'll have time to race back home to check on Sophie for a few minutes after our lunch. 'Is twelve too early?'

'Twelve is perfect. Thanks, Kels. I really do appreciate it.'

An older lady comes up to the counter asking to try on a dress.

'I'll leave you to it.' Tia kisses my cheek and tries to coax Leo away from the toys. Eventually she waves goodbye and I receive a sticky hug from Leo. I'm panicking about how I'm going to fit everything into my forty-five-minute lunch break, but I'm soon forced to turn my attention back to work. The shop appears to have filled up and there are people everywhere, rummaging through the rails and peering in all the baskets. I manage to make a few decent sales, so at least Derek will be pleased. It makes me happy too. The more money we raise, the better it is for our little community.

Half an hour later the shop has emptied out again. It looks like a tornado has whipped through the place. Why did I agree to have lunch with Tia today? There's no way I'll be able to make it home to see Sophie as well as having time for a chat with my friend. I'll have to skip the home visit and trust that Sophie will be okay on her own all day. I'm sure she'll be fine. I had to leave her alone yesterday and nothing bad happened. I should stop worrying about it.

Sophie doesn't have a mobile phone, but I gave her my number and told her to use the landline to call me if she needs to. I wonder whether I should call the landline now to let her know that I won't be home until later. But I'm not sure she'd even answer it. And what if she gets freaked out by the phone ringing? No. I'll leave it.

I tidy the shop, check my watch and see that it's already eleven thirty. I'm antsy, fidgety. I feel useless, which is ironic because I volunteered here to feel *more* useful. I nip into the stockroom and fetch my phone. Hopping up onto the stool behind the counter, I do a Google search for missing persons called Sophie. I don't even know her surname. As I type in her first name, I realise that it could very easily be fake. I never asked to see any ID. Although it didn't look like she had anything on her anyway. She wasn't carrying a bag or a purse. In fact, the more I think about it, the chances are that she probably *has* given me a different name.

The Google search results show quite a few missing people called Sophie. There are Facebook posts and tweets of missing girls, and online news stories of families searching for loved ones all over the world. I click on the Images results and scroll through all the photos. It's heartbreaking to see so many missing people. Where could they all have gone? But there are no pictures of the Sophie I know.

The girl is still a mystery.

CHAPTER FOURTEEN

FIONA

Molly's at the reception desk updating the online diary. 'Marion Scott called this morning about her bedroom curtain material. She wants you to go over with the swatches. But I can go instead, if you like? And the Carmichaels have rescheduled next weekend's appointment. I told them a week tomorrow at three is fine. Hope that's okay?' She's being surprisingly helpful and perky. In fact, Molly's been acting like a different person all morning, humming and walking around with a bounce in her step and generally being super-helpful.

'Sounds good.' I peer over her shoulder at today's schedule. 'Yes, if you could go over to Marion's that would be a real help. She lives up at—'

'It's okay, I've got her address. Milham Drive, out by the lake.'

'That's right. She'll probably want to go for the voile, but steer her towards something heavier – she'll thank me once winter hits.'

'No problem.'

I think that's the first time Molly's ever said 'no problem' to me. How come she isn't always like this? I would have loved to work with *this* Molly. I guess she's excited about her pregnancy and upcoming wedding. Although, call me cynical, she also said she wants to carry on working once she's settled into her new town and had the baby, so she'll be needing a good reference from me.

That's possibly the most likely reason for her sudden turnaround in attitude.

Well, I shouldn't complain. At least I'll have a willing assistant for the next four weeks. After that, who knows? I should probably start advertising for someone new, but I don't even know where to start. There's so much else going on that finding a new employee is the least of my worries. I slope reluctantly back into the showroom, glancing across at my two biggest problems – namely Cathleen and John. I wonder again if Molly might be the reason they're here. Would she really be that vindictive; to jeopardise my whole career just because I can be a bit of a hard-ass at work?

Cathleen and John are still beavering away in my office, periodically calling me in to answer questions about various transactions and receipts. Thank goodness I've been efficient at filing things away properly. But that still doesn't stop my stomach lurching in fear every time one of them pops their head out of the door to speak to me, worrying about what they may have stumbled across. So far, there have been no nasty surprises. Touch wood.

As expected, they commandeered my office all day yesterday, leaving work at the same time as me. I even stayed a bit later than usual in the hope that they'd knock off at five and I could have some time to myself, but they showed no sign of departing until *I* did. Consequently, I went home and then returned an hour later to have a snoop. I was paranoid they'd be camped outside the showroom waiting to catch me out, but there was no sign of them or their car. I don't know what I expected to find in there, but my nose around the office didn't yield anything. I wasn't really that surprised. It's inevitable that they'd keep all their notes on their laptops and not lying around for me to discover.

Molly bustles into the showroom, distracting me from my thoughts. 'Okay, that's all the messages answered, and your appointments are all up to date. You don't have any appointments today until your meeting with Kay Clarke at four.'

'Who?'

'You know, she's that local furniture maker who emailed asking to talk to you.'

'Oh, yeah, I remember. That's great, Molly. Thanks.'

'Is there anything else you want me to do before I get on with sorting out the curtain swatches?'

I almost want to laugh at Molly's new helpful persona. Can't she see how absurd this is after her complete apathy and indifference to the job? We both turn at the sound of the main door opening.

'Hello! Anyone around? Fifi, you here?'

Ugh, I recognise that voice.

'Want me to speak to him?' Molly asks, continuing to be uncharacteristically helpful. 'I could tell him you're not here, if you like?'

I can't say I'm not tempted to take her up on her offer. 'No, it's fine. He'll keep coming back to bug me if I don't see him now.' Taking a deep breath, I leave the showroom and walk into reception with a tired smile. 'Hello, Paul.'

In his late forties, Paul Barton is sporting a blue-check shirt, chinos and loafers, a bit of a change from his usual white coat. 'Fifi, you've been avoiding me. Don't think I didn't see you sneaking off down that side street yesterday. I'm offended.' He puts his hand to his heart, then runs a hand through dyed-brown hair that looks like it belongs on a Lego character.

I give him what I hope is my most bemused look whilst swearing in my head.

Paul owns the dental surgery next door. If it were possible, I'd ban him from ever coming in here. He irritates the hell out of me. Unfortunately he's been my dentist since I was a kid and still insists on calling me Fifi, as that was what my parents used to call me – and often still do. It's one thing for my mum to call me by my childhood nickname, but it's another for this twerp to use it. I've told him countless times to call me Fiona, but he just won't – I think he takes a perverse pleasure in winding me up – so I've given up correcting him. He's only sixteen years older than me but because he knew me as a child, he still treats me like one.

'Now, Fifi, have you had the opportunity to think about what we discussed?'

'Look, Paul, I'm really quite busy today. Could we talk about this some other time, do you think?'

He flashes me a polar-white grin and slicks his hair back again. 'That's what you told me last time. But this is a time-sensitive deal, sweetheart. You're going to miss out if you don't act quickly. Bet you haven't even mentioned it to that husband of yours. He'd tell you to snap my hand off. It makes good financial sense. You know it does.'

A few months ago, Paul told me he wants to expand his dental practice and take over half of my premises. He said he's prepared to pay me a lot for it. On the one hand, the money would be nice, and I don't really need all this space. But the thing is, I like having room in which to spread out. It looks good for a prestige business like mine. Plus, my rent isn't actually that high considering I'm smack bang in the centre of town. I can afford to keep the whole space, but if I took Paul up on his offer, I'd certainly save money. Only I might regret such a drastic decision.

'Honestly, Paul, I'll give it some serious consideration.'

'You said that last time.'

'How about I let you know by the end of the month, okay?'

He pouts. 'Fine. But come the first of August I'm withdrawing my offer and moving to the other side of town where there's a nice big property just waiting for me to move in. And then it'll be too late for you, *capiche*?'

'Yeah, sure.'

'Who are that lot in there?' Paul nods in the direction of my office.

That's all I need – Paul Barton getting wind of my tax audit.

His eyes narrow. 'Hmm, grey suits going through your stuff.'
He wags his finger at me. 'You been a naughty girl, Fifi?'

Right now, I want to punch Paul Barton. Molly, who's standing behind him, starts making violent stabbing motions at his back. She reads my mind so clearly that I choke back a giggle.

Paul smirks, thinking I'm laughing at his poor attempt at humour. 'Better put you on the naughty step.'

'It's nothing,' I lie. 'I've hired a firm of accountants to streamline the business, that's all.'

'Have you indeed? Well, you can tell them about my plan to lease half your showroom. That'll streamline things for you. Having a bit of a cashflow problem, eh?'

'Not at all.' Although if those tax inspectors find out what I've done, I'll have more than cashflow problems. Paul would love that. He'd be able to get his hands on the whole premises if my business went bust.

'That's a fancy-looking coffee machine, Feefs. Fancy firing her up? I could murder an Americano.'

How am I ever going to get rid of this bloody man? I glance at my watch. 'Look, Paul, I'd love to chat over a coffee, but I have to go out now. Got a lunchtime meeting.'

'Oh.' He thrusts out his bottom lip, like a sulky overgrown child. 'Fine, I'll walk out with you. We'll take a rain check on that coffee.'

I give Molly a shrug and grab my bag. Now I'm going to have to go out just to keep up the charade that I have a meeting. I leave the showroom with Paul at my side, tuning out his non-stop chatter about his proposed expansion into cosmetic dental surgery. Once we reach the pavement I ask him which way he's going.

'Back to the surgery, Feefs, where else?'

'Okay, well, I'm going this way.' I point in the opposite direction. 'I'll see you.'

'See you later, Fifi. And remember, end of the month is D-Day.'

'Yep.' I make off in the opposite direction, relieved to have got our encounter out of the way.

I always keep a selection of salads in the fridge at work, but today I'm really craving carbs so I think I might treat myself to a cheese roll from Ida's. As I approach the bakery, I see that there's already quite a queue out the door. I recognise a few familiar faces in the queue so if I join them, I'll have to make small talk. What am I even doing here? I should be back at the showroom getting on with my designs for the Carmichaels' place. I can't let the likes of Paul Barton and those tax inspectors put me off doing my job. I'm better than this. If I'm not careful, I'm going to drive myself out of business without the aid of anyone else.

I stop where I am and take a breath. I'm going to forget about the cheese roll. If I bump into Paul again, I'll just tell him the truth – that I'm too busy to talk. That I have work to be getting on with. I'm fed up of being polite to the man. As I turn to head back to Salinger's, I glance in through the bay window of Ida's. Beyond the cake display, I spot Tia and Leo seated at one of the tables. They're looking up, talking to someone. It's Kelly. She hangs her bag over the back of the chair and sits down at their table. Looks like they're all about to have lunch.

My chest constricts a little. I can't help but immediately feel hurt that they didn't ask me to join them. I know that's silly – I often meet up with one of my friends without the other. Okay, maybe not Tia, but I do see Kelly a lot on her own. It's just that Ida's is less than a minute away from where I work. Would it have been so hard for Kelly to pop her head in and ask me to come along too? Unless they're discussing something they don't want me to know about... No. Screw it. I'm not having a good day. I need to see my friends. I'm going in to have lunch with them. If they don't want me there, they can tell me to my face.

CHAPTER FIFTEEN

They've led her back to school. She thought it would be okay. Her friends sounded so adamant that this was the right thing to do. They wouldn't take no for an answer. So she let them persuade her to come back. And now the stink of the place has caught in her throat and snaked its way into her mind. It's crept beneath her clothes and infused her skin. She never knew that a smell could infect your whole body.

She's shaking as she walks back down the warm corridor, her limbs soft, her brain soggy. Her friends are kind and soothing, but she can't make sense of the words. They're fading in and out of clarity. She catches fragments of comforting phrases interspersed with a hushed, frantic conversation.

'It's okay' … 'We're nearly there' … 'She looks really pale' … 'Should we call her parents?' … 'I can't believe it' … 'He might not even be there' … 'Horrendous' … 'Shhh.'

They stop outside a door. A quick glance up shows it's the headmaster's office. One of her friends clears her throat and knocks.

'Come in!' Mr Williams' voice is brusque and authoritarian.

She wants to leave so badly now. To run back down the corridor and out of the main doors. To keep running forever. Instead, the headmaster's door opens, and she walks in, her friends flanking her like armed guards.

They talk to Mr Williams while he gives quiet rumbling responses. He leaves the room for a short while before returning with Mrs Bonnington, the deputy head.

Mrs Bonnington ushers her over to a chair where she sits, mute.

Her friends explain what happened on her behalf. She told them what happened in great gushing detail. But now she never wants to speak of it again. She wishes the whole thing could be erased from her mind. But it's lodged in there like a tick sucking out fresh blood and leaving behind disease.

She hears her friends going over it all. Speaking a version of her original words. First there was the thing itself. Then there was her own retelling. And now there's yet another iteration. Another layer of the truth being laid down as the birds outside sing and the warm wind sighs through the trees.

She listens to them tell of how Mr Lawson kissed her. How he touched her, and he wouldn't stop. How his hands were everywhere, all over her body, beneath her clothes. How she had to fight him off and run away.

But the thing she hasn't told them is that she thought she liked him. She thought she wanted him to kiss her. Only, the thing is, as soon as he had bent to kiss her, she realised that this wasn't what she wanted at all. The fantasy in her head was different to the reality of here and now. This grown-up man wasn't what she wanted. She got scared and told him to stop. She'd tried to pull away. She had told him 'no'.

But he hadn't listened. He hadn't listened at all.

CHAPTER SIXTEEN

Friday

TIA

Kelly arrives at the café at noon on the dot. I've already been here for fifteen minutes, which was probably a mistake because Leo's already finished his milkshake and now his sugar rush is kicking in. He's fidgeting in his chair and whining about being bored. I should have got him to burn off some energy in the park first, but I wanted to arrive in plenty of time in case Kelly managed to get here early. I feel a bit bad asking her to give up her lunch break to meet me when it was clear she had other stuff to do. But I wouldn't have asked if I wasn't desperate.

'Mummy, I want a sausage roll.' Leo points to the counter.

'*Please*,' I admonish.

'Please. I want a sausage roll.'

'The lady will come in a minute and you can tell her what you want. But you have to say *please*, all right?'

'Aw right.'

'Hey, Tia.' Kelly sits down opposite me and leans closer, speaking quietly so no one else can hear. 'Everything okay? You seemed a bit upset earlier. I wanted to come and see how you were, but I couldn't leave the shop.'

Her kindness is going to undo me. Now that she's here, I'm desperate to tell her what's been going on, to unburden myself, but I'm not even sure where to start. She doesn't have a long break, so I think I'm just going to have to launch straight into it. I wipe Leo's hands with a napkin and give him my iPhone to play on. That's probably the only thing in the known universe that will keep him occupied for more than ten minutes. I also give him my earbuds to keep him from eavesdropping. Once he's settled, I lean forward in my chair. I realise my heart is thumping in my ears. I'm nervous about telling my friend.

What if she doesn't believe me? Or, worse, what if she saw me going off with a man at the club but hasn't said anything? Maybe she and Fiona have been discussing that night behind my back. But that's ridiculous. Kelly isn't like that. She would tell me straight. She would ask me outright. Anyway, I'm almost positive that those photographs are fake.

'Well…' I begin.

Kelly waits for me to go on.

'Hi.' A familiar voice interrupts my attempt to explain what's been going on. I look up and try not to let my disappointment and annoyance show when I see who it is. It's Fiona. What's she doing here?

'Hi, Fi.' Kelly turns and gives her a warm smile.

'Hey,' I say quietly, hoping she's just here to say a quick hello and then leave.

She seems a little unsure of herself, which isn't at all like Fiona. She's usually so self-possessed and confident. 'I was just walking past and saw you guys through the window.'

'We're just having a quick sandwich,' Kelly says, flushing. I can tell she feels bad for not asking Fi to join us. 'But I know you don't usually eat carbs.'

'Actually, I'm craving a cheese roll.' Fiona gives a nervous laugh.

'Sounds good, you should let loose and order one,' I say, trying to keep my voice light. Trying not to blurt out that I want her to leave because I'm in the middle of a really important conversation.

'Actually, do you mind if I gatecrash your lunch? I need cheering up.'

My heart sinks.

Kelly flashes me a blink-and-you'll-miss-it apologetic smile. 'Of course you can. They haven't taken our order yet. Come and sit.'

'Is that okay, Tee?' She turns to me and looks for a moment like a lost little girl.

I feel like a total cow for having such mean thoughts about her. 'Of course it's okay. That would be lovely.' I try to push my disappointment away. 'We haven't caught up for ages.'

Fiona sits in the empty chair and I resign myself to the fact that my problems will have to remain unspoken for a while longer.

'How are things with you, Tee?' Fiona asks.

'I'm okay.'

'She was just about to tell me something,' Kelly says, oblivious to my discomfort, which isn't like her at all. She's normally pretty sensitive to other people. She turns back to me. 'Maybe we could both help with whatever it is?'

'No, it's fine. It's nothing.'

'I've interrupted something.' Fiona's face reddens again, and she stumbles to her feet. 'I'll leave you two to chat.'

'Fi!' Kelly cries. She and I exchange another fleeting look. 'Fi, sit down.'

I put a hand on her arm. 'Stay, Fiona. You haven't interrupted anything. You're my friend too. I just didn't want to bore you with school stuff.' I decide that there's no way I'm telling Fiona about the photos. Maybe I'll tell her about the incident with Rosie instead. That way, she won't feel like I'm keeping something from her. I'm also still not entirely convinced that it isn't Fiona behind the photos. For all I know, her uncharacteristic nervousness might be due to a guilty conscience.

'I…' Fiona stands for a moment, not making a move to either leave or sit back down.

'Fiona, don't be silly, sit down.' I give her the warmest smile I can muster.

'Are you sure?'

'Yes!' Kelly and I chorus.

She sits back down, and we all relax a little. Leo hasn't even noticed the drama; he's wrapped up in his video game.

'Thanks, guys,' Fiona says, waving a waitress over. 'I've had a crap day and could do with a bit of girl talk.'

'What's happened?' I'm keen to deflect the conversation away from myself.

'You know Molly, my assistant? She's just handed in her notice. She's pregnant and she's moving away.'

'Sorry to hear that,' I say, thinking that's nothing compared to a possible blackmailer sending incriminating photos that have the potential to blow apart your marriage. But I have to stop thinking such uncharitable thoughts. Fiona doesn't know what's going on with me, so it's not her fault. Unless she does know what's going on with me and this is all an act.

'That's a shame,' Kelly says, 'but I thought you said she wasn't that great at her job?'

'Yeah, I know. I guess she's probably done me a favour in the long run, but it's going to be such a pain trying to find someone to replace her. Ashridge isn't exactly awash with interior-design assistants. Plus Paul Barton is hassling me about wanting to take over half the studio.'

'Creepy Barton?' I give a shudder.

'Yes. I've told him I'll think about it. But anyway, I didn't mean to make this all about me. What's happening with you guys? Tell me some good news. Something cheerful, or funny.'

Kelly and I both look blank. There's certainly nothing cheerful going on in my life at the moment. I wrack my brains to think of something. 'We've got the regatta tomorrow; that should be fun.'

Fiona nods. 'You're right. Nathan and Ed are both racing, which will be great to watch.'

I glare at Fiona and shake my head. She instantly bites her lip. We both turn to look at Kelly. She must be feeling weird about the regatta – Michael always used to race too. Kelly didn't feel up to attending last year as it was too soon after he died, so it's a big deal that she's even going this year.

'Oh, Kelly, I'm so sorry.' Fiona puts a hand on her arm. 'That was really insensitive of me.'

'No, no, don't be silly. Yes, Michael used to race, but it'll still be fun to watch Nathan and Ed. I'm looking forward to it. In fact, we should treat it like a mini holiday. A break from all the stresses of everyday life. Why don't we all meet up and have a group picnic like the old days? All three families together.' Her voice is upbeat, but there's a forcedness about it. As though she's trying to convince herself that everything's fine.

'Sounds good,' I reply awkwardly.

'Yep, count me and Nathan in.'

'Can I take your order, ladies?' A waitress stands by my side with a notepad in her hand. She takes Kelly and Fiona's order and begins to walk off.

I call after her. 'Excuse me, I haven't ordered yet.' But she doesn't appear to have heard me. Before I have a chance to catch her, she's gone back out to the kitchen. 'Can you keep an eye on Leo a sec?' I go up to the counter where they're serving the takeaway customers. 'Hi, Ida…'

She holds a finger up. 'You'll have to get to the back of the queue.'

'Yes, but—'

'Uh-uh, back of the queue.'

'I'm at a table.'

'Then it's waitress service. Sit down and they'll get to you.'

In all the years I've been coming here, I've never known Ida be so rude. What's going on? I slouch back to the table and sit down.

'What happened?' Kelly asks.

'That waitress acted like I wasn't here. You saw that, right?'

'I don't know…' Fiona says. 'I think she's just busy and got distracted.'

'So I went up to Ida to give her my order and she told me to get to the back of the queue or sit back down. Like I'm some sort of school kid.' Normally I wouldn't take that kind of rudeness from anyone. I don't know what's up with me. Or rather, I do know what's up with me, and I don't like it. I don't feel at all like myself.

'Let me go and have a word.' Kelly gets up. 'What do you want, Tee?'

'A sausage roll for Leo and a chicken salad wrap for me.' But, actually, I feel like telling them to stuff their business up their arses before storming out.

Kelly goes up to the counter. I see her talk to Ida who gives her a warm smile and a nod.

'Did she take the order from you?' I ask when Kelly gets back.

'Yeah, no problem.'

'Thanks.' I shake my head in disbelief. What the hell was all that about? The waitress deliberately ignored me and then Ida was downright rude.

'You okay?' Fiona asks.

I want to yell, *No, I'm not okay!* I really wish I'd never pushed Kelly into coming to meet me for lunch. It's been a total waste of time. Rather than making me feel better, I now feel ten times worse. I want to cry with stress and frustration. Someone's sending me disturbing photos, there are rumours going around that I'm a murderer, and, to top it all, everyone in town and at school seems to hate me. *What the hell is going on?*

'Yep, fine,' I reply, not wanting her to see that I'm rattled. But I'm not sure how long I can keep all this bottled up.

CHAPTER SEVENTEEN

KELLY

I push open my front door. Luckily Derek agreed to let me close the shop early so I could be home when the kids get back from school. Normally they walk home and let themselves in when I'm at work, but because Sophie's here, I'm not comfortable leaving them all together without me. Just in case something happens.

They shouldn't be back for at least another half hour, which is perfect, as that will give me enough time to talk to Sophie about what she plans to do next. I'm not sure how much good a talk will do, but she can't expect to stay here forever. I want to help her, of course I do, but hiding away in my attic isn't going to fix whatever's been going on in her life.

I'll also have to call Tia later. I feel bad that she didn't get a chance to talk about whatever it is that's upsetting her. I thought she might open up to me and Fiona, but it was clear that she didn't want to say anything in front of Fi. Not sure why because Fiona's always been good at giving out advice. True, it's not always the advice people want to hear – I guess she can sometimes be a bit too honest. But Tia's also quite straight talking. I sense there might be some awkwardness between those two. Maybe things will settle down after our group picnic at the regatta tomorrow. I hope so. And I also hope Ryan isn't going to be difficult. I have this niggling feeling he might refuse to come, and I really don't want to leave him at home while we're all supposed to be there having fun. Especially if Sophie's still going to be here.

I step inside the house and close the door behind me. And then I freeze. My nerve endings prickle. There are voices coming from the kitchen. I cock my ear. There's music playing, and it sounds like someone's laughing. It must be Sophie. Has she let someone else into the house? I don't think I'm very comfortable with that. No, I'm definitely not happy. In fact, my palms have begun to sweat. What if it's her abusive partner who's discovered where she is?

There's another short burst of laughter. I know that voice. It sounds like…

I stride into the kitchen and throw open the door. Despite it being a bright day outside, the blinds are closed, and the lights are on. I realise that Sophie is still wary of anyone spotting her through the windows.

Right now, she's leaning against the kitchen counter with a cup of tea, while Ryan and Sonny are seated at the kitchen table, their homework spread out before them. The radio's playing some dance track while a DJ talks about tomorrow's breakfast show. Sophie immediately straightens up when she sees me, her eyes wide and suddenly fearful.

'Hi, Mum!' Sonny waves. 'Sophie's helping us with our home-work. She's really good at it.'

'Hello.' I'm not sure what to make of this scene. 'Why are you two home so early?'

Sonny rolls his eyes in an exact imitation of his brother. 'It was a half day, Mum. Teacher training. You forgot.'

'So how long have you been back?'

'Ages,' Sonny replies. 'Sophie helped us make lunch.'

'Uh, I hope that's okay.' She's almost cowering. I hate to think that I'm the reason for her uneasiness.

'Of course that's okay.' I smile, trying to put her at ease. 'I'm grateful to you for helping them.'

'Oh, I'm happy to do it. They've been telling me all about the regatta. Sounds great. I'd love to be able to sail. It sounds like such good fun.'

'I could teach you, if you like?' Ryan says, reddening.

I realise he might have a bit of a crush.

'I'd love to take you up on that one day,' she replies. 'I didn't realise you were a sailor.'

'He's really good,' Sonny pipes up. 'He used to win all his races.'

'Used to?' Sophie gives Ryan a questioning look.

I walk over to the kettle, gasping for a cup of tea.

'It's just boiled,' Sophie says.

'Great. Dying for a cuppa. Do you want a top up?'

'No, I'm fine thanks.' She turns back to Ryan. 'So, does that mean you aren't racing tomorrow?'

Ryan's face clouds over and he shakes his head.

'That's a shame. Why not?'

'He doesn't sail anymore,' Sonny says.

'Shut up, Sonny,' Ryan mutters.

'Hey!' I turn to my eldest son. 'Don't talk to your brother like that.'

'Why don't you sail anymore?' Sophie asks. 'Sorry, don't mean to be nosy. It's just, if you're so good at it, it seems a shame not to carry on.'

I wait for Ryan's rude response. I can't even mention sailing these days without him snapping my head off. But to my surprise, he slumps down in his chair and sighs. 'I wish I *was* sailing tomorrow.'

I have to play it carefully now. Too much enthusiasm from me could put him off. I try to sound as casual as possible. 'It's not too late. I can get you entered if you like?'

'Really?'

My heart swells at the hopeful light shining in his eyes.

'Yes, of course.'

'But I haven't practised in ages.'

I check my watch. 'There's normally a Friday training session at four. Why don't you go and get changed and join them. Then, if you feel up to it, you can ask if they can put your name down for the under twelves.'

'Do you think?'

'I just said so, didn't I?'

'Thanks, Mum, you're the best!' Ryan gets to his feet and races out of the room, his feet pounding up the stairs.

I'm the *best*? This is a Ryan I haven't seen for months. How come it's taken a virtual stranger to turn my sad and moody child into a boy who's almost excited about life again? Offering Sophie some temporary shelter may just have been the best decision I ever made. I glance over to see her talking to Sonny about his science homework. He's really listening to her, totally engaged. I shake my head in wonder. She's a regular Mary Poppins.

Sophie and I are sitting in the lounge, with the blinds and curtains drawn, eating cheesy pasta off trays on our laps. The kids ate earlier, as Ryan was ravenous after he got home from training. Turns out one of the juniors got sick and had to pull out of the under twelves race, so Ryan managed to nab their spot. He's on cloud nine, and I'm pretty sure it's all down to Sophie. I managed to persuade him to have an early night so he's fresh for the race tomorrow; he didn't take too much convincing, as he was shattered from his time out on the lake.

Conversation between Sophie and I has been a little stilted so far. She said she was fine having her dinner in the attic, but I thought it would be weird with her up there and me down here, so I said she should come down. I also need to broach the subject of what she's going to do next.

I chew my food slowly and try not to dwell on the silence of the room. I usually read or watch TV in the evenings, followed by an early night. It's strange having company. 'I don't know what you said to Ryan earlier, but I haven't seen him this happy in ages.'

'Really?' Sophie's feet are pulled up under her as she delicately spears a broccoli floret with her fork and pops it into her mouth. 'I didn't do or say anything special. The three of us just chatted while they did their homework.'

'Well, whatever you did, thank you. I can't tell you how much it means to have him actually talk to me without grunting.'

She shrugs. 'He's a teenager, I guess.'

'Nope. He's only eleven. Tall for his age though. And another thing, how did you get them to do their homework? They usually leave it until the last minute on Sunday evening.'

'I don't know. I was up in the attic and I heard the front door slam. I thought it was you so I came down. When I saw it was your children, I wasn't sure what to do. But Sonny was really cute and friendly and asked what was for lunch. So I thought I'd make them something – hope that was okay? I couldn't think of what to talk to them about at first, so I just asked about school. Ryan said he had some really hard maths homework. I offered to help him with it after lunch.'

'Well, I'm grateful.'

'Not as grateful as I am.' Sophie looks down at her barely touched pasta and sets down her fork. 'Actually, I'm not really very hungry. Do you mind if I...?'

'No, that's fine. Leave it if you don't want it.'

'Sorry. It's a waste.'

'No, it's...' I shake my head. I seem to have lost my appetite too. I put my tray on the coffee table. 'Actually, Sophie, we should probably have a chat about what you want to do next.'

She gives a brief nod and stares down into her pasta bowl.

'Have you managed to have a think about it?'

'I don't know.' Her voice is small and wavery.

I feel like such a bitch for pushing her. But she can't stay here indefinitely. Especially as I don't even know what it is she's running from. 'Can you at least tell me what kind of trouble you're in?'

'It's complicated. It's better if I don't tell you.'

I don't like the sound of that. By helping her out, could I have put myself and the kids in danger? 'Look, you know I'm taking Sonny and Ryan to the regatta tomorrow, so you're welcome to stay here another day. And then it's Sunday, so you may as well stay here for the weekend. But let's work out a plan for Monday, okay? We'll ring round a few shelters and get you fixed up with some proper help.'

Sophie nods again without looking up. 'Thank you.'

I feel guilty for putting a timescale on this, but I can't have her living with us permanently. 'So you're okay with me contacting a shelter?'

She shrugs.

'I think it's for the best.'

'I don't know. But you've been really kind letting me stay. There aren't too many people like you in the world.' Sophie's tone suddenly turns bitter.

'I'm sure there are.'

Her lip curls into a cynical sneer and she shakes her head. I notice her fists are clenched. 'People are mainly horrible. And that's me being nice about them.'

'Well, hopefully your life will get better and you'll meet some good people.'

'I doubt it.'

A series of heavy thumps on the front door makes me sit up.

'Are you expecting visitors?' Sophie asks, her eyes wide.

'No, I'm not. Unless… it could be my friend Tia, but she's never thumped on the door like that.'

'Don't answer it!' Sophie slides her tray off her lap and onto the sofa cushion next to her before jumping to her feet. 'We should go upstairs. Hide.'

My heart starts racing at the fear in her eyes. '*Hide?* This is my house. Whoever it is can't get in. The doors and windows are all locked.'

'That won't stop him.'

'This is ridiculous.' I stand and try to think what to do. There's another series of thumps on the door. 'I'll have to answer it. Whoever it is, is going to wake the boys up and I don't want them involved or frightened. You go on up to the attic and don't come down until I tell you.'

'Aren't you coming with me?'

'No. I'll get rid of them.'

'How? Don't let them in, will you?'

'Quick, go on upstairs.' I walk out of the lounge and turn off the hall light, ushering Sophie out and up the stairs. She starts to say something else, but I give her a stern glare and wave her away. I think I must look braver than I feel.

Once her footsteps have receded and I hear the distant sound of the attic door closing, I take a breath, put the chain across the door and pull it open.

CHAPTER EIGHTEEN

FIONA

I slip on the oven mitt and slide the salmon en croûte out of the oven. It's far too hot to be cooking, but Nathan is fond of home-cooked meals whenever he manages to make it back in time for dinner, so I always keep a few standby meals in the freezer.

Right now, Nathan's sitting at the table out on the deck. He's sipping a glass of wine and scrolling through his phone. I won't say anything, even though he always has a go at me if I ever dare to look at my phone while we're eating. His short brown waves are perfectly swept back off his face by insanely priced hair wax. Even his relaxing-around-the-house clothes are smart – a pale-grey short-sleeved shirt, designer shorts and sunglasses. Beneath my apron I'm wearing an Issey Miyake green crepe dress that Nathan bought me last month. He said it looked perfect with my chestnut hair and hazel eyes. My hair is naturally wavy, but Nathan prefers it when it's straightened.

I dish up the salmon, remove my apron and take the plates outside. There's already a bowl of mixed salad leaves and a bottle of chilled wine on the table. Nathan looks up and smiles, setting his phone down next to his plate.

'This looks and smells amazing, Fi. So do you.' He looks me up and down appreciatively.

'Thanks. Hope it tastes as good.'

'I'm sure it will. You're a fantastic cook. I'm so lucky to have such a talented wife.' He leans back in his seat. 'Successful in business, incredible in the kitchen and spectacular in the bedroom.'

Normally I'd lap up his praise, but today I don't feel anywhere near as wonderful as he's making out. I feel like I'm barely holding it all together.

Nathan's expression darkens at my lack of response. 'Everything okay, Fi? I just complimented you, you know.'

'Sorry, Nath. Thanks. I'm not quite with it. Got some stuff on my mind.'

'What stuff?' He cuts into the salmon en croûte, and stabs a chunk with his fork, blowing on it gently.

'Molly handed in her notice.'

Nathan takes his first mouthful and chews. 'Delicious. You could give Ed a run for his money, Fi. Set up a rival gastropub.'

'Thanks. It's quite easy to make though.'

'Don't run yourself down. I've told you about that before. You're a bloody good cook.'

'Yes, okay, you're right. Sorry. Did you hear what I said about Molly?'

My plan is to mention the fact she's pregnant and see what his reaction is. The thing is, if *I've* started having maternal thoughts, maybe *his* mind has changed too. Maybe he'll be open to the idea of having a family. Although part of me knows that if this was the case he'd have let me know straight away. I've never known Nathan to shy away from saying what he thinks. I always used to love that about him. His directness.

When Nathan and I first met it was refreshing to have a man tell me he liked me without playing all those ridiculous dating games. He actually called me when he said he was going to call, rather than waiting an arbitrary amount of time so as 'not to seem too keen'. It felt like I was being wooed by a proper man, not some stupid kid who didn't know his own mind. Nathan certainly wasn't afraid of commitment. He knew what he wanted, and he went for it. And what he wanted was *me*. But how might he feel about the idea of children now? I need to plant a seed without being too obvious.

'So Molly's leaving.' He shrugs. 'So what? Big deal. Assistants like Molly grow on trees. She's not exactly winning any employee of the year awards.'

I need to play this carefully. 'It's nice she's pregnant though. Her boyfriend proposed as soon as he found out and they're moving away to be closer to family. It's exciting for them. Starting their own family. A new adventure…'

Nathan takes a few more mouthfuls and then breaks to pour some more wine. I've barely touched my food. My appetite seems to have disappeared. I blame cooking in the heat, but deep down I know it's more than that. Nathan is deliberately not engaging with my conversation. It's boring him. He doesn't want to talk about assistants and babies. He isn't interested in starting a family, and I don't feel brave enough to tell him how I really feel.

I briefly think about mentioning the tax officers, but those words stick in my throat too. Instead, I pick up my wine glass and take a few large gulps. The cold liquid feels good sliding down my throat. I like the way it blurs my thoughts and dulls my anxieties, blocks things out, allowing me to gaze out across the water and imagine I'm a bird skimming across the surface of the lake, heading out somewhere far from here where there are no worries.

'How's the Carmichael job?' Nathan asks.

'Good. They're going super contemporary.'

'Sounds expensive. That'll be good for your portfolio.'

'Although they do like to change their minds, so who knows what we'll end up with.'

'You need to be firmer. Show them your design and make them stick with it. Don't take any shit.'

I nod. 'You're right.'

'You know it.' He raises his glass to mine, and we clink.

Although it's not as simple as telling clients what they want. You have to tread carefully around people like the Carmichaels. They need to feel like they're in control. Like it's their own vision and I simply carried it out for them. They want all the creative glory for themselves. That's why I'm so successful – I praise and flatter my clients for their impeccable taste, even though the ideas are all mine. I won't try to explain this to Nathan. He'll tell me I'm being ridiculous.

I take another sip of wine. 'Paul Barton called round today.'

'What does that dickhead want? Is he hassling you about taking over the showroom again?'

'It's fine.' I put my glass down. 'I've told him I'll give him my decision by the end of the month.'

'Fi, there is no decision. Tell him to piss off. Better yet, I'll tell him.'

'No, no, don't worry, it's fine.'

'It's not fine. You need to keep hold of that showroom. Salinger's is a prestigious business. It'll send out the wrong message if you downsize. And I won't be able to recommend you to any of my colleagues if you run a poky little shop rather than an impressive showroom.'

Nathan has never recommended Salinger's to a single one of his work colleagues, but sometimes, especially after a few drinks, he likes to take credit for keeping my business going, even though he has absolutely nothing to do with it.

'Don't forget, that's *my* name attached to it.'

'Hello.' I give him a little wave. 'Fiona *Salinger* here.' I grin to show him I'm teasing.

He smiles back. 'You know what I mean, Fi. Everyone knows who I am. They know that's my name. I didn't mind you naming your business Salinger's, but you have to realise that because it has my family's name, it has to keep up a certain reputation.'

I don't remind him that *he* suggested I change the name of my business from *Fiona's* to *Salinger's*, because he said it sounded more premium. He was right, of course. The surname is much better. But it irks me when he acts like he did me this huge favour letting me use the name.

I suddenly realise that if Nathan finds out about the tax audit from someone else – someone like Paul Barton, who has a way of discovering everyone else's business – he'll be absolutely furious. The thought chills me. I don't think I have any choice but to say something about it. I take another huge sip of wine and decide to launch straight into it.

'Nathan, there's something else I need to talk to you about.'

His head snaps up. Under his steady gaze, I really feel like chickening out, but I can't risk not telling him. His eyes narrow. 'Well? What is it?'

I spoon some salad leaves onto my plate for something to do. 'It's probably nothing. Just a random spot-check thing, but… I'm having a tax audit.'

He frowns and nods. 'A tax audit? Okay, that's fine. When are they coming?'

'They're already here. Two of them. They arrived on Wednesday, but I didn't get a chance to tell you.'

'What? So they're already at Salinger's?'

'Yes. They've taken over my office.'

'Hmm, that's not good.' He leans back in his chair and scratches his cheek. 'How long are they going to be there for? Did they give you an idea of timescales?'

'It can take days or weeks. They can't be more specific unfortunately.' I know I should tell him the rest, but I can't bring myself to do it. Maybe the inspectors won't find anything, and they'll simply leave. Then things can go back to how they were before. But I realise I'm kidding myself. I'm in a financial mess and there's no way to get out of it without telling Nathan the whole story. Just… not tonight.

'Right, well, you've got nothing to hide, have you?'

I shake my head. 'Nothing that springs to mind.'

'Good. So it'll be fine. Just do everything they ask. Be really helpful, and they'll eventually leave. Do they work evenings?'

'No. They leave when I leave.'

'Good. That'll give you a chance to go and check what they've been up to.'

Nathan seems remarkably calm, for which I'm grateful. I thought he might blame me. I thought it might lead to us getting into a fight and him getting angry. I allow my shoulders to relax and unclamp my jaw. My appetite has even come back. I try a small bite of the salmon – not bad, though I say it myself. I allow myself a few more mouthfuls before setting my knife and fork down on the plate.

'You've got such a tiny appetite, Fi.' He gives me an appreciative smile. 'Not like your friends – Kelly and Tia eat like pigs.' He chuckles. Even though Nathan likes home-cooked meals, he isn't too keen on me eating them myself. Not that he says anything specifically. It's more a feeling I get. Consequently, I've trained myself to eat really small portions.

'I really don't know what you see in those two,' he continues. 'I know you were all friends at school, but they don't really fit into your life any more, do they?'

'They're my oldest friends,' I protest. But, thinking about it, he's right about Tia. We have nothing in common any more.

'Well, I think you should cut them loose. Make some new friends – ones who'll be good for your business.'

'Maybe… but it's nice having friends who aren't linked to work.'

'If you say so.' He shrugs.

I wait for him to finish his plate and start clearing the table while he goes through to the lounge and switches on the TV. Once

I'm done and the kitchen is immaculate once more, I slip off my heels and follow him through to the lounge, where I snuggle up next to him on the sofa.

'What do you fancy watching tonight? A series or a movie?' I ask.

Nathan leans away from me and gives me an enquiring look. 'What are you doing, Fi?'

A chill slides down my back. I know that tone. I knows he's trying to catch me out. *Think, think.* What have I done to annoy him? What have I forgotten? 'I… Sorry, Nath, did you want something else? Tea? Some dessert?' Even though Nathan never eats dessert, I try to think what I could whip up. Maybe a fruit salad… or I could nip to the shops. Maybe Kelly's got something. She's bound to have a freezer full of desserts for the boys.

'You don't think you get to sit and watch TV when you've screwed-up so badly,' Nathan sneers.

My heart is pounding now. Knocking so violently against my ribcage that it actually hurts. Nathan's eyes are stony. I'm so stupid. Why did I have to tell him what's going on with the tax audit? I should have kept it to myself. 'No, of course not.' I jump to my feet. 'I'll… I'll go to bed.'

'Bed?' He shakes his head and smiles incredulously. 'No time for sleep, Fi. You're going to have to head back to the office and go through your accounts with a fine-toothed comb. You need to make sure your business is squeaky clean.'

'It is, Nathan. You don't need to worry on that score.' I can't think about the reality of the situation. I can't give Nathan a hint of the truth – that the legitimacy of my business is balanced on a knife edge. That any day now the auditors could come across a receipt that will tip them off to what I've been doing.

'It better be clean. Because I can't afford any hint of a scandal. I work in finance, Fi. *Finance.* I won't have us the subject of gossip. I won't have my reputation dragged through the mud. Is that clear?'

'Of course.'

'*Of course.*' He mimics my nervous tone, shakes his head and laughs. 'Go on then. Off you trot. And don't think about coming back until you've checked and double-checked every single piece of paper in that office.'

I stumble out of the room with the taste of salmon en croûte in my throat and the acidic burn of white wine in my gullet. Nathan isn't going to let this drop until the auditors have given my business the all clear. *But I'm not sure that's ever going to happen.*

CHAPTER NINETEEN

KELLY

With trembling fingers, I open the front door as far as it will go with the chain attached. I peer out to see a man standing a couple of paces back, illuminated beneath the security light. Despite the warmth of the evening, he's wearing a navy hoodie and a baseball cap. His eyes are blue, and he looks to be somewhere in his twenties. His face isn't one I recognise.

'Hello?' My voice sounds calmer than I feel.

'Hi.' He shifts from one foot to the other and rubs at the dark stubble on his chin.

'Can I help?' I smile but it feels fake, so I stop.

'Sorry to disturb you.' His voice is soft and deep. 'I'm looking for someone.'

This must be the man Sophie has run away from. I wonder what he did to her. 'Oh?'

'It's my wife…'

I wait for him to go on. Looking closer, I notice that his eyes are a little bloodshot.

'It's just… she's missing. She's been missing for a few days… so I've been knocking on doors all over town asking if anyone's seen her.'

I wasn't expecting this. I thought the person looking for Sophie would be somewhat rougher. Angrier. More intimidating somehow.

But maybe that's his plan. Maybe he's trying to appear nice to lull me into a false sense of security, so that I'll give Sophie up.

I flinch as he pulls something out of his hoodie pocket. But then I realise it's just a phone. He taps the screen a couple of times and holds it out. 'This is my wife. This is Sophie. Don't suppose you've seen her?' He swallows. 'I'm really worried for her safety. She has a few issues.'

Issues? The photo on the phone is indeed one of Sophie. She's standing in a sunny garden, the light shining on her face. She's radiant; smiling at the person taking the photo. I really want to ask him about the issues he's talking about. I want to question this man about Sophie and what he's done to make her so afraid of him. But I can't let him know that I've seen her. That she is, in fact, staying in my attic. So I frown and shake my head. 'She doesn't look familiar. Is she from around here?' I wonder if my lies are convincing.

He looks disappointed, his shoulders sagging. He massages his temple. 'We live just outside town. Sophie disappeared some time during Tuesday night. It was weird – I woke up and she was gone. But she wouldn't just leave like that, not without saying anything. We're in love. We have a great relationship. Something must have happened…' He puts the phone back in his pocket and starts scratching his forearm. 'So? Are you sure you haven't seen her?'

'Sorry, I don't think so, no.'

'Think hard. Maybe you passed her in town, or on the street. She's not a forgettable person.' His eyes are boring into mine. I'm convinced he must know I'm lying.

'Like I said, I'm sorry, but I've never seen her before. Have you been to the police? Reported her missing?'

'They're useless. I know they don't believe me. They think she must have left willingly. But she wouldn't do that.'

I find it interesting that he's saying he's reported her missing to the police. I wonder if he really has. Because if he's been abusive towards her, then would he really go to the police? But then again, other people's issues are often more complicated than they first seem. There are always two sides to every story. Not that there's any excuse to treat another person badly, but the man before me seems so sincere.

He pulls something else out of his pocket. It looks like a piece of scrunched-up paper, but then I see it's actually a small pile of paper slips. He hands one to me. 'Here's my name and phone number, in case you see her. Even if you're unsure whether it's my wife or not, will you call me? Because I can't eat, I can't sleep, not until I know she's okay.'

'Uh, sure.' I glance at the slip and see the name *Greg* followed by some scribbled digits.

'Greg.'

He nods.

'What's your last name?'

'Jones.'

'Greg Jones? And your wife is called Sophie? So, Sophie Jones, yeah?'

His eyes narrow.

'In case I see her.'

His shoulders relax. 'I'm really worried for her safety. I feel like I'm in a nightmare.'

If I didn't know better, I'd swear he was telling the truth. 'If I see her I'll call you.' The lie catches in my throat and I cough.

'Thanks,' he mutters.

'Good luck.' I swallow.

He fixes me with a final, piercing stare that quite unnerves me. Then he nods and walks away.

I close the door and realise that my whole body is shaking. That I can hardly breathe. I only hope I managed to keep my nerves hidden well enough from him, because if he suspects Sophie's here, I don't know what he'll do. Maybe everything he said about going door to door was a lie. Maybe he already knows she's here. He could possibly have spotted her through the window at some time over the past day. I rush back into the lounge and stare critically at both windows – the curtains are fully drawn with no gaps, and the blinds are closed behind them. I'm sure there's no way he could see anything through there.

But what about while I was out at work? Perhaps Sophie walked past an exposed window without thinking. Or maybe one of the kids let something slip at school? This is stupid. My imagination is running away. If he's a dangerous person and he knows she's here, he would have tried to force his way in. Surely he would have seemed more threatening and mean, but he just seemed worried and exhausted.

I'm tempted to peer out of the window to see if Greg really is going door to door. But I'm too nervous to look. What if he's standing outside and watching the house? The thought makes me shiver.

'Kelly…' It's Sophie calling down quietly from the top of the stairs. 'Was it him? Has he gone?'

'Stay up there,' I hiss. 'He could still be outside.'

'Oh my God, it *was* him wasn't it? How did he know I was here? How did he find me?'

'Shh. Let me just check the back door's locked and then I'll come upstairs.'

'Be careful, Kelly. He's not a nice man.'

At her words, my heart knocks uncomfortably in my chest and I start to think that I must be crazy for inviting this drama into my home. But then my mind swings back to Sophie and how, without my help, Greg might have found her and taken her back to whatever it was she's trying to escape from.

I wish Michael was still alive. He'd know exactly what to do. Ever since he died, I feel like every decision I've made has been the wrong one. Like my judgement is off. I never used to feel like this. Then again, I know that he wouldn't have approved of taking in this girl in the first place. But Michael is gone. And Sophie needs my help. So I'm going to have to live with my decision and continue doing what I think is best.

The back door is locked, as I knew it would be. I go from room to room checking the ground-floor windows, and they're all locked too. So unless Greg tries to smash his way in, I think we're secure. I'm hoping he doesn't know for sure that Sophie is here, and that it's like he says and he's simply knocking on doors, trying his luck. One thing's for certain though – this situation can't continue. I'm going to have to persuade Sophie to either call the police or seek help elsewhere. Now that a potentially dangerous man has shown up on our doorstep, I can't risk exposing my children to harm.

I take a determined breath and walk upstairs to the attic room, where Sophie is sitting in the dark, on the edge of the bed, a hunched figure chewing at her fingers. She looks up as I walk in and switch on the light.

'Does he know I'm here?' She squints against the light.

'I honestly don't know. He said he was going door to door asking about you. He thinks you're in danger.'

Sophie scowls.

'He said he's your husband and that he's scared for your safety. Is he really your husband?'

She shrugs and then gives a reluctant nod.

'And you want to leave him?'

Another nod.

'Has he been hurting you?'

'I really can't… I don't want to talk about it.' Her voice cracks.

I sit on the bed next to her and take one of her hands in mine, giving it a squeeze. 'I know this must be hard, but it's possible he knows you're staying here. It's probably not safe—'

'I get it.' She snatches her hand away from mine. 'You want me to leave.'

'Hey, I didn't say that.'

Sophie stands and swipes away a tear from her cheek. 'It's fine. I'll go.'

'Sophie, I didn't say that at all. And anyway, Greg's probably still in the vicinity, so it really isn't a good idea to leave the house right now. Especially not while you're upset and it's dark out there.' I'm trying to keep my voice quiet so as not to wake Ryan and Sonny. The last thing I need is for them to come upstairs and ask what's going on.

'But me staying here isn't fair on you. On your kids. You don't know me. You don't owe me anything.'

'Listen, Sophie.' I get to my feet again and try to stay calm. 'Obviously you can't stay here indefinitely. It's not practical. And now that Greg may well have found you, it's not necessarily safe. But it's also not a good idea for you to go running off into the night with no plan to speak of.'

She takes a deep breath. I can see it's costing her everything to try to keep herself together.

'The only alternatives I can see are to call the police and report your husband for whatever abuse he's been inflicting on you.'

'Not going to happen,' she mutters.

'Or, you let me find you a shelter where they're used to helping people in your situation.'

Her shoulders droop.

'Look… let's leave it for tonight. It's getting late and I doubt there's anything I can do right now. We'll sort something out tomorrow, okay?'

But tomorrow is the regatta and I can't not go to that when Ryan is so looking forward to racing. This is the first time he's shown enthusiasm about anything since his dad died. I have to give him my full attention tomorrow. This could be the start of getting my happy son back. And, actually, I may have Sophie to thank for that.

'Why don't you try to get a good night's sleep. Things might seem clearer tomorrow. But I think it's probably best if you don't go downstairs or near any windows. Just in case anyone's looking at the house. I can bring any food and drink up here for you.'

'Are you sure you don't want me to leave now? All I've done is bring trouble to your door.'

'Not true,' I insist. 'The boys seem to like you, and you're actually no trouble at all as a house guest.' The truth is that things would be simpler if she wasn't here, and I can't deny that the appearance of her husband has unnerved me more than a little. But what harm can one or two more days do? Although it's risky, the urge to help this girl won't go away. I'll sort out alternative accommodation for Sophie on Sunday or Monday and that will be that. In the meantime, I'll simply have to hope that Greg doesn't show his face again.

I'm just going to assume that he doesn't already know Sophie is staying here. Because if he does, then we could *all* be in danger.

CHAPTER TWENTY

TIA

Ed's at work and the kids are watching *Toy Story*. I'm squashed in between them on the sofa, trying to block out the TV noise while I attempt to straighten out my thoughts. But my mind is still a terrible jumble. I have no idea what to do or who to turn to for help over these hideous photographs. And I can't ever seem to get any time to myself to make sense of it all. I tried escaping to the kitchen earlier, where it's quieter, but Rosie and Leo took it in turns to come and ask me for one thing or another. So I figured I'd have fewer interruptions if we all sat together in the lounge. The TV could keep them entertained, giving me some time to think. I was wrong.

'Mummy, my toys are naughty. They're very messy all the time.' Leo holds out his Buzz Lightyear figure and waggles his finger at it. 'They make a big mess in my room so we have to tell them off.'

'Well, then you'll have to help Buzz tidy up,' I reply.

'It's not Buzz,' Rosie says knowingly. 'You're the one who makes all the mess, Leo.'

'No I don't! It's Buzz. Not me!'

'All right, you two. Are you going to be quiet and watch this film? Or shall we turn it off and have an early night?'

'Watch the film,' Leo says with a scowl, wriggling his bottom deep into the sofa.

'Rosie?'

She folds her arms across her chest and mumbles something about watching the film.

Putting my arms around their small bodies, I edge them both in towards me and take a breath, confident that they're about to settle down at last.

'Mummy, can we have a snack?' Leo suddenly springs away and gets to his feet.

'You've just had your tea, Leo. Sit back down.'

'Mummy!' Rosie cries. 'He's in the way, I can't even see the telly.'

'Right, that's it!' I stand up and click the TV off.

'Mummy! Don't turn it off!'

'Put it back on, Mummy, put it back.'

'We're going out,' I declare. I can't sit here doing nothing with these thoughts flying around my head and the children constantly clamouring for my attention. I need to do something. I tried to confide in Kelly earlier, but that didn't work with Fiona gatecrashing our lunch. And even though I've texted Kelly a couple of times since, she still hasn't replied. I guess she's busy with work and the kids, but I did think she'd have made a little bit of time for me, her best friend. And I won't even be able to talk to her tomorrow at the regatta, because Ed and the children will be there, not to mention Fiona and Nathan.

There's only one other option I can think of right now… 'Okay you two, how would you like to go out and see your Uncle Ash?'

'Unkash! Unkash!' Leo cries and starts bounding around the lounge.

'I'm going to tell Uncle Ash about those mean boys at school so he can put them in prison.' Rosie folds her arms and nods.

This is the first time today that Rosie's mentioned those boys at school. I wonder if I should ask her about them. See whether they've been persisting with their story.

'Can I bring Shorty?' she asks.

'Quickly then.'

Rosie races up the stairs to fetch her toy giraffe. She's obviously not upset anymore, so I decide to leave it. There's no point talking about those boys if she's happy right now. I'd only be dredging it all up, and the last thing I want is Rosie in tears again.

'Right, let's go. Leo, get in your pushchair.'

'No.'

'Okay, you can stay here then.'

Leo immediately runs into the hall and plonks himself into his pushchair where I strap him in. He's getting way too old to be pushed about, but his buggy is so handy for keeping him contained when I don't have the time or energy to manage him. Does that make me a bad mother? Maybe, but that's a guilt trip I'll save for another day.

Rosie thunders back down the stairs with Shorty and the three of us leave the house. Stepping outside, I instantly start to feel more positive, the warm evening air a balm on my skin. The simple act of walking and pushing Leo's buggy makes me feel proactive, less trapped. I've always had a hard time sitting still and doing nothing.

'This is like an adventure, Mummy!' Rosie cries, skipping along by my side.

'It is, sweetie. It's a lovely evening adventure.'

'Unkash!' Leo cries again, pointing to the road ahead.

'Yes, we're going to see Uncle Ash. You sit nice and quietly and we'll soon be there.' My cunning plan is that the motion of the pushchair will eventually lull Leo to sleep. In fact, I'm going to walk the long way around to give him more of an opportunity to get snoozy.

My big brother Ash is a local cop. He always wanted to join the force and it suits his personality down to the ground. He's a straight shooter, a real good guy who isn't afraid of anything. His only flaw is that he tends to look down on me, his tearaway sister. When we were younger, I was always the one getting into scrapes, blaming him, and landing us both in trouble with our parents. I love Ash, I really do, but it's hard living in his perfect shadow. However, the one thing I do know is that he'll always be there for me. As long as I play by the rules.

Twenty minutes later, Leo is fast asleep in his pushchair, his mouth wide open, a line of drool down his chin, while Rosie walks sedately by my side, yawning, her thumb in her mouth, all her earlier enthusiasm having faded after our long walk in the warm evening air. I get the feeling I'll be carrying her all the way home.

We stroll along the high street past the silent shops and the lively pubs, past Salinger's, where I notice that Fiona's left a light on at the back. I think about texting her to let her know, but immediately change my mind. Maybe she's working late. And if she is, she might feel obliged to come out and start talking to me. I pass Ida's Bakery – which is closed for the night – and stick my middle finger up at the window, subtly so Rosie can't see, but it's satisfying, nonetheless. I still don't know why the staff were so rude to me earlier. It's weird.

There's something odd going on that I can't quite put my finger on. Like everything in my universe has slightly shifted. I think it could have something to do with the crazy rumour at Rosie's school about me being a murderer. As long as it's nothing to do with the photos. My skin tingles. What if I *did* do something with that man in the photograph? What if it's common knowledge and lots of people saw me that night? They might think I'm carrying on behind Ed's back. If that's the case, then Ed is sure to find out. Someone will tell him. Maybe he already knows…

I can't think like this. No one knows. Of course they don't. I'm just being paranoid. They're probably fake images anyway. Please God, let them be fake. I haven't heard anything more from the person who sent them – not since they texted Ed. But I'm sure it's only a matter of time until they get in contact again. And when they do, it'll be worse than last time; I'm convinced of that. Whoever it is wants to ruin my life. But why?

Rosie stops and holds her arms up to me. I hoist her onto my hip and she rests her sleepy head on my shoulder. I've become adept at carrying her while pushing Leo in the buggy; it's second nature. But I know that soon my arms will start to ache. Quickening my pace, I stride along the rest of the high street, turn right after the library and head towards the police station. If Ash isn't working tonight, his house is only around the corner. I don't like to turn up unannounced, but I don't want to text either, to give him the chance to say he's too busy to see me.

I push Leo's buggy up the ramp into the police station. It's Friday night so things will soon be busy with drunken fights and lovers' spats, but for now it's empty in here. Just Sally Payne on the front desk, her blonde hair pulled back into a neat bun at the back of her head. She's a couple of years older than me and has worked for the local police force since leaving school.

She looks up briefly with the beginnings of a smile on her lips. But when she sees me, the smile dies.

'Hi, Sally,' I say tentatively.

'Tee. Can I help?' I'm taken aback by the lack of warmth to her greeting. Maybe she's had a stressful day.

'I'm here to see Ash.'

'Oh. Well, he's only just clocked on.'

'Is he free for a quick chat? I won't keep him long.'

She gives a barely suppressed huff. 'Fine, I'll see if he's got a minute.'

'Don't do me any favours,' I mutter under my breath as she ducks into the back office. I set Rosie down on one of the vinyl chairs where she immediately curls up and resumes sleeping. Leo is also still sound asleep. Poor babies, they'll be disappointed that they missed seeing their uncle. But at least it'll make it easier for me to chat to him without constant interruptions.

The door to the back office swings open with a squeak and my brother walks through in his uniform, a hesitant smile on his face with an accompanying raised eyebrow. He's tall and broad, dark and handsome. My brother used to be the school heartthrob, only he never knew it. He got married really young to Lyndsay Daniels, a quiet girl who lived up the road from us. They now have three kids, aged fourteen, twelve and nine.

'Hi, Tee. Everything okay?' He comes around the front and gives me a hug. I squeeze his shoulders a little too hard and a little too long, my eyes beginning to fill up. I sniff and try to compose myself before he sees my face again. But he obviously senses something's up. 'Hey, Tee, you okay?' He pulls back and stares at me.

I tut and roll my eyes to throw him off the scent. 'I'm fine. How's things with you? Lynds and the kids okay?'

'Yeah, all good.' He nods in the direction of my two. 'I see my niece and nephew are out for the count.' His baritone reverberates through the small reception area.

'What's up with Sally?' I note that she hasn't come back to the front desk yet.

'Sally? How do you mean?'

'She was a bit off with me just now.'

'Really? She seemed okay to me…'

'Oh, okay, never mind. Sorry to drop in on you at work. I just have a quick question.'

'Sure.' He gives me a look that says he's wondering why I had to walk all the way over here on a Friday evening to ask him a quick question when I could just as easily have called or messaged.

The thing is, I don't want to tell my brother exactly what's going on. I'm not too sure how he'd react if I actually showed him the photos. He might believe they're real and the last thing I need is my brother's disapproval. And even if he didn't think they were real, he wouldn't have approved of me going out clubbing with the girls while I have a husband and kids at home. Don't get me wrong, Ash is a lovely husband and he believes in equal rights for men and women. He's a good guy. The same ethical code would apply to him as to his wife – basically he would never in a million years want to go out with his friends while his wife was at home. They do everything together as a family. Which is lovely. I adore spending time with my family too. But sometimes, every once in a while, I get the urge to cut loose for a night. Doesn't mean I love my husband any less or that I want to do anything with anybody else, it simply means I enjoy having a laugh with my friends every so often. But Ash wouldn't understand this. And I can't face his judgement right now. So I'm going to be a little bit economical with the truth.

'I was just wondering… how easy is it to fake photographs?'

'What do you mean?' His brown eyes narrow.

'I mean, is there a way of telling whether a photo is real or fake? Like if someone else's face was put onto a different photograph, are there ways to spot that?'

'You'd have to show it to an expert.'

'Isn't that something you lot would be able to work out? Like, do you have special software or something?'

'What? In Ashridge Falls Police Station? Most days we're lucky if we can find the stapler.'

'Okay, I get your point.'

'What's this about? Has something happened?' His stare intensifies. My brother always has the ability to make me feel instantly guilty. There's no way I'm telling him about the actual images and what they're of. I feel sick at the thought of him or anyone else seeing them. But maybe he's right. I probably need to get them checked out by an expert.

'So how would I go about finding someone who can tell if the images have been faked?'

'Tee, are you going to tell me what this is about? If someone's uploaded images of you online without your permission, you can get them taken down, you know. Give me the link and I can investigate – or is it something you don't want me to see?'

'No, it's nothing like that. This is just a hypothetical situation.'

He folds his arms across his chest. 'Yes, Tee, you came halfway across town with two sleeping kids to ask me about a hypothetical situation.'

His radio beeps, and a male voice starts talking. Ash holds a finger up at me. He frowns. 'I have to go, but this conversation isn't over. We'll speak later, okay?'

'Can you give me the name of someone who could help?'

'I don't know off the top of my head. Google it. I'll call you after my shift. You need to tell me what's going on.'

I sigh and turn away to collect my sleeping kids. As Ash disappears into the back room, talking into his radio as he goes, I instantly feel more anxious and less secure. I don't visit Ash enough. We need to make more time for one another.

Heaving Rosie into my arms, I realise I'm still no further on in my quest to discover who's behind the images, and now I've also made my brother suspicious. He's not going to let this drop. I didn't think this through properly. I probably shouldn't have said anything to him, and I should have warned him not to mention any of this to Ed. I'll text Ash, just in case. Except that's bound to make him doubly suspicious.

The walk home is slow and tiring. Rosie is a dead weight in my arms, and my mind and body are leaden. Ed won't be home till late, so it will be just me alone at home with my thoughts. I only hope I don't receive any more unwanted photos or messages. Maybe I'll do what Ash suggested and try to find a photography expert online. But how will I have the courage to show the photos to a total stranger? To have someone judge me like that. This whole situation is hopeless.

CHAPTER TWENTY-ONE

Lying on the floor, she flicks idly through the magazine her friends brought round, but the pictures are a blur and the articles may as well be written in Chinese for all the sense they're making. She hasn't been out of the house for three days. She's been holed up in her bedroom trying to forget about what happened. But it's not working. The walls feel like they're closing in and no matter how many times she brushes her teeth, she can still taste his sour mouth on hers. It makes her gag.

She closes the magazine and eases herself up onto her feet. Walks over to her dressing table and looks in the mirror at her thin face and limp hair. She needs to get out of here and breathe in some fresh air.

She tiptoes down the stairs, hoping to sidle out the front door without disturbing her mum. Because, since it happened, her mum has barely stopped crying. And it's exhausting having to cope with that on top of everything else.

Too late.

'Are you going out?' Her mum comes out of the kitchen into the hall.

'See you in a bit, Mum. Won't be long.'

'Shall I come with you?'

'No, I'm just going for a walk.'

'I think I should come with you. Hang on, let me get my bag.'

'No!' She says it a little too forcefully. 'Sorry, I just want to be on my own for an hour or so.'

'You've been on your own in your room for days. Why don't you call one of your friends to go with you?'

'I'll be fine. I'll be back soon.' She makes her escape and jogs quickly away from the house before her mother has the chance to come after her.

Once she's a couple of streets away, she slows to a walk and tries to catch her breath. Her body feels sluggish and weak. The jog has made her a little light-headed. She comes to the bus stop and sits on the empty bench for a moment, closing her eyes as the sun warms her face and the breeze ruffles her hair. She should get up and head down to the lake, but she doesn't want to move. It feels nice to just sit here for a while.

'Liar!'

Snapping open her eyes, her heart sinks as she sees a group of five or six teens walking down the street towards her. They're chewing gum, their mouths working furiously. She recognises one of them as being a couple of years above her at school – Sally something or other. But she's guessing that the one who called out is the girl with the dark hair who's swaggering up to her now with an accusing scowl.

'You know he's been suspended, right?' The dark-haired girl's eyes bore into her own. 'Because of you.'

'I…'

'It's in the Gazette. Mr Lawson's the best teacher in the whole school. I've got my exams next year and you've screwed my future up by being a lying bitch. You need to go to the police station and own up. My mum says he would never have done what you said. She says you're an attention seeker.'

'I…' But she doesn't know what to say. Tears prickle at the back of her eyes, but she can't give them the satisfaction of seeing her cry. It's what they want. Some of the boys are nudging each other and laughing. She doesn't know what to say. What to do.

'Well?' The dark-haired girl raises an eyebrow.

'I wasn't lying.' Her voice is weak and shaky. She wishes she sounded more certain.

'Come on,' one of the boys says impatiently, 'let's go, we're gonna be late.' The group slowly moves on down the road, an amorphous *mass of hate, but not before the dark-haired girl throws her another sneering glare and calls her a whore.*

She lowers her head, scared to look after them in case they see her staring and come back. Her body is numb. Does everyone think she made it up? Does everybody hate her now?

CHAPTER TWENTY-TWO

Saturday

FIONA

I stand on the deck beneath the shade of the pergola, sipping my double espresso and staring out across the water. For now, the lake is empty, just a few silver ripples disturbing its silent depths. By contrast, up by the boathouse the shore crackles and pops with excitement and activity, the morning air shot through with scattered laughter and coloured bunting flapping in the warm breeze. Later, the surface of the water will be teeming with launches and sailboats, but for now the view ahead is calm and serene.

Today is regatta day and, quite honestly, I can't wait until it's over. It's already hot as hell, and the thought of having to be happy and sociable with everyone is making my head hurt. If it wasn't for Nathan racing later, I would cry off, cite a migraine or too much work. But my husband is really looking forward to his race, and he needs my support.

Right now, he's upstairs getting ready, changing into his sailing gear. He woke up in a really good mood, kissed me, slid his hands all over my body and acted as though last night never happened. But it did happen. His cold fury frightened me, so I stayed at the showroom going through receipts and invoices until I couldn't keep my eyes open any longer – which ended up being somewhere around 2.30 a.m. I eventually crept home, terrified of waking Nathan. Wondering whether he would even allow me back into the house. I debated whether to even come home at all. But then, what if he grew angry because I'd stayed out all night?

No matter how many times I go through the paperwork at the office, there's nothing I can do to change what I've done. The auditors are either going to pull me up on it, or they're not. The transactions are already there in black and white on my bank statements.

In the end, Nathan didn't even stir as I slid into bed beside him, and this morning he's been so focused on the race that he hasn't mentioned the tax audit or my late night. I'd like to think that's the last I'll hear of it, but that's highly unlikely. Nathan is nothing if not unpredictable. He'll wait until I've been lulled into a false sense of security before bringing it up again. I find myself praying that he wins his race today. That everything goes well. That nothing happens to put him in a bad mood.

Even with my late night, I got up super early to prepare our picnic. Which meant I only managed about three hours' sleep last night. It'll be fine though; hopefully I'll be able to have a nice early night tonight.

'You ready?' Nathan's voice is so soft I barely hear him.

I turn to see him step out onto the deck, appraising my outfit. I'm wearing a floral shift dress with high wedge heels and Jackie-O sunglasses to hide the dark circles beneath my eyes – there's only so much an illuminating highlighter pen can do. I'd rather have worn flip-flops or deck shoes than heels, but I didn't dare risk wearing anything that wouldn't have made it into the pages of an editorial fashion shoot; not to such a public event. 'Ready when you are,' I breathe, draining the last of my espresso.

'You look beautiful, Fi.'

I glow under his praise. 'You don't look half bad yourself, Mr Salinger.' He's wearing his blue-and-black Ashridge Falls kit, which consists of shorts, a rash vest and wraparound sunglasses. It all fits his toned physique perfectly. His firm partially sponsored the regatta this year, so the name Black Sky Financial is emblazoned across everything.

'I'll grab the cool box and then we'll go, yeah?' He kisses me and then pulls back and grimaces. 'You better do something about that coffee breath.'

I flush. 'Give me two secs, I'll run up and brush my teeth.'

'Maybe use some mouthwash too!'

Eventually, we leave the house via the deck and through the garden gate, strolling along the shoreline towards the boathouse. As we draw closer, we stop to chat to various friends and neighbours. It might be my imagination, but everyone we talk to seems to be a little off with me, focusing all their attention and conversation on Nathan and virtually ignoring any comments I make. Or am I simply being paranoid? Nathan hasn't lived in Ashridge as long as I have, but I swear he knows more people than I do. It helps that he regularly donates to local good causes and makes time to personally hand over the cheques. Nathan's known locally as an all-round good guy. Maybe that's all it is. Maybe I'm just being a little oversensitive.

'Fiona!' I turn to see Kelly waving from behind the cake stall. She's with Sonny, who's helping her to arrange cupcakes onto patterned china plates. She looks like a pre-Raphaelite painting in a long flowered dress, her blonde curls tumbling down her back.

Nathan and I walk over and give her a hug.

'Hey, Sonny, how are you?' I ask. 'You seem to have grown again.' I groan inwardly, feeling like that's such a lame thing to say to an eight-year-old boy. I've never really been great with kids. Maybe it's for the best that Nathan doesn't want any.

'I'm okay, thanks, Fi. How are you?'

'I'm fine.' He's such a sweet, polite kid.

'Aren't you racing today?' Nathan asks him.

Sonny shakes his head. 'Ryan is though.'

'Good for him.' Nathan nods his approval. 'The wind's really getting up now, so it should be a fun race.'

'Ryan's racing?' I ask, surprised. 'That's great news, Kelly.' She's been terribly worried about Ryan these past few months. The fact that he's sailing again must be a good sign.

'I know, I can hardly believe it. He only decided to enter yesterday. It's a miracle. I'm so pleased.'

'Everything else okay?' I ask. She looks decidedly pale and not as happy as her words suggest.

'Yeah, fine. Just a bit nervous about Ryan's race.'

'He'll be great,' Nathan says. 'What's his time slot?'

'Eleven fifteen.'

'We'll be cheering him on, won't we, Fi?'

'Of course.' I nod.

Nathan puts a hand on Kelly's arm. 'I know today must be difficult for you. I'll be thinking of Mike while I'm out on the water today.'

Kelly bites her lip. 'That's so lovely of you, Nathan. Thank you!' Her eyes glisten for a moment and then she gives herself a shake. 'Anyway, these cakes aren't going to eat themselves. Can I interest you in buying some? My stint here only lasts an hour and I'm determined to sell a few at least.'

Nathan pays way over the odds for a box of cupcakes that I help him select, and we promise to meet up in an hour's time to cheer Ryan on. Kelly says she'll look after our picnic things, so we continue wandering around the grounds, checking out all the stalls and saying hello to everyone. It's a beautiful day, despite the wind, and everyone is happy and relaxed. Everyone, that is, apart from me. Although I'm going through the motions, I feel separate from it all. Distant. Excluded.

I greet friends, dismissing their perceived coldness as a symptom of my own insecurity and sensitivity. Instead, I smile and laugh with Oscar-worthy conviction as the dark blot in my chest spreads, weighing down my limbs and slowing my mind. If you asked me to talk about how I'm feeling, I couldn't even begin to put it all into words. This deep, black dread started long ago, and I've managed to keep it contained for years. But recent events have brought everything bubbling to the surface. If I'm not careful, it will spill over and ruin everything. Yet, even as I have that thought, I wonder if there's actually anything left to ruin.

'Come on, Fi.' Nathan takes my arm. 'Ryan's race will be starting in a minute. Let's go down to the clubhouse.'

'Yes, you're right.' I smile into his eyes, even as bile creeps up my gullet.

Nathan stops dead and frowns, peering at a spot above my forehead. 'Is that a grey hair?'

I pat the top of my head. 'A grey one? I hope not!'

'Better get yourself down to the hairdressers next week. Looks like you might have got your dad's genes in the hair department. He went grey early, didn't he?'

'I don't think one grey hair's anything to worry about,' I reply. 'Lots of my friends have them.'

'Hold still.' Nathan grips my shoulders to stop me moving. He peers at my head and runs his fingers through my hair, staring. I begin to feel queasy under his scrutiny.

'Ow!'

He's yanked out a couple of strands and is staring at them critically, running his fingertips along their length before he bursts out laughing. 'It's icing sugar from the cupcakes!'

'Icing sugar? You mean you pulled out my hair for nothing?' I rub the sore spot on my head and grin to let him know I'm not really annoyed. The churning in my belly subsides.

'Come on, let's go.' Nathan takes my arm once more and we make our way over to the clubhouse, where I spot Kelly and Sonny standing next to Tia and Rosie. Ed is close by chatting to

Ash while trying to keep hold of little Leo. I'm nervous about going over, as I get the feeling Tia isn't too keen on me these days. And Nathan always gets this macho competitiveness whenever he talks to Ed. Not sure why, as Ed is the most easy-going person I know. I think somehow Ed's laid-back personality riles Nathan in some way.

I inhale deeply, needing to let go of all this anxiety. If Nathan has a problem with Ed, there's nothing I can do about it. Same goes for Tia. If she has a bee in her bonnet about something that I may or may not have done, she should just tell me what it is. I wish I could run home and sit on the deck on my own. Maybe read a book or paint. That would be a real luxury right now.

'Hey, Fi, Nathan.' Kelly smiles and beckons us over. Her warmth is infectious, and I feel myself relaxing a little.

'You managed to bag a great spot,' Nathan says, nodding appreciatively at the view over the lake.

'We saved you some chairs!' Sonny says proudly.

'Hello, Tia.' Nathan nods at her. 'Is Ed ready to get his arse kicked this afternoon?'

'You'll have to ask him.' I cringe at the flirtatious wink Tia gives my husband. She just can't help herself, and Ed is only standing a few feet away. She's not even properly dressed for a regatta, in very short cut-off shorts that highlight her long brown legs, a silk leopard-print vest top and trainers. Yet somehow she manages to look relaxed and stunning. I feel overdressed by comparison.

'You're not racing?' Nathan asks her.

Tia pulls a sad face. 'No time to train. My little monsters keep me too busy.'

'That's a shame. Be good to see you up at the clubhouse again.'

'Maybe I'll get back into it some day, once they're older.'

Ed catches my eye and waves. I give a half-hearted wave back, aware that Nathan still has hold of my arm and is squeezing it quite tightly.

I catch the eye of a woman whose kitchen I designed last year – Lucinda Blethin. She's standing with a group of local women, most of whom I recognise and grew up with. I smile and wave. But instead of smiling back, Lucinda turns to her friends and says something. They all glance over at me and then they look at Kelly. A couple of them curl their lips in what looks like disgust. Their unfriendly scrutiny makes me anxious and I wonder whether I should mention it to Kelly. Maybe she knows why they're being so rude.

'They've started!' Sonny cries, a pair of binoculars glued to his eyes.

I'll have to wait until later to speak to Kelly about Lucinda. I realise she needs to focus on the race right now.

'How's Ryan doing?' Nathan asks.

'Not sure, hang on.' Sonny twists the dial on his binoculars.

A line of white sails slices across the surface of the lake like paper cut-outs. Kelly's boss Derek is on the PA system commentating. I'm not too sure what's going on, but I hear Ryan's name mentioned a couple of times. We watch for a while, but I still can't make out who's who.

'Ryan's out in front!' Sonny cries.

'Go, Ryan!' Tia yells, her confident cry ringing out across the water.

The crowd along the shoreline are cheering and waving, even though there's no way any of the competitors would be able to hear from so far away. They're getting closer though, and as they do, their speed takes my breath away. I wonder why I've never got involved in sailing. It's such a big part of Ashridge life and it looks like something I would enjoy – a real adrenalin rush. Nathan would probably laugh if I suggested it though. He'd tell me I wasn't suited to it. That I'd end up hurting myself or making a fool of myself. He's probably right.

'Oh no!' Sonny's cry draws our attention. 'I think… I think Ryan's in trouble.'

'What do you mean?' Kelly takes the binoculars from her son and swears under her breath as she attempts to refocus them and get the boats in her sight. 'Which one is he?' Kelly cries.

'Number seventeen,' Sonny replies, his eyes full of fear. 'He'll be okay, won't he?'

'He'll be fine,' I say, taking Sonny's hand and giving it a rub. Although I have no idea what's actually happening out there. I glance over at Kelly's white features and pray that Ryan's okay. She can't have another tragedy in her life. Not after losing Michael.

CHAPTER TWENTY-THREE

FIONA

I strain my eyes to try and work out what's happening out on the lake. But all I can see are a mass of white sails and churned-up water.

'It looks like Ryan turned too sharply!' Kelly's body is rigid as she follows the progress of her son through the binoculars.

A few spectators on the shore are pointing. Even without binoculars I can see that one of the boats is in difficulty; it's keeling over. The other boats have all overtaken it and a couple of race stewards in a speedboat are heading out across the lake towards number seventeen.

'I should never have let him enter,' Kelly cries. 'He hasn't sailed in over a year. He's out of practice, and it's so windy out there. What was I thinking?'

'Kels…' Tia puts an arm around her before I can get to her. 'Don't worry. Dinghies capsize all the time. He knows what to do. He'll be fine.'

'But he'll be so scared. What if he's hurt?'

Lucinda and her cronies are openly staring at us now and I really want to tell them to get lost – not that I would do that, because that would mean losing control and making a scene and I don't feel strong enough for that. Not today anyway. Their sideways glances are making my cheeks heat up and my chest constrict. I feel like a child again. Their whole pathetic behaviour is all too reminiscent of a time I'd rather forget. I force myself to look away. To ignore them. To not let all those old feelings well up and paralyse me. I have more important things to worry about right now. Like whether Ryan's okay.

Derek's tinny voice on the PA cuts through our growing panic. '... and I'm being told that Ryan Taylor is safe and well. If a little wet!'

A cheer goes up, and Kelly starts to cry. 'Oh, thank goodness.'

Tia and I wrap our arms around our friend. I put Lucinda out of my head. She's not important.

Derek's commentary continues. 'What a shame! If he hadn't tacked quite so sharply he might have been picking up a gold medal. Better luck next time, Ryan!'

'I better go down to the jetty and see if he's okay,' Kelly says, extricating herself. 'Sonny, you stay here with Tia and Fiona.'

'But, Mum, I want to—'

'Sonny, can you help me find a good spot to set up the picnic?' I interrupt, trying to distract him. 'Ryan will be hungry when he gets here.'

Kelly throws me a grateful glance and rushes off.

Forty minutes later, we're all set up on the grassy bank with picnic rugs, chairs, hampers and cold boxes laid out in an enticing spread. Ryan's changed into dry clothes and is being treated like royalty by everyone who passes – offering him their commiserations, asking if he's okay, and telling him what a hero he is for capsizing so spectacularly – but the scowl hasn't left his features. The poor boy feels humiliated and embarrassed. I know from personal experience that when you're down, the more someone asks if you're okay, the worse it can feel.

'Can we go home now?' he keeps asking Kelly in a low mutter.

'Let's enjoy the picnic first.'

'I'm not hungry.'

'We've got cupcakes,' Nathan offers.

'No thanks,' Ryan replies.

'Don't worry, you'll smash it next year,' Nathan says.

Ryan nods, unable to be rude to my husband.

I can tell that Kelly's almost at the end of her tether with him. Ryan just won't be consoled. I think the best thing is probably to leave him be for a while.

After lunch, it's Nathan and Ed's turn to race.

'Good luck, guys!' I kiss Nathan and pat Ed on the back.

'Are you going to win the race, Daddy?' Rosie asks Ed.

'I'm going to try, pickle.'

'Just do your best, okay?' she says seriously, making everyone laugh.

They finally leave us to go and get prepared. After they've gone, I manage to relax a little and eat a few mouthfuls of the avocado salad I prepared. Kelly's appetite is as lacking as mine, while Tia's getting stuck into the champagne and strawberries. There's no way I could drink anything alcoholic right now. I'm hovering on the edge of exhaustion; a glass of champagne would finish me off.

The kids are loving the picnic though, and I even spot Ryan wolfing down a couple of sandwiches when he thinks no one's looking.

The afternoon ticks by and soon we're all back down on the shore, cheering the men's race. My paranoia from earlier is back in full force and, although I can't spot Lucinda anywhere, I'm aware of people looking over at me and then sliding their gazes away. I feel as though I have a sign stuck to my forehead. Do they know about the audit? I wouldn't be surprised. It's such a small town and rumours spread so quickly. Once again, I try to shrug off my anxieties. To tell myself I'm overtired and stressed and imagining things. It doesn't help that I'm really hot and my shoes are killing me. I take a breath and tell myself to calm down and try to enjoy the day. I'm an adult having a lovely day out by the lake with my friends. I should focus on that, and not on some ridiculous gossipy locals. Even if they do know about the audit, *so what?*

I take a few more steadying breaths and turn my attention back to the speeding boats on the lake, forcing myself to focus on the race. I love how Ed was nervously excited at competing in his first event. And yet a win by Ed would be devastating to Nathan's ego, which would mean he'd be in a bad mood all evening. So, much as I don't want Ed to do badly, I hope with every fibre of my being that Nathan bags the gold medal. I've never been this nervous about the outcome of a race before.

I didn't have to worry. Nathan won easily and he's now on a high, charming everyone and even being gracious towards Ed, who came third from last. But Ed doesn't seem upset or disappointed. He seems genuinely happy for Nathan.

Back in our early twenties, when I used to go out with Ed, his laid-back attitude used to frustrate me. I perceived it as laziness, as a lack of ambition. But I realise now that it's what makes Ed such a lovely person – he works hard, but he isn't obsessed with winning. His career comes second to his family and he isn't afraid to wear his family-man badge with pride. He doesn't see it as a weakness, but as a strength.

While Nathan regales us all with a blow-by-blow account of the race, Ed slings his arm around his wife and gathers his kids in towards him, dropping kisses onto their heads. I swallow down the bitter taste that I might be just the tiniest bit jealous of Tia.

Nathan finally brings his race story to a close. 'Bad luck, Ed. Better stick to cooking.'

'There's always next year,' Ed replies.

Nathan grins. 'Bring it.'

I catch sight of Kelly, who's hanging back from all the banter. She's gazing out across the lake and I realise how hard today must have been for her. Aside from all the earlier drama with Ryan, the regatta always used to be about Michael. He was an accomplished sailor who used to win every race he entered. If he was still alive today, it would have been him with the gold medal, and not Nathan. Not that Kelly ever cared about who won, but I wouldn't blame her if she left before the prize-giving ceremony. So many painful memories.

Kelly catches me staring and I give her a smile.

She returns it half-heartedly. 'Guys, I think we're going to head off now.' She glances around to locate Sonny and Ryan.

'Finally,' Ryan mutters.

'Do we have to go?' Sonny asks. 'I want to stay till the end.'

'It's almost the end,' I say. 'That was the last race.'

Sonny sighs. 'I wish it could last forever. I like it when everyone's here together. It feels really nice. Like it used to be with Dad.'

This brings a lump to my throat and I turn away so the kids can't see the tears that are threatening. Michael was a lovely man. Steady and calm. He was a great dad to his boys and it's heartbreaking that he's no longer around. I feel like I probably haven't been a good enough friend to Kelly over the past few months. She's one of those people who never asks for anything, but always tries to be there for everyone else. I resolve to do more for her. To help out with the boys. I know I'll probably never have any children of my own, but I love Ryan and Sonny, so I'll get more involved with them. I'd love to be the sort of person who they feel they could talk to about anything. Another grown-up who has their back.

We all help Kelly gather up her things and then kiss her goodbye. I manage to give Sonny a quick hug, but Ryan hangs back, so I just give him a short wave and a smile. I'm gratified that he returns it. That kid is so angry, yet so adorable. When he smiles, you feel as though you've won a prize.

After Kelly and the boys have gone, Ed ropes Nathan into going with him to the mini funfair with Leo and Rosie, and I find myself left alone with Tia. I sit on one of the camping chairs and start rummaging through my handbag for my phone, just for something to do.

Tia comes over with the remains of the champagne and two plastic glasses.

'Not for me, thanks.'

'One glass won't hurt, Fi. Live a little.'

I grit my teeth and try not to huff out loud as she pours two measures and hands me one.

'Cheers.' She knocks her glass against mine and pulls up another camping chair, plopping down heavily into it. 'Today must have been rough on Kels.'

I nod in agreement. 'How do you ever get over losing the love of your life, the father of your kids? Everything today must have reminded her of him.'

'I'd die if I lost Ed.'

'Yeah.' I think about how I'd feel if Nathan died. And then I try desperately to think about anything else.

'So, what's been going on with you, Fiona?'

I sense an element of snark in her voice. Something that's been let loose by the champagne she's consumed.

'Same old.' I don't particularly want to share my troubles with Tia.

'So, there's nothing you'd like to tell me?'

'Like what?' I turn to look at her. She's staring at me with some kind of accusation in her eyes, but I can't work out why. In fact, she's acting extremely strangely. Could she have something to do with what's been going on at work? Could she be the one who reported me to the tax office? She's always been envious of my career, and of my closeness with Kelly. Does she still hold a grudge against me for having been Ed's girlfriend? She has so many reasons not to like me, but would she go so far as to try to ruin my life?

Tia drops her gaze and leans back in her chair, gulping down half her glass of champagne. 'You know, you're a great designer, Fi.'

A compliment? 'Thanks.'

'Are you any good at photography?'

'I'm okay, why?'

'Just okay?'

'Yes, I'm not a professional. If you need a decent photographer I can give you a couple of names. Is it a family portrait you want?'

'No, I don't need a photographer. I've got enough photos for now.'

'Oh, okay.' I have no idea what she's talking about. But I'm pretty sure she's drunk.

She wobbles to her feet and her camping chair falls over. 'Photos of me, Fiona. Know anything about them?'

There's definitely something weird going on with her. I'll have to speak to Kelly about it; see if she knows anything. 'Maybe you should go home and have a lie down, Tee. I can let Ed know you've gone, if you like?'

'A lie down? Ha! Good one. You think I had a lie down with someone else, but I didn't.'

I stand up and pull out a bottle of water from my bag. 'Drink this while I go and get you a coffee.'

'Don't need any of your water or coffee. I'm going home.'

'Shall I come with you?'

'No. I can walk home on my own, thank you very much.'

I think about going to fetch Ed to look after his wife, but he's with the kids and it's better if they don't see Tia like this. Maybe I could get Ash. I glance around but can't spot him or his family anywhere. And anyway, Tia wouldn't thank me for letting her brother know she's had too much to drink.

'See you, Fi.' Tia gives me a wave and starts marching off up the bank towards the path. She's still talking to herself and I consider going after her, but I can't deal with more of her drama right now. I have enough on my plate.

Instead, I sit back down in my chair, sip my glass of warm champagne and try to block out the myriad anxieties that are vying for attention in my mind. I focus on the blue lake and the hazy sky. On the warm wind and the friendly atmosphere of the regatta. Before I'm even halfway to relaxing, my phone pings with a text.

It's from an unknown number, so it's either spam or a potential new client. I open up the message and start to read:

Hello Fiona. If you think things are bad now, you're wrong. Soon you're going to get everything you deserve.

My skin prickles uncomfortably. Is this some kind of *threat*? I re-read it and realise with a sickening lurch that it is. Maybe it's something to do with the tax audit. Is this the person who reported me? Could it be Tia? Surely not. With clumsy fingers, I text back:

Who is this?
It doesn't matter who this is. What matters is what you DID.
What am I supposed to have done?
Your sins will find you out.

Shit. Whoever this person is, they're not all there. I drop my phone into my lap and glance around, suddenly feeling exposed and vulnerable out here in the open air. What the hell do they want with me? My heartbeat skitters around my chest as I realise I might just understand what they're referring to. But that can't be it. Surely not. That was all so long ago. It's finished. Done with.

My phone rings, making me almost jump out of my skin. What if it's the texter wanting to speak to me? There's no way I'm going to have an actual conversation with them. No way, no how. I'll just let it go to voicemail. Gingerly I lift my phone from my lap, holding my breath as I look at the screen. I exhale when I see that it's only Kelly. Maybe she's calling to say she's left something behind.

'Hi, Kelly.' I'm so shaken up that I decide I'm going to tell her about the text. But as she starts talking, it's obvious something's very wrong.

CHAPTER TWENTY-FOUR

TIA

Walking back along the lakeside path, my head starts to pound, and my stomach feels decidedly unsettled. I can't exactly remember what happened back at the regatta, but I think I just made a gigantic idiot of myself in front of Fiona. I was rambling about the photos, and she didn't seem to have the faintest clue what I was talking about. Unless she was just pretending of course. That's a strong possibility.

She always seems to get my back up. I saw her looking down her nose at my cut-off shorts. Probably thought I was showing off too much leg. Probably thought I was dressed like a teenager. Well, I like how I dress. I'm not going to change what I wear because of snooty Fiona and her immaculate designer wardrobe. Some of us can't afford to dress like a princess.

And it wasn't just Fiona making me feel like crap. Lucinda Blethin and some of the other school mums were giving me the evil eye over something or other. I'm wondering if it was to do with that stupid rumour. Rosie hasn't talked about it again, but that doesn't mean that other kids aren't gossiping about it. And if they told their parents then it'll be all over town by now. Great, that's all I need. Those bloody women could have at least tried to be a little more subtle about it instead of pointing and whispering like bitchy teenagers. I shudder, thinking back to the last time I was the subject of gossip. A time I wish I could forget.

I fumble in my bag for my phone and text Ed to tell him I'm on my way back home, although Fiona's probably told him by now. I bet she's also told him that I had too much champagne. She'll make it sound like I'm drunk. My phone vibrates with a message. It's Ed. He's telling me not to worry. Says he'll stay on at the regatta with the kids for another hour or so.

Thank goodness for Ed. He's quite literally the most perfect husband in the universe. I don't deserve him. I love him so much. My eyes fill with tears, which is ridiculous. I realise that maybe I *am* a bit tipsy, but so what? It's what you do, isn't it? You go out, have fun and have a few drinks. Ed doesn't mind. He knows I like to enjoy myself. It's what he loves about me. My fun-loving attitude.

But what's he going to say when he finds out about the photos? I can't even prove that they're fake because I don't remember what went on that night. It's all still a blank. I know I'm burying my head in the sand about the whole thing. Hoping it'll all go away of its own accord. I still haven't even attempted to look for an expert to examine the photos. And I've been avoiding my brother's calls. He's pushing me to tell him what's really going on, but I don't want him to know. I should never have gone to see him about it. That was a big mistake.

My phone vibrates once more. Must be Ed again. But when I look at the screen, I see it's a text from an unknown number. I stop walking and take a breath before opening the message:

Make the most of it Tia, because your marriage will soon be over.

A wave of panic hits me.

I knew they'd be back in touch, and I knew I wouldn't like what they had to say, but as I read the text again, my fingers are trembling with shock.

I clumsily tap out a reply:

Who is this? What do you want?

There's no response, so I send another one:

***If you don't tell me what you want, I'm going straight to
the police to show them your messages.***

Of course I'm bluffing, but I don't know what else to do.
Whoever it is seems intent on intimidating me. They still haven't
asked for anything specific or said what all this is about. I realise
that the effects of the champagne have suddenly worn off, and
I'm stone-cold sober, like someone has chucked a bucket of icy
water over me. Although my head still throbs, and my throat is
so parched I can barely swallow. My phone vibrates with a new
message, and I'm suffused with a queasy dread.

*I wouldn't go to the police if I were you. Your brother can't save
you now.*

My *brother*? So they know my brother's a police officer. Did
they see me go and speak to him? Have they been following me?
I type angrily:

***Why shouldn't I go to the police? You can't keep harassing
me like this.***

*I can do whatever I want. After what you did, you deserve a
lot worse.*

What am I supposed to have done?

You know what you did. The rumours about you are true.

The *rumours*? My heart begins to pound and my mind buzzes with fear.

Tell anyone and the photos will be forwarded to every person on your contact list.

I go rigid. The thought of them sending out the photos to my contact list doesn't bear thinking about. Aside from ruining my marriage, there's my family to consider, the other parents from school, teachers, friends, everyone… I'll never be able to hold my head up again.

Why are you doing this? Who are you?

I wait, but there's no response. I try calling the number, my heart in my mouth as I listen to the ring tone. But no one is picking up and the number doesn't seem to be connected to an answering service. After twenty rings I end the call and tap out another text:

Hello
Answer me
Please

But they've obviously said all they're going to say. Thank goodness I received the message while I'm alone and not back at the regatta with everyone else. Did whoever it is do that on purpose? Do they know I'm by myself? I try to survey the area without making it too obvious, but I'm in too much of a state to be subtle. There are a couple of families dawdling up ahead. Behind me, the regatta is winding down and emptying out. But it's still reasonably busy. The noise from the funfair carries on the breeze. Derek is still talking non-stop into the PA system, but his words are blurred and unintelligible, a monotonous drone. As I glance around like a frightened rabbit, I don't even know what I'm looking for – a lone man or woman hiding behind a tree, staring at me… I shake my head and keep walking. Maybe I'm still drunk. There's no one paying me any attention out here. Whoever it is, they're hiding behind their phone. Too cowardly to face me.

Again, I get the feeling that it could be all Fiona's doing. For a start, she knows I'm on my way home alone. I left her sitting by herself, so now would be the perfect time for her to send a text. I did try mentioning photographs this afternoon to gauge her reaction, but either she's a really good liar or I'm way off the mark. Would she really stoop to doing something so awful? The thing is, I can't think of anyone else who might have a reason to want Ed and I to split up. Maybe she still loves him. Although she's always going on about how she and Nathan are blissfully in love. Unless she's lying, but I can't see it somehow; they're so well suited.

Fiona and Nathan Salinger think they're some kind of super-couple. It always gets so competitive when those two are around. It's like, who can be the most successful, the most beautiful, the most in love. It's annoying. But is that Fiona's doing or Nathan's? He's one of those guys who has to win at everything. I honestly don't get what Fiona sees in him. Sure, he's rich and good-looking in an obvious way, but he's also a bit of a dick.

The texter also mentioned 'the rumours'. Could they be talking about what happened at school with Rosie? Surely not. That's just kids making stuff up. Isn't it? Unless… *No.* That was all too long ago. It can't be anything to do with that, surely.

Ugh, my head hurts. I don't want to think about this anymore. I just want to get home, crawl into bed and sleep.

CHAPTER TWENTY-FIVE

KELLY

'You know you did amazingly out there today, Ry.'

My son grunts in response. We're walking home and I'm trying to bring him out of his gloomy mood, but it's hard work – we're all hot and tired. Sonny is walking by my side humming to himself and yawning. He'll sleep like a log tonight. We all will.

'Your speed was incredible. Everyone was so impressed.' I pause. 'Your dad would have been proud.'

He stops walking for a moment and turns to me. 'Do you think so?'

'I *know* so.'

'Even though I capsized?'

'All sailors have capsized at one time or another, even your dad. It was exciting to watch,' I lie – it was terrifying. 'And brave.'

Ryan kicks at some loose gravel, but his face goes pink and I can tell he's pleased. I know today wasn't perfect. That he's angry with himself for falling in. But it's a start on the road to getting my boy back.

'So, shall we have a celebration dinner tonight?' I don't want to overdo my gushing, but I can't help it. I'm happy that Ryan is finally showing an interest in life again.

'Yeah, okay, but I came last so it's not exactly a celebration.'

'We're celebrating your spectacular return to the world of sailing.'

'*Mu-uum.*' Ryan rolls his eyes.

'What? I'm just teasing. It's what parents do.' I'm echoing Michael's words. He used to tease the boys mercilessly, but they loved it and would always give as good as they got. It's time I brought some light-heartedness back into our lives. 'So, pizza or sushi?'

'Pizza!'

We turn into our road and my eye is caught by something flashing up ahead…

Blue lights. There's a police car and an ambulance parked outside our neighbours' house. I hope it's nothing too serious. They're an elderly couple – Bob and Margo – and Bob had a fall a few weeks back and broke his wrist. And then I'm gripped by panic as an alternative explanation occurs to me. I quicken my pace, wishing the children weren't here… just in case. I debate whether to send them back to the regatta.

'Mum.' Sonny points. 'Look, there's a police car in our road.'

'Do you think Sophie's okay?' Ryan asks, his face suddenly pale.

'I'm sure she's fine,' I say, trying to keep my voice even. 'If the police are here, then whatever's happened, they'll have it under control.' I'm saying this as much to reassure myself as the children. 'Can you two just wait here under this tree while I see what's going on?' I take hold of both boys' arms and steer them to a leafy sycamore at the end of our road. They're both too distracted to protest. 'Ryan, stay here and look after your brother. Don't move.'

Ryan nods and takes Sonny's hand. This in itself is unheard of, but I don't have time to marvel over my eldest child's mood reversal.

I leave them beneath the tree and walk quickly towards the house, hoping that the emergency services are here for someone else and that this has nothing to do with Sophie. That we'll be able to walk into our house, order pizza and have a nice relaxing evening. But I know that's wishful thinking.

As I draw closer, I see that my front door is wide open. In fact, it's falling off its hinges and looks like it's been forced. There's broken glass on the driveway. I look around but can't see where it's come from. My mind flits to the image of Sophie's husband, Greg. Is he responsible for this? Has he been here and forced his way in? Has he hurt Sophie? I should never have left her alone. I should have insisted that we get her settled into a shelter. I'm so stupid. She must be in the ambulance, but I can't tell from this angle as the back doors are facing away from me. Please, God, let her be okay. Thank goodness the kids weren't here when it happened.

I quicken my pace and take in more of the scene. There's a male police officer in the driver's seat of the car talking to someone on his radio, and a female officer in the passenger seat. And then I see Ash come striding around the side of the ambulance. Good. He'll be able to fill me in on what's happening. He's wearing his uniform so he must have just come on duty; I only saw him at the regatta an hour or so ago, and he was wearing his civvies back then.

I wave.

He gives me a strange look.

Oh no, what's happened? 'Ash, what's going on?' I'm going to have to explain about who Sophie is and what she's doing in my house. He'll think I'm stupid for welcoming her into my home, but I can't worry about that. I hope he hasn't arrested Sophie, thinking she's some kind of trespasser. Ash still hasn't answered my question, although he is coming towards me.

The male officer gets out of the car – I don't recognise him, but he's joining Ash. The female officer also exits the vehicle, but she stays by the car and watches me. I vaguely recognise her from school; I think she was in the year below me. I nod, but she doesn't react, which is a little rude. Maybe she thinks that because she's a policewoman now she doesn't have to be polite.

'Kelly,' Ash says as I draw closer, 'I'm sorry to have to do this, but I'm arresting you on suspicion of false imprisonment of another person.'

I think I must have misheard him. But now he's doing that thing you hear on TV where they caution you and read you your rights, like I've done something wrong! 'Ash, what's going on? Is this a joke? It's not funny, my kids are here.'

'Ryan and Sonny?' He frowns and glances around. 'Where?'

'I saw the ambulance and police car, so I told them to wait at the end of the road.' I crane my neck to peer into the house to see if I can spot Sophie. 'There's a girl staying with me at the moment – Sophie. Is she okay?'

Ash gives me another strange look.

'Tell me what's going on, Ash. You can't really be arresting me? You said something about false imprisonment. Was it *Greg*? Was he here? He's the one you need to speak to.' I'm not taking his threat of arrest seriously because there's obviously been a mix-up. Some misunderstanding where Sophie's husband has tried to pin something on me so he looks innocent.

'Who's Greg? Look, I'm sorry, Kelly, but I have to follow procedure. I have to take you in, and then you'll get a chance to tell us your side.'

'My side of *what*?' I feel like I've stepped into an alternate universe. And I still can't help thinking that this is some elaborate prank. Although who on earth would think this was funny?

Ash speaks into his radio and the female officer gets out of the car. He points down the road and she starts heading in that direction.

'What's she doing? Why is she walking towards my children? Ash, talk to me.'

'I'm sorry, Kelly.' He doesn't look me in the eye.

'You're my friend! And anyway, I don't even know what I'm supposed to have done.'

'We'll look after the kids while you come down to the station with us.'

'What do you mean, you'll look after them? You mean you personally?'

'Uh, no. We'll place them in temporary care.'

'What! No you will not!' Tia would be my natural go-to person to look after the kids, but being Ash's sister, I'm reluctant to get her involved. 'Let me call Fiona. She'll have them for me while I sort this out.'

Ash shakes his head. 'You can make a call when we get to the station.'

'Please, Ash! They're my kids. At least let them have some normality while this is being straightened out. I don't want them going off with some stranger.'

He sighs and nods. 'Okay, quickly.'

With trembling fingers, I take my phone from my bag and call Fiona's number. She answers immediately, thank goodness. 'Fi, it's me.'

'Kelly, are you okay?'

'No. I need your help.'

'My help? Of course, what do you need?'

'Can you come over to mine right now and pick up the boys.'

'Uh, sure, what's happened?'

'I'm being arrested.'

'Ha! For a minute, I thought you said you were being arrested.'

'I am. I did. Ash is here to take me into custody.'

'*What?!*' Fiona's outrage is loud enough for Ash to hear. I give him a look that says, *You see?* He frowns and makes a winding-up motion with his finger.

'Fi, can you take the boys back to yours while I try to straighten this out?'

'Shit. Are you okay? Don't worry, I'll pick up the kids right now. Are they at yours?'

'Yes.' My voice breaks. Hearing Fiona's concern is undoing me.

'Kelly, don't worry. We'll sort this out, okay? And the boys can stay with me for as long as you need.'

'Hopefully it won't be for long.'

'Don't worry about that. Why were you arrested? Surely it's a mistake. Shall I call someone? A lawyer?'

Ash is holding his hand out for my mobile.

'Look, Fi, I have to go.'

He finally takes my phone from me and puts it back into my bag. 'PC Shales will stay with the boys until Fiona gets here.'

'Thanks.' At least that's something, I suppose. At least I don't have to worry about my boys for now. 'I can't believe you're doing this, Ash. After what happened with Michael last year. After what the kids went through. And now you're putting us through whatever charade this is!' I'm not normally an angry person. I'm calm, even-natured, gentle. But right now, I want to yell at Ash and pummel his chest in frustration. This is ridiculous. Whatever I'm supposed to have done, I bloody well didn't do it.

At that moment someone steps out from the back of the ambulance. It's Sophie. She's red-faced, like she's been crying.

'Sophie! Are you okay? What happened? Was it Greg? Did he come looking for you?' I turn to Ash. 'Is she under arrest too? Did Greg report her to the police, is that it? Because you should know that Sophie's hiding from him. She's scared. He's been abusive—'

'Okay,' Ash says firmly, 'that's enough now. Save it for when we're at the station.'

Sophie has stopped dead in her tracks. I notice her wrists and ankles have red welts around them, as though she's been tied up.

When she spots me, her face drains of all colour. She lifts her arms slowly and points in my direction.

'That's her,' she says, her eyes sharp with fear. 'That's the woman who drugged me and locked me in her attic. I… I thought she was going to kill me.' Her breathing is ragged, and she sounds like she's about to have a panic attack.

I stare back at Sophie in mounting confusion and horror. 'What are you talking about? Sophie, it's *me*, Kelly.'

But she turns away and is led back into the ambulance by a paramedic.

I look at Ash. 'What did she say to you? I don't understand. I was helping her! You can ask my kids. They'll tell you.'

Ash leads me to the police car and puts a protective hand over my head as I duck into the back seat. He's now avoiding all eye contact with me. Can he really believe I'm guilty of what Sophie's accused me of? Before he closes the door, I try to appeal to his paternal instincts. 'Can I just go and tell Ryan and Sonny not to worry? Won't you at least allow me that?'

'You don't want them seeing you upset like this, Kelly. It's better if my colleague explains.'

'But what will she say?'

'She won't make you look bad.'

'Bit late for that.'

'She'll tell them you need to answer some questions.' Ash closes the door and all I can do is look out the window. But I can't even see my two from in here. I wish I could at least give them an encouraging smile, so they'll know I'm not upset.

Embarrassingly, several of my neighbours are out in the street, and while they're not overtly gawping, I can tell they're fascinated by what's happening, giving me sideways glances. No doubt they'll all get together when I've gone to have a good speculative gossip. But I don't care about any of that. I'm still totally bewildered by Sophie's accusation, and I'm devastated that my children have had to witness their mother being arrested. We were on our way home to have a nice family evening. How did it turn into *this*?

It hits me now how stupid I've been, letting this stranger into my home. I was arrogant and self-righteous, thinking I was doing this good thing. Helping a girl in distress. Being kind. When all I've really done is put my family in jeopardy.

CHAPTER TWENTY-SIX

FIONA

By the time I turn into Kelly's road there are blisters forming on my heel and toes, and I'm cursing my choice of footwear. The street itself is empty and quiet, but there are still sounds from the regatta floating around on the wind. Cries and laughter from the funfair, and the whine of jet skis bombing around the lake now that the sailing is over.

Aside from the shock of Kelly being arrested, I'm still shaken up by the texts I received earlier. I can't bring myself to re-read them yet. The thought makes me feel physically sick. In fact, just knowing they're sitting there in my inbox makes me want to throw the damn phone into the lake. I guess I could erase them. But that would mean looking at them again. I give myself a shake. I can't think about that now. I have to pull myself together for the sake of my friend and her boys.

When I reach Kelly's front door, I'm shocked to see that it's been boarded up. What on earth has gone on here? Kelly forgot to mention that fact on the phone. Or maybe she doesn't know. I ring the doorbell. If the boys don't answer, I'll go around the back.

Kelly said she'd been arrested, but she didn't mention anything about her house being damaged. Maybe there was a break-in. But why on earth would they arrest Kelly if someone broke in? A female voice startles me.

'Hello?' A young uniformed police officer appears around the side of the house. I'm a little taken aback to see a police officer, but I guess I shouldn't be surprised – neither Kelly nor Ash would have wanted to leave the boys on their own.

'Hello, my name's Fiona Salinger. Kelly asked me to come and pick up Ryan and Sonny.'

'Hi.' She gives me a smile. 'I'm PC Lynette Shales.' She walks over and we shake hands.

'What happened here?' I point at the front door.

'Afraid I can't say.'

'But you know, right?'

She gives me an apologetic, businesslike smile. 'So, you're here to pick up the Taylor boys?'

'Yes.'

'Do you have any ID on you?'

'Uh, yes, hang on a minute.' I root through my bag, pull out my wallet and show her my driving licence and some credit cards. I hope she can't smell the champagne on my breath. I'm not driving, but still, it doesn't look great to pick up someone else's kids when you've been drinking.

'Okay, that's fine.' She hands me back my ID. 'Shall I bring the boys out to you?'

'Actually, can I come in? I'm dying for the loo and a glass of water. And if they're staying over, I'll need to pack some spare clothes, toothbrushes and pjs, that sort of thing.'

'Okay. I'll come back inside with you.'

'There's no need. I can lock up when I leave.'

'That's okay,' she replies, letting me know that there's no way she's leaving me here on my own.

We go in via the back door. If PC Shales wasn't here I'd have a snoop to see if I could spot any clues as to what's gone on. But the policewoman is following me around, watching my every move, so I guess a nose around is off the cards. The boys aren't in the kitchen, so I nip to the downstairs cloakroom, have a pee and splash my face. Noticing a shoe rack on the floor, I reach down and undo the straps on my sandals, kicking both of them off with a sigh of relief. I slip on a pair of Kelly's trainers to walk home in, hoping PC Shales doesn't notice or say anything. But there's no way I could walk another step in those instruments of torture.

When I return to the kitchen, the boys are standing next to the policewoman like a couple of lost puppies. I want to hug both of them tightly but decide that now isn't the time to get emotional. Instead, I clap my hands. 'Hey, guys. Lucky me, I get to see you twice in one day.' It sounds forced and patronising even to my ears.

'What happened to Mum?' Ryan grunts.

'Tell you what, let's get your stuff together, and we can talk about all that back at my place.'

'Our *stuff*?' Ryan frowns. 'What do you mean?'

'Where's Mum?' Sonny's face is pale, and he looks like he's about to cry. I notice that Ryan is holding his hand, and my heart melts. I take a breath.

'Your mum called and asked if you could stay with me and Nathan, just until she gets home. So let's go and pack an overnight bag, okay?'

For a moment, I think they're going to protest and refuse, but after a couple of seconds' hesitation, Ryan nods and I follow them both upstairs. PC Shales watches as they throw a few things into some bags. It doesn't take too long and eventually we're ready to go. The policewoman gives me a card with a number to call if there are any problems with the boys, and we leave her to lock up Kelly's house.

The walk back to my place is quiet and a little sad. The boys must be utterly confused and more than a little scared, so I decide not to add to their anxieties with more questions. Despite Kelly being one of my best friends, I realise the boys haven't visited my house much. She and Michael used to come around for dinner quite regularly, and Kelly pops over for coffee now and then, but it's not really a kid-friendly house. It's not warm and cosy – it's sleek, with hard expensive surfaces in marble and glass, black and gold. When Kelly and I meet up, it's usually me who goes to Kelly's place. I guess it's more relaxed there. More homely.

I hope I'm up to the job of looking after her boys. I've never had them to stay before. Does that make me a terrible person? I mean, Kelly lost her husband last year, she's a single parent, and I'm supposed to be her best friend. I remember offering a few times, but never anything concrete. It was always vague statements where I would say, *If you need anything, just ask.* But she's never asked. I should have been more specific. I should have said, *Hey, Kelly, how about I have the kids next weekend so you can relax?* That's what I should have said.

And Kelly's had a tricky time with Ryan. He misses his dad. Both boys do. I glance at them as they walk by my side, subdued, tired, their clothes rumpled, their hair a little messed up. I resolve to really pamper them while they're with me. Spoil them. Make the most of having them to stay. Maybe… maybe Nathan will see how lovely it could be to have kids around the place.

I texted him earlier to let him know what was happening. It was with some nervousness that I waited for his reply, but thankfully he messaged back to say he'd pick up dinner for the four of us. As we walk down the driveway, I see Nathan getting out of the car with several takeaway bags. Good; he didn't forget. Although I don't feel remotely hungry.

'Hello, you two.' Nathan nods at the boys. 'I picked us up a Chinese takeaway, so I hope you're hungry – there's a lot of food here.'

'Thanks,' they mumble.

Nathan looks questioningly at me, over the top of their heads. And then he frowns. 'What the hell are you wearing on your feet?'

'Huh? Oh, they're Kelly's trainers. I got blisters so I had to take off my sandals.'

'Well, they look awful.'

'I know, sorry.' I turn back to the boys. 'Let's go inside. I'll show you to your rooms… unless you'd prefer to share?'

Ryan shrugs and Sonny doesn't respond so I decide to take charge and put them together in one room in case they feel strange or homesick during the night.

Nathan opens the front door and disables the alarm. 'I'll get plates and put the food out while you settle them in, Fi.'

'Okay, great. Come on boys, kick off your shoes and follow me.' I lead them up the wood and glass staircase, deciding to give them the best guest suite, which has views over the lake.

'Wow,' Sonny says, his eyes drawn to the balcony.

'Be careful out there,' I warn. 'No leaning over the balcony – I don't want any accidents.' I open the sliding doors. 'Let's get some fresh air in here.'

Both boys step outside and stare out across the water.

'Why don't you take a few minutes to get washed and changed and I'll meet you downstairs, okay?'

They look at me, their expressions still dazed.

'Okay?' I repeat, trying to sound as comforting and kind as I can.

They nod.

I leave them on the balcony, wondering whether they'll actually do as I asked. Nathan won't be too happy if they come down to dinner still sweaty and crumpled from a day's racing. Taking heed of my own advice, I make my way up to our master suite on the top floor, which sits above the boys' room. I shower quickly and change into a loose-fitting linen dress. A couple of my blisters have already split, so I apply some antiseptic before forcing my feet into a pair of raw-silk mules which are the least painful option after bare feet. But I don't want to risk Nathan's disapproval by going barefoot to dinner, not when he seems to be in such a good mood.

*

Fifteen minutes later, the four of us are seated on the deck with a mountain of Chinese food laid out in the centre of the table. Thankfully, the boys took up my suggestion of getting showered and changed, and they sit next to me with damp hair and pink cheeks, smelling of Bamford shower gel.

Nathan's given us all chopsticks, but I notice the boys are struggling with theirs, so I nip back into the kitchen to fetch them each a fork, avoiding Nathan's eye.

'It's a great Chinese, right?' Nathan says. 'It's from an award-winning place just out of town. You should try some of the noodles; they're amazing.' He holds out the carton, and I watch Sonny attempting to scoop a portion onto his plate, but most of them end up slithering onto the table.

I get to my feet again. 'Let me…' I help him dish out a portion, then use a napkin to scoop the runaway noodles off the table and wipe up the stain. I don't dare look at Nathan. Sloppy eating is one of his bugbears.

Nathan tuts at me. 'Leave it, Fi, it's just a bit of sauce. Nothing to worry about.'

Surprised and relieved at my husband's new laid-back attitude, I sit back down and take a small mouthful of egg fried rice.

Sonny puts his fork down. 'Mum said we were going to have pizza tonight. Do you think they'll give her any supper at the police station?'

'Of course they will.' I shoot a worried glance over to Nathan. 'She'll be having a lovely dinner there; don't you worry about that.'

'How do you know?' Ryan asks.

'Because Ash will be there making sure your mum's okay,' I reply.

'Why did they take her to the police station anyway?' Sonny asks, his chin trembling. 'She didn't do anything wrong. Is it because of Sophie?'

Ryan glares at his brother. 'You weren't supposed to tell anyone.'

'Who?' I wrack my brain to think of anyone I know called Sophie, but my mind comes up blank.

Sonny's cheeks flush. 'But—'

'She's Mum's friend,' Ryan says through a mouthful of food. 'She's been staying with us.'

'Why is it okay for *you* to tell them about Sophie and not *me*?' Sonny cries. 'Anyway, she was in the ambulance when we got back from the regatta. I saw her.'

'Who was in the ambulance?' I ask. 'Your mum or this Sophie person?'

'Sophie,' Ryan replies.

Nathan gives me an indecipherable look before turning back to Ryan. 'And you're sure Sophie was actually staying in the house with you and your mum?'

'Yeah, she was staying up in the attic.'

'And it was supposed to be a secret,' Sonny adds.

'Don't worry,' I say more brightly than I feel, 'I'm sure we'll find out exactly what's going on tomorrow.'

'Why don't we go and see Mum now?' Sonny asks. 'We can ask her about it.'

'We won't be allowed,' Ryan says, scowling. 'Because we're kids.'

'Fiona's right,' Nathan interjects. 'We'll be able to find out more tomorrow. For now, it's best if you both have an early night so you're fresh for tomorrow. Your mum won't want to see you with bags under your eyes.'

'It's only six o'clock,' Ryan says. 'Only babies go to bed at six. Mum usually lets me stay up till at least nine.'

'Do you want some more Chinese?' I ask. 'There's lots left.'

'No thanks.' Sonny puts his fork down on the plate. Ryan does the same.

They've hardly eaten anything. Maybe they didn't like the food. Or maybe they're too worried to eat.

'What about some dessert?' I turn to my husband. 'Did you bring those cupcakes home from the regatta?'

'No, I binned them. You know we don't keep that sugary crap in the house.'

I incline my head towards the boys to let him know not to use that kind of language in front of our guests, but Nathan screws up his nose at me as if I'm making too big a deal of it.

'It's okay,' Ryan replies, catching on at my unsubtle attempt to shield him and his brother. 'The kids at school say way worse than that.'

'You see, Fi.' Nathan grins at Ryan. 'I'm down with the kids.'

'Fair enough.' I give a wry laugh, pleased that the ice has broken a little. It's funny that we've known these boys since they were born, but we don't really know them at all. I feel a little out of my depth. At least Nathan seems to be at ease with them.

After dinner, despite the early hour, the boys seem keen to go up to their room. I show them the TV hidden in the armoire, but they turn their noses up, preferring their phones and earbuds.

'Nathan and I will be just downstairs if you need anything. There's a mini fridge up here, with drinks and snacks, but make sure you brush your teeth after, okay?'

They nod.

'Our bedroom is on the next floor up if you need anything during the night, okay? Oh, and close the balcony doors if you switch the light on or you'll be bitten to death by the bugs.'

Again, they nod.

I really want to hug them, but I also don't want to make them uncomfortable, so I settle for tousling their hair and blowing them each a kiss. I leave the room, thankful they have each other to talk to. They must be so confused, poor mites. I wonder what on earth Kelly can have done to get herself arrested. It's bound to be a misunderstanding. Kelly wouldn't hurt a fly. And who on earth is this Sophie woman the boys were talking about?

Downstairs, Nathan has ensconced himself in the lounge and is on his phone scrolling through social media. I clear away the remains of the Chinese, clean down the surfaces and set the dishwasher going before joining him.

He pats the sofa and I sit next to him. 'Thanks for getting the food in.'

He doesn't look up. 'I didn't really have much choice, did I, Fi?'

At his words, I hold myself very still. I had thought Nathan was cool with us having Kelly's children to stay, but I obviously misread the situation.

He continues looking at his phone for a while, and I wonder if I should leave him to it. I'm just about to get up and leave the room when he shifts around in his seat and looks directly at me. 'You knew how much I'd been looking forward to today,' he says through gritted teeth, tossing his phone down on the sofa. 'This race was the one day I got to relax and do something I love. My chance to show this town who I am. And then I actually win the race and hope that my wife might be a just a little bit excited for me. Just a little bit proud or pleased or whatever. I hoped that we could come home and relax, or maybe even go out and celebrate together. But, no. You couldn't give a shit about my feelings.' He curls his lip in disgust. 'You're more concerned with your hippy friend who's managed to fuck up her life with no thought for her own kids and is expecting everyone else to pick up the pieces.' He shakes his head.

My stomach has descended to the floor and I can hardly breathe. I don't know what to say to make this better, so I say nothing. The only saving grace is that he's speaking in a low whisper so at least the boys won't be able to hear him.

'And what were you *thinking*, offering to look after her kids? We don't even know how long she'll be held in custody. It could be days, weeks, *months* even. We're not taking on that responsibility. Not with everything else we've got going on in our lives.'

I want to defend myself. To say that Kelly is my best friend. That if the tables were turned she would do the same for me. But instead I stay silent, my heart thumping, the egg fried rice congealing in my throat, the noodles slithering around in my stomach like worms.

The way he was acting around Ryan and Sonny – all jovial and light-hearted – I thought he liked them. But I realise now it was all an act. Nathan wants everyone to love him. Deep down he's insecure. He's like a little boy himself. I should have known that having Ryan and Sonny to stay was a bad idea. But what else could I do? I couldn't turn down Kelly's request.

'You'll have to get rid of them tomorrow,' Nathan hisses. 'And keep them out of my way. You know how I feel about kids.'

Right on cue, Sonny calls out to me from the staircase – it turns out we forgot to bring his homework with us and he needs to have done it by Monday.

'Don't worry, mate, Aunty Fi will pop back for it,' Nathan calls out to him. He turns back to me and drops his voice. 'Just as well you're going out; I can't stand to look at you right now. Just get out of my sight.' His eyes have grown so dark I can no longer see my reflection in them.

I stand as if in a dream, as though my mind is removed from my body. Nathan has only ever hit me a couple of times before and I don't want to give him an excuse to do it a third time. I keep my eyes trained on the ground and I leave the room, closing the door quietly behind me.

CHAPTER TWENTY-SEVEN

TIA

Lurching in through the front door, I close it behind me and lean back against the cool wood, shutting my eyes and enjoying a momentary feeling of safety. Although I'm kidding myself. It isn't safe here, or anywhere. The person behind the photos can contact me whenever they like. They know where I live, they have my phone number. They're toying with me. Enjoying their little game, whatever it is.

It has to be Fiona. She didn't want to talk to me at the regatta – avoiding my gaze and acting awkwardly around me. She's guilty as hell. I know she is. I want to scream with frustration. I wish I could block all of it out and go back to how my life used to be, before the photos. There's half a bottle of white wine in the fridge that I could quite happily polish off right now. That would go some way to helping me forget.

Snapping open my eyes, I march into the kitchen, stride past the fridge, and pour myself a tall glass of water. I gulp it down and wipe my mouth with the back of my hand. Then I pour myself another glass and sip this one more slowly. It soothes my parched throat and lessens the pounding in my head. Now is not the time to get drunk and wallow. Ed will be back with the children soon and then I'll be caught up in bathtime and bedtime and I won't have the headspace to think about anything.

I need an ally. A friend. Someone to help me look at this clearly. To help me to decide what to do. I need to speak to Kelly and tell her the whole truth about what's been going on. I sit at the kitchen table and call her number but, annoyingly, it goes straight to voicemail.

'Hey, Kels, it's me. Hope Ryan's okay after today. He did so well, bless him. Look, I really need to talk to you. Would it be okay if I came over just for half an hour or so? Call me back and let me know, okay? Or message if easier. Love you.'

I get up and start pacing the length of the kitchen, clutching my phone and waiting for Kelly to call me back. Maybe her mobile's run out of battery. She might not check her messages until tomorrow and I really can't stand the idea of waiting all night to speak to her.

After a few more minutes of pacing and staring at my silent phone, I go upstairs, shower and get changed into a comfy track-suit. Then I come back down, busy myself with some household chores and begin getting supper ready for when Ed gets in with the kids. They eventually bustle in through the front door in a whirlwind of laughter and excitement. My heart fills with love as they burst into the kitchen with tales of carousels and candy floss. Their presence only strengthens my resolve. I can't lose my family because of some horrible vindictive person out there.

'So you had a terrible time at the fair, then?' I tease.

'No, silly.' Rosie giggles. 'It was a *good* time not a terrible time.'

'Yeah, silly Mummy!' Leo pretends to be cross and waggles his finger at me. 'We went round on the big wheel really high up in the sky like we was flying.'

'You were flying?'

'We weren't really flying, Leo,' Rosie says.

'Yes we was!'

'How was Nathan?' I wind my arms around Ed. 'I hope he didn't go on too much about winning. You did amazingly seeing as it was your first ever race.'

'I was terrible, Tee, but thanks for stroking my ego. Nathan was all right. Just giving me a bit of friendly banter, you know. He didn't actually stay too long; had to rush off to pick up some food or something.' Ed's gaze lands on the table and he makes a big deal of sniffing the air. 'Something smells good. Shepherd's pie?'

'I know it's not the right weather for a hot meal, but after all that picnic food today I thought it would be good to have a proper dinner. And, as you've got the night off, I didn't think it was fair that you should cook.'

'I love you, Mrs Perry.' Ed comes over and gives me a kiss. 'Shall I make a salad?'

'Already done and in the fridge. Sit down, I'll go and bath the kids.'

'You sure?'

'Yep.'

An hour later, the children are in bed and the dishes are soaking in the sink.

'Fancy watching a movie?' Ed asks as he comes down the stairs having kissed the children good night. 'It's our lucky night – both of them have zonked straight out. All that fresh air and excitement.'

'Actually, Ed, would you mind if I popped over to see Kelly? I want to make sure she's okay after Ryan's meltdown.' I feel bad stretching the truth, but I can't very well tell Ed why I really want to visit my friend.

'Uh, yeah, sure.' He looks a little disappointed and I feel bad.

'You can have full control of the remote, maybe watch an action movie.'

He grins. 'Now you're talking. Okay, send Kelly my love, won't you.'

I give my husband a quick peck, fetch my handbag and head out into the warm evening air. Kelly still hasn't replied to my message, but I figure if I show up on her doorstep she won't have the heart to turn me away. I feel a faint stirring of optimism in my chest.

Kelly will help me sort this out, I know she will. As I walk, the scent of barbecues wafts over painted fences and fragrant hedges. Snatches of teenage laughter and the ebb and flow of pumping basslines from passing cars reminds me of what life used to be like when I was younger.

As I draw closer to Kelly's house, doubts begin to flare up. Will Kelly believe that the images have been faked? I stuffed the envelope of photos into my bag to show them to her. But the thought of another person – even Kelly – seeing them makes me feel nauseous. I can't back out of this now. Even if my friend is disapproving, at least I can trust her not to say anything to anyone else.

I turn into Kelly's road, my hand resting protectively on my bag. I'm paranoid that someone's going to mug me, take my bag and find the images. When I reach Kelly's drive, I'm shocked to see that her front door has been covered over by a huge sheet of plywood. *What the hell?* Has she had a break-in or something?

I ring the doorbell, but it's obvious she can't open the front door with it boarded up like that, so maybe I should go around the back. Before I turn to go, the curtain at the lounge window twitches, making me jump. I swallow down a dart of fear. This is ridiculous. It was obviously Kelly or one of the boys. I walk over to the window and rap on the glass. 'Ryan? Kelly? Are you there? It's me, Tia!' Cupping my hands around my face, I peer in, but I can't see anyone inside; it's too dark. I ring the doorbell again, but I'm beginning to get really creeped out. Despite Kelly's car being parked in the drive, it feels as though the house is deserted. Abandoned. Which is crazy, because Kelly would've told me if she was going away.

'Tia? What are you doing here?'

I turn to see Fiona coming around the side of the house. My fear dissolves and my hackles rise. Why is *she* here? 'Fi... hi. I've come to see Kelly.'

'Oh.' She doesn't look herself. She seems somehow smaller and a little crumpled, her hair not as shiny as usual.

'Why are *you* here?' I ask, sounding sharper than I mean to. 'Is Kelly in? What happened to the front door?'

Fiona sighs. 'It's a bit of a long story.'

'What do you mean? Are they okay?'

'The boys are staying at my place. Nathan and I are looking after them while Kelly is… well…'

'While Kelly is *what*?'

'Uh…' Fiona turns one way and then the other, like she doesn't know what to do with herself. She seems to have lost all of her usual poise. 'Why don't we go inside?'

I follow Fiona around the back of the house and into the kitchen, which seems somehow more forlorn than usual. It smells stale, and feels chilly and strange, as though the heart has been ripped out of it. I wonder what can have happened so that Kelly's boys have gone to stay at Fiona's place. She isn't exactly the maternal type. I would have had them to stay with me, if only Kelly had asked.

We sit at the kitchen table and I wait for Fiona to tell me what's going on. It's all so strange that I wonder if this has anything to do with the photos I've been sent. Is it more than a coincidence that Fiona is here – at the scene of another strange situation?

'Well?' I prompt.

'Okay, so after you left the regatta, I had a call from Kelly to tell me that she was being arrested.'

My mouth falls open. Of all the things I expected her to say, this wasn't one of them. 'You're joking, right?'

'I'm not. I wish I was.'

'Arrested for what, exactly?'

'She didn't say.'

'Didn't you ask?'

Fiona arches an eyebrow. 'Of course I asked, but she couldn't really say anything at the time. She was in the middle of it all.'

'So what happens now?' I know it's selfish, but I'm hurt that Kelly called Fiona to look after Ryan and Sonny instead of me.

'Well…' Fiona's wearing a sheepish expression.

'What?'

'I think your brother was the arresting officer, so maybe you could give him a call and get the lowdown.'

'*Ash* arrested Kelly! What the hell did he think he was doing?'

'His job, I presume.'

I scowl.

'Sorry, but it's true. Anyway, that's beside the point; we have to find out what's going on.'

'I'll give Ash a call, but you know what he's like, he won't tell me anything he's not supposed to. It's more than his job's worth.'

Fiona nods in agreement. 'Ryan and Sonny told me they had some woman staying with them – a friend, Sophie, I think her name was. Did Kelly mention anything to you about her having a friend to stay?'

'No. I don't know any Sophie.'

'Me neither.'

'Are you absolutely sure that's her name?'

'Definitely.'

'What about a last name?'

Fiona shakes her head. 'They didn't mention a last name. But they did say that it was supposed to be a secret. They weren't supposed to tell anyone she was staying. Kelly made them promise. In fact, they said she was staying in their attic, which is really strange, don't you think?'

'Very. Do you think Sophie is a criminal, and somehow Kelly's got herself caught up in it?'

Fiona points at me. 'Yes! You're right. That must be it. That must be what's happened. I knew Kelly wouldn't have done anything illegal.'

'But who is this Sophie? And what did she actually do?'

'No idea.' Fiona takes a breath. 'Hate to say this, but it does sound just like something Kelly would do. She's always helping people who've got themselves in trouble and they take advantage of her. She's too soft-hearted for her own good.'

'I know.' I sigh, thinking about my own predicament and how I was coming here for the very same reason – to ask for her help. 'What's going to happen to her now?'

'No idea.' Fiona picks at her nail polish. 'I called the station about half an hour ago, but they wouldn't let me speak to her. They said to try again tomorrow.'

Something occurs to me. 'Why are you here anyway? I thought you said the boys were staying at your place.'

Fiona looks away and blinks a couple of times. She looks like she might start *crying*.

'Fi? Are you okay?'

'I'm fine,' she snaps.

I bristle at her tone. 'Sorry, I was only asking.'

'No, I'm sorry for biting your head off. Sonny forgot his homework, and then Nathan and I… we had a bit of a bust-up, so I came round to get it – the homework.'

'Sorry you're having a crappy evening.' I offer up a lukewarm smile. 'I'd have thought Nathan would be in a great mood after his win today.'

'Yeah, well, he wasn't too thrilled at having visitors to stay. He wanted to go out and celebrate.'

'You mean because you've got Kelly's boys?' I think Nathan's a bit of an arsehole, but I'm still surprised that he would be so churlish – he always seems desperate to be the good guy.

Fiona flushes. 'Sorry, that came out wrong. He's fine with the boys, just cross with me for springing it on him.'

'But that's hardly your fault!' I find myself annoyed with Nathan on Fiona's behalf.

'It *is* my fault. Look, I haven't told you the whole story. I've made Nathan out to be the bad guy, but he's not. It'll be fine. I'll go back home, and we'll make up. It's no big deal.'

But I can tell she's covering up for him. There's something else in her voice. Something she's not telling me.

We agree to keep in touch over the next day or so and I offer to look after the boys if she needs me to. She waves away my offer, but I have a feeling she'll change her mind if Nathan's got any say in the matter. We agree that Fiona will go to the station tomorrow and if she doesn't have any luck getting more information, then I'll call Ash and try to get him to spill the beans. But I already know it'll be a waste of time.

Fiona and I leave Kelly's at the same time, parting ways at the end of the road as she heads to her multi-million-pound lakeside mansion, and I head home to my beautiful family in our modest home.

On the walk back, I realise that I'm still no nearer to working out what I'm supposed to do about the photos. And it doesn't look like I'll have a chance to discuss it with Kelly any time soon. She has far more important issues on her mind – like why she's being held in police custody overnight. Poor Kelly. I hope she's okay. And now, after tonight's conversation with Fiona, I'm starting to doubt my theory that she's behind the images. She didn't seem at all threatening this evening. In fact, she seemed quite vulnerable.

Afternoon shifts into dusk and, despite being a Saturday, the roads are empty. This is a quiet residential area; all the regatta celebrations will have transferred to the pubs and bars in town. The organisers used to set up a marquee by the lake with a bar and disco that played on until the early hours, but that was vetoed several years ago after the lakeside residents' committee complained about the noise.

I'm halfway home when I hear the soft shuffle of footsteps behind me. I want to turn around to see who it is, but that would look too paranoid. I remember having a conversation with some friends about women's safety when walking alone. Ed said that if he ever finds himself walking behind a lone woman, he'll always cross over to the other side of the road and fall back a little way, to make them feel less threatened. Whoever is behind me now obviously doesn't have the same level of thoughtfulness. I speed up to a brisk walk, trying not to let my imagination run away with me. But after everything that's been happening, it's hard not to.

But it's definitely not my imagination when I hear the footsteps behind me grow louder and faster, matching my own. My pulse quickens and I pray for someone to step out of their house, or for a car to pull up, for *anyone else* to come along. But there's nothing other than our two sets of footsteps, my fast-beating heart and my ragged breath. Without slowing, I reach into my bag and fumble for my keys, arranging them between my fingers like a jagged knuckleduster.

I cross over the road, and now I know I'm not being paranoid because the footsteps are still behind me. Getting closer.

I can either turn around. Or I can run.

Suddenly, I don't care about how stupid I look, I'm going to turn around and see who's behind me. I stop walking, my heart in my mouth, my right hand still clutching my bunch of keys.

As I turn, the person behind me speaks.

'Excuse me, do you know if I'm going in the right direction for Hazelmere Drive?'

My heart rate slows and the sick feeling in my stomach starts to melt away as I come face to face with a slim, pale-haired young woman wearing scruffy jeans and a long-sleeve T-shirt.

'You scared me half to death!' I exhale with a relieved smile. 'Thought you were a mugger.'

Her face falls. 'Oh, sorry, I didn't think.' She puts a hand on my arm, an oddly intimate gesture.

'S'okay. Hazelmere Drive? You need to turn around and then take the second turning on the right. We passed it just back there.' I point down the road.

'Okay, thanks.' She gives me an odd little smile before walking away.

I watch her for a moment before turning around and heading home. But rather than feeling relieved that it wasn't a mugger, that strange encounter has made me even more unsettled than before.

CHAPTER TWENTY-EIGHT

KELLY

A shout from the cell next to mine makes me jump. It's a man's voice, slurred and aggressive, swearing at one of the police officers. Everything echoes here – the doors opening and closing, the voices, the footsteps. It's how I imagine hell would be – not boiling infernos, but cold and detached and clinical. Lonely.

My own cell is a small rectangular box with a built-in bed, rubber mattress and a metal toilet in the corner. The walls are a dirty cream, and there's a grid-like window way up high letting in a weak glow of fading daylight, supplemented by two ceiling strip lights that illuminate every depressing aspect.

All I can think about are my boys and what they must be thinking right now. Are they scared? Angry? Do they even know I've been arrested? Did I make the right call asking Fiona to look after them? Ryan and Sonny are more comfortable around Tia and Ed, but how could I have asked Tia, when her own brother is the person who arrested me?

Ash barely said two words to me on the drive to the station. He wouldn't answer any of my questions about Sophie. About why I'd been arrested. The only thing he did say was that I was entitled to my own legal representation. But it's Saturday night and I can't get anyone here until at least Monday. My only other option is to use the duty solicitor. So that's what I've agreed to do.

I can't afford to waste hours or days looking for my own lawyer. Ash said the duty solicitors are pretty good. Despite him being the one to arrest me, I still trust him. Ash isn't the type of person to twist the law to his own advantage. At least I hope not.

A jangling of keys and the creak of the door handle jolts me from my thoughts, and I sit up straighter in anticipation of what's next. The door opens. It's Ash.

'Hi, Kelly. The duty solicitor is waiting to see you. Do you want to come with me?'

I stand up on shaky legs and follow Ash down a brightly lit, blue corridor, past several more cell doors. I have so many more questions to ask him, but it would be a waste of time. I'll save them for my solicitor.

Ash knocks on a door and opens it. Inside the interview room, seated at a table, is a dark-haired man in a grey suit. I'd guess he's around my age, but his confidence and stature makes him seem infinitely older and wiser. He stands when I come in and holds out his hand to shake mine. Ash nods at us both and leaves the room.

'Hi, Kelly. I'm Saul Barker, your solicitor. Officer Dewan has been filling me in on your case. Please, have a seat.' He gestures to a chair across from him and I do as he asks. 'There's a cup of tea for you on the table.'

I notice the mug in front of me.

'Do you take sugar?'

I shake my head. I have so many questions that I need to ask him, but I don't know where to start. It's as though my whole body has gone numb and my brain has floated off somewhere else.

Saul takes a sip of his tea and straightens out the notepad and sheaf of papers on the table in front of him. 'So, Kelly, just to let you know, I'm the duty solicitor on call tonight; I'm a criminal defence solicitor and I'm here to ensure that your legal rights are observed.'

'Okay. Thank you.'

He gives a curt nod. 'You've been arrested for the false imprisonment of Sophie Jones.'

'Which is ridiculous,' I say.

'Okay, so you're denying it?'

'Yes I am. Absolutely. I don't even know how they came to that conclusion.'

Saul looks down at the sheet in front of him. 'Sophie Jones claims that she was being held captive in your attic, tied to a chair by her wrists and ankles. She says she managed to shuffle over to the window and smash it, calling down to a passer-by for help. Whereupon a neighbour spotted her and called the police.' Saul is reeling off this information as though it's some kind of boring shopping list. There's no judgement or emotion in his voice. Which is more than can be said for how *I'm* feeling.

My face is heating up and my throat has gone completely dry. I take a sip of the tea in front of me. It's lukewarm and really strong but at least it lubricates my vocal cords. 'Are you kidding me? She actually said all that?'

'Yes. She says she's been held against her will since Wednesday. She also inferred that you're mentally ill. How do you know Sophie Jones?' Saul's grey eyes meet mine for the first time.

I realise my mouth is hanging open as I try to process what he's telling me. I close my mouth and swallow. 'I don't really know her at all. She showed up at my house on Wednesday morning. She was scared out of her mind so I said she could stay for a few days.'

'And had you met her before this?'

'No.'

'So, let me get this straight, you invited a stranger to stay in your house?'

I take a breath. 'When you phrase it like that it sounds a bit crazy, I know. But she was terrified. When I found her in my garden, she was literally shaking with fear. It was obvious that she was trying to get away from someone. I felt sorry for the girl so I said she could come in for a few minutes to catch her breath and have a cold drink.'

'Did she tell you that someone was after her?'

'Not at that point, no. I think she said that she was in danger and needed somewhere to hide.'

'Did you not think it would have been better to call the police?'

'Of course. That's the first thing I suggested. But as soon as I said that, she started heading out the door.'

'So why didn't you let her go?'

'I felt sorry for her. I told her that I wouldn't call the police if she didn't want me to. I also suggested contacting a shelter, but she wasn't keen on that either. She just seemed kind of shell-shocked and I thought it would be nice to give her the chance to catch her breath without putting pressure on her to contact the authorities.'

'Did you take her up to your attic?' Saul asks.

'Not straight away. First, she helped me to make some cakes for the regatta.'

'You made cakes?' Saul's expression is sceptical.

'I'd just got out the ingredients when she arrived. It was all laid out on the table, so I asked her if she wanted to help me bake. I thought it might help her to open up if we were doing something normal together.'

'And did she open up?'

'Not really.'

'So after you made the cakes, that's when you took her up to the attic?'

'Yes. I said she could stay up there until she figured out what she wanted to do.'

'And did she want to go up there with you?' Saul asks.

'What do you mean, *did she want to*?' I don't like what his question is implying. 'I didn't force her to go up there, if that's what you mean. I offered the room up there as a place to stay.'

'Sophie Jones claims that she knocked on your door to ask for directions. She happened to mention that she was thirsty, so you offered her a drink of lemonade. She said she noticed that it tasted funny. The next thing she remembers is being shut in a room where she was tied to a chair.'

'Are you joking?' I don't know whether to laugh or cry at this utter fabrication.

'Unfortunately not. She also has rope burns on her wrists and ankles consistent with being tied up.'

'But I never tied her up! I certainly never spiked her drink if that's what she's implying. She was completely free to wander around the house.'

'You let a stranger wander around your house?'

'It wasn't like that.' I push at my forehead with my fingertips, trying to think how best to word this. But it all seems to be coming out wrong.

'Look, Kelly, your story isn't making too much sense. Can you help me to understand what happened here? I'm on your side, but right now, it isn't adding up.'

'I know, I know.' There's a lump in my throat and my brain is spinning out. I need to try to calm down and make this man understand what happened. 'Okay, so this girl – Sophie – showed up at my door, scared and upset. I offered her a drink. She came in and we got talking. She said she had nowhere to go and no one who could help her. I wasn't about to turf her out onto the street, so I let her stay in our loft. She seemed really grateful. It was only supposed to be for a few hours, but then I didn't have the heart to kick her out. So I said she could stay for a day or two and we'd talk about what to do.

'Anyway, I found that I liked her and decided to help her – is there a law against that?'

Saul shakes his head, but I can tell that he's not impressed.

I square my shoulders, determined not to feel guilty for helping another human being. 'Last night there was a knock on the door.

It was a man who said he was her husband; he said his name was Greg Jones. He showed me a photo of his wife, Sophie, and said he was going door to door looking for her after she disappeared in the middle of the night on Tuesday. He said he'd reported her missing. So the police should have a record of that…'

Saul makes a note in his pad. 'I'll check.'

'After he'd gone, Sophie was terrified. She was worried that he knew where she was. I decided that whatever happened, I was going to contact a women's shelter on Monday to see if they could take her in. But then when I got home from the regatta this afternoon, the police arrested me. It's all completely surreal. I mean, how long will I have to stay here? My kids are at a friends' house, but I need to get back to them. My eldest is going through a few things at the moment. He needs me. I'm a single mum, my husband died last year.'

'I'm sorry to hear that.' He clears his throat. 'Did your children meet Sophie at all?'

'Yes, they did, and they both really liked her. She was lovely with them. I can't believe she's accusing me of all these things.'

'So she wasn't tied to a chair when she spoke to them?'

'She wasn't tied to a chair ever! Not unless she tied her*self* to the thing!'

'Okay, I understand.' His voice is calm, gentle, bringing me back from the brink of a near-meltdown. I realise I'm shaking. I can't lose it. I need to stay focused. I need to do everything I can to make them believe I'm telling the truth. The quicker I prove my innocence, the quicker I can get back to Ryan and Sonny. I take a breath.

'So, when can I expect to get out of here?'

'They'll want to interview you tonight. But I advise against answering any of their questions at this point.'

'*What?* Why? I've got nothing to hide.'

'Your story isn't straightforward. There's far too much you could say to incriminate yourself.'

'But I'm not guilty.'

'Doesn't matter. For now I would advise you answer all their questions with a strict "no comment".'

'Won't that make me look even more guilty?'

'It will make you less likely to say something that can be used against you. They're going to interview you shortly, which won't give us enough time to prepare.'

'Okay… So I just say "no comment" every time they ask me a question? That seems wrong. What will they do? Will they let me go home after?'

'They'll probably bail you tomorrow with conditions.'

'Bail me?' I can barely breathe. 'But I didn't do anything wrong! This is a nightmare. Surely I should just tell them everything I know, explain what happened so they can release me.'

Saul gives me a stern look. 'Kelly, I know this is hard to take in but try not to worry. One thing in our favour is that your children spoke to Sophie. How old are they?'

'Eight and eleven.'

'Good. Children that age are generally truthful, or at the very least bad liars. When the police question them—'

'They're going to question my children?'

He makes a calming motion with his hand. 'Trust me; in this instance, it's a good thing.'

'I still can't believe this is happening. And you said they won't let me out until tomorrow?'

'I said they'll *possibly* bail you tomorrow. But that's not guaranteed.'

My brain is buzzing, and the brightness of the room is giving me a headache. All I want is for this to be over. To go home and hug my children before sinking into a warm bath. But right now, that feels like an impossible fantasy.

After a few more questions and some administrative details, Saul stands up. 'I know this seems scary and strange right now. But I'll do everything I can to clear your name, okay?'

I nod, not trusting myself to speak. The thought of going back to that antiseptic cell is filling me with dread. But I don't want to lose it while I'm in here. That will only make things worse. I need to stay calm and try to think positively. I need to focus on the strong possibility that tomorrow I'll be able to go home – even if it is just on bail. I can cope with one night in here, can't I?

CHAPTER TWENTY-NINE

Sunday

FIONA

'But, Kelly, what were you thinking, letting a total stranger into your house? Letting her *stay* with you?'

'Please, Fi, I've spent the last twenty-four hours either answering questions about it or thinking about it. Could we save your questions for later?'

It's early afternoon and Kelly and I are walking out of the police station. I parked around the corner and Ryan and Sonny are anxiously waiting in the car to see their mum. They wanted to come into the station with me, but I thought it best if I went in without them. I figured Kelly wouldn't want her children to see her in there. And besides, I didn't know what kind of state she'd be in.

While she was being processed out, and picking up her things, Kelly briefly filled me in on what's been happening, and I have to say I'm shocked. Kelly's always been a sweet, kind-hearted person; generous with her time and going above and beyond. But what she did – taking that girl in – was just plain stupid, in my opinion. And now it's come back to bite her on the backside.

Although, if we're talking stupid, then I guess I can't really talk. I'm still burying my head in the sand about the tax audit.

'Kelly, I'm sorry for firing loads of questions at you. It must have been awful having to spend the night in a cell. And I'm so mad at Ash for taking that awful girl's word over yours.'

'It's not his fault, Fi.' She runs a hand through her messy blonde waves. 'He was just doing his job. He can't very well turn a blind eye just because a friend is involved.'

'Yes, but he's Tia's brother. He knows you'd never do anything like what that little witch is accusing you of. I mean, she must be unstable, delusional. It's crazy! And now you have to go to court! What a joke. What an absolute waste of taxpayers' money.'

'How are the boys?' Kelly neatly changes the subject. 'Thanks for looking after them. I hope they weren't any trouble.'

'They were lovely, Kelly. No trouble at all. Maybe just… a little subdued, but that's understandable.' I don't mention Nathan's attitude towards them. He didn't show his true feelings to Ryan and Sonny, but I'm worried that they might have picked up on his reluctance to have them to stay. Luckily, Nathan was all smiles today. He seems to have forgotten about yesterday's outburst. When I got back from Kelly's place yesterday evening, he was still in the lounge, so I crept upstairs to check on the boys, who were out for the count, bless them, so I turned off their light and crawled off to bed too. Nathan came up a while later. He whispered my name and didn't sound cross, but I didn't want to risk a repeat of earlier, so I pretended to be asleep.

'I can't wait to see my boys,' Kelly says, picking up her pace. 'This whole thing has been such bad timing — not that there would ever be a good time for something like this. But Ryan was finally cheering up after his disastrous race and we were planning on spending a lovely family evening together. I was feeling so optimistic yesterday.'

'You can still pick up where you left off,' I say, realising that it won't be the same. That Kelly won't be able to relax. She'll be worrying herself sick about what's going to happen next.

'What if I go to prison, Fi?' Kelly stops in the middle of the road and I have to nudge her forwards. 'What if I'm found guilty of this false imprisonment thing?'

'Never gonna happen.'

'You don't know that.'

'Mum!' Sonny has jumped out of the car and is running towards us. Ryan follows suit. I watch the three of them hug as though they've been parted for centuries, and I feel a pang of envy at their closeness. I don't think I've ever loved anyone like those three love one another, and I'm not sure I ever will. I walk to the car and wait for them to join me. Through the windscreen I see them talking nineteen to the dozen. Kelly still looks exhausted, but the light has come back into her eyes. She sees me looking and gives me a smile, ushering the boys back to the car.

'You know you didn't need to pick me up.' Kelly gets into the passenger seat. 'It's lovely of you, but it's not exactly miles to walk.'

'Are you kidding?' I reply as Ryan and Sonny get into the back seat. 'As if these two would have waited patiently for you to walk home. They've been antsy all morning waiting to hear when you were coming back.' I start the engine and pull off down the road.

'Yeah, Mum,' Sonny agrees. 'We missed you. What was it like at the police station?'

While Kelly fields more questions from the boys, my mind wanders back to my own problems. The tax inspectors will be coming back to Salinger's tomorrow, and they still haven't given me any information about anything. Any hint about what they might be looking for. The only time they ever speak to me is to query paperwork or ask what certain receipts are for. They're stern-faced and completely unapproachable, and I'm seriously worried. Especially as I've reassured Nathan that everything is fine and above board. What will I do when it all comes out into the open?

Maybe I should confide in Kelly. It would take her mind off her own problems. But that's just selfish of me. I can't burden her with my issues. Not now.

'Fi... Fiona? Are you okay? You missed the turning.' I realise Kelly's talking to me, and that she's right. I've been so caught up in my thoughts that I've taken the turning towards my house instead of hers.

'Oh, sorry. I'll turn left here.'

'Is everything okay?' Kelly puts a hand on my arm.

'Yeah.' I take a breath. 'Yes, everything's fine. I just zoned out for a minute.'

'Oh!' she cries suddenly. 'Slow down! Slow down!'

At her outburst, I hit the brake, swerve slightly and almost hit a parked car. 'Kelly, what is it? What's wrong?'

'Mum!' Sonny calls from the back seat.

'Are you okay, Mum?' Ryan asks.

'Sorry, Fi, but is that Tia?' Kelly turns and cranes her head. 'On the other side of the road, back there on the corner. Who's that she's talking to?'

I glance in the rear view and see Tia talking to a youngish, dark-haired man. 'Yes, that's Tia. Do you want to go and speak to her?'

'Who's that man she's with?'

I realise I've stopped in the middle of the road, but there are no cars behind me so I'm all right for the moment. I put my hazards on anyway and turn around to get a better look. The guy looks to be in his twenties, but it's not anyone I recognise. 'Is he someone you know? Do you want me to pull over?'

'Yes! I mean, no! Keep driving, keep driving!'

I turn off the hazards and continue down the road, wondering what it is that could have got Kelly so spooked about that guy.

The boys are still looking out of the back window. 'What's the matter, Mum?' Ryan asks.

'Nothing, Ry. I just thought it was someone I know, that's all.'

'Everything okay?' I mouth at Kelly.

Her face has drained of colour and she's wearing a worried expression.

'Who is that guy?' I hiss, trying not to let the boys hear me.

'It's him,' she says in a low voice so the kids can't hear.

'Who?'

'He's the man who called round to my house asking about Sophie. He said she'd gone missing and that he was her husband. His name's Greg Jones.'

'So what's he doing talking to Tia?'

'I don't know.' Kelly fidgets with her hands in her lap.

'That man's not called Greg Jones,' Sonny calls out from the back seat. Obviously we weren't speaking quietly enough to keep our conversation private.

'What do you mean he's not called Greg Jones?' Kelly turns to look at her son. 'How do you know what he's called?'

'Because that's Rosie's teacher, Mr Jeffries.'

Kelly tuts. 'No, I think you must have got it wrong, Sonny.'

'It's definitely Mr Jeffries, Mum,' Ryan chips in. 'He sometimes teaches us PE, if Mr Nichols is off.'

'Are you absolutely sure?' Kelly asks.

Both Ryan and Sonny make noises of agreement.

With one eye still on the road, I glance across at Kelly, whose face is now even paler than before. I wonder what on earth this could mean.

CHAPTER THIRTY

TIA

The plastic handle is digging into the skin on my fingers, so I transfer the shopping bag to my left hand and roll my right shoulder back and forth. I should've divided the groceries between two bags and evened out the weight. I'm debating whether or not to set the bag down on the pavement, but that might give Mr Jeffries the idea that I want to linger and chat, when actually I'm dying to get these groceries home before the hot sun curdles the milk and wilts the vegetables.

I bumped into Rosie's teacher a couple of minutes ago on my way home from the supermarket. I nodded and smiled and gave him a quick hello, but then he started talking to me about the weather and it would have been rude to cut him off, so here we are on the corner of the empty street in the middle of a stilted conversation. I would have thought the last thing a teacher would want on his day off is to talk to one of his pupil's parents.

He pushes his dark fringe out of his eyes. 'I saw your husband at the regatta yesterday. He put in a good performance on the lake.'

'Thanks, I'll tell him you said that. He'll be pleased. Do you sail?'

'Used to when I was a kid, but haven't done it for years.'

'Well, if you want to get back into it, let me know and I'll give you Ed's number. They're always looking for new members at the club.'

'Thanks!' He seems genuinely thrilled. Great, this would be a good point to slope off. 'Well, it's been nice talking to—'

'Look, I'm glad I bumped into you, Mrs Perry—'

'Please, call me Tia.'

'Thanks, Tia. I'm glad I bumped into you because I wanted to ask how Rosie's been getting on at home… you know, after the incident last week with those boys calling you a murderer.'

I feel the blood rush to my cheeks. Mr Jeffries' facial expression is sympathetic, but the starkness of his question has shocked me a little. Using the word *murderer* like that. And just when I had started putting that unpleasant incident behind me. 'Uh, yes, Rosie's fine now. It was probably like Mrs Lovatt said – just children getting carried away and making things up.'

'Yes, that'll probably be it.' He smiles and straightens. 'Well, I'm glad Rosie's okay now. She's such a bright child – a real pleasure to teach.'

'Thank you.'

'Sorry, Tia, I really can't stay and chat any longer, I've got lots to get on with today. It's a busy time, you know.'

I can't help thinking it's a bit rich that he's acting like I'm the one keeping him here when it's actually *him* who's been keeping me talking. 'Yes, you must be rushed off your feet with it being nearly the end of term. Well, enjoy the rest of your day.'

'I'll do my best.' He nods and walks off, whistling.

Who on earth whistles these days? I always thought I liked Rosie's teacher, but I can't help feeling just a little creeped out by our encounter. I shiver and tell myself not to be so sensitive. I'm probably still a bit on edge after last night's episode, when I thought someone was following me home.

I hoist up the shopping bag and carry it in my arms. That feels much more comfortable, even if I am still hot and bothered. Finally I reach home, and put the bag of groceries down on the doorstep while I reach into my handbag for my keys. As I pull them out, they catch on a scrunched-up piece of paper. It tumbles onto the ground and I pick it up, thinking it must be a receipt. But it feels more weighty, like a crumpled sheet of copier paper. Curious, I straighten it out and try to make sense of what I'm looking at.

It's a poor-quality copy of a photograph. I recognise it – it's a picture from my old photo album of me, Kelly and Fiona back when we were teenagers, our arms around one another. But, troublingly, someone has used a red marker pen to scribble out our faces.

My body goes cold and then hot when I realise this must be from the same person who sent the photos.

I was only this minute with Mr Jeffries! Could it have been him? But he wasn't anywhere near my bag. Also, my keys were sitting on top of the crumpled photo, so it must have been put in my bag some time before today. Who had access to my bag? Fiona. She would also have a copy of the photograph. But why would she scribble out her own face? Perhaps to throw me off the scent?

'There you are!' I shove the photocopy back into my bag as Ed opens the front door, barefoot in shorts and a T-shirt. 'I was worried about you, Tee. You've been gone ages. I thought you were only nipping out for milk.' He picks up the bag of shopping and kisses me as he stands back up, his blonde stubble grazing my chin.

As he does so, I'm suddenly struck by how much I love this man. By how lucky I am to have him in my life. He loves me and I love him, and I realise that I can't keep this terrible secret from him any longer. I need to show him the disturbing photocopy as well as the other photos, and make him understand that they're fakes. That I have no recollection of kissing anyone or sleeping with anyone. That I would never do that to him. To *us*. I need to tell him that someone is messing with me. Trying to come between us, to break up our relationship.

Ed frowns. 'What's wrong?'

I follow him into the hall, trying not to let my emotions get the best of me. I need to do this quickly, before I chicken out and change my mind. 'Where are the kids?'

'In the garden. Rosie's making Leo have a tea party with her and her cuddly toys.'

Normally this would melt my heart and we'd both talk about how cute our kids are, but I can't focus on them right now. 'Can we talk?'

'Sounds serious.' Ed takes the shopping through to the kitchen and dumps the bag on the counter. He puts the milk away in the fridge.

Through the window I spy Rosie and Leo sitting cross-legged on a picnic rug on the grass in the shade of the neighbour's overhanging tree. All Rosie's toys have been arranged in a circle with a plate and cup in front of them. Miraculously, Leo is sitting fairly still and seems to be enjoying himself – probably because each plate contains a tiny piece of cake and Leo will get to eat some of it if he goes along with Rosie's game.

Ed sits at the kitchen table. I should probably join him, but I'm far too wound up to sit down. A trickle of sweat runs down my back and my guts twist at the thought of what I'm about to say.

'Tee?' Ed gives me a worried stare. 'You're starting to freak me out.'

'Sorry, sorry.' I push an imaginary strand of hair out of my eyes and take a breath.

My phone buzzes in my bag, but I ignore it.

'So?' Ed prompts.

My phone buzzes again.

'Do you want to get that?' he asks.

I sigh. 'Maybe I should check, just in case it's Kelly.' I pull my phone from my bag and see that there are two new text messages. I stop breathing for a moment. They're both from the same unknown number.

Hello Tia.

...

I'll destroy the photos if you'll agree to meet me.

I take a breath and try to decide what I should do. Should I show the texts to Ed? Or is there now a way I can resolve this without involving my husband?

'Everything okay?' Ed asks.

'It's just Kelly.' The lie trips off my tongue easily and I feel ashamed. 'Can you hang on a minute while I text her back?'

'Sure.' Ed gets to his feet. 'Is she all right?'

'Not sure.'

'Send her my love. I'll put the shopping away while you're doing that.'

'Thanks.' I don't dare look up at him in case he can read the lie on my face. I leave the kitchen and go into the lounge, my heart pounding. I read the messages again and try to decide what I should do. But my fingers take over and I text back:

When?

The reply is almost instant:

Tonight.

CHAPTER THIRTY-ONE

***Ashridge Falls teacher faces
multiple charges of sexual assault***

***Married father of two, Brian Lawson (41) – who teaches
history at Ashridge Falls Senior School – appeared in court
today, just two weeks after his arrest.***

*Lawson is charged with committing sexual offences against three
girls under 16. One of these offences is alleged to have taken place
last month. The other two incidents are alleged to have happened
last year. However, the previous victims have only recently had
the courage to step forward and speak out.*

*Mr Lawson appeared before Ashridge Falls Magistrates Court
on 24 July and was released on bail until 20 September, when
he is due in the dock at Portreach Crown Court. His bail was set
with conditions that prevent him going near the school. He has
also been ordered not to attempt to contact his alleged victims.*

*Presiding magistrate Penelope Fitz told him: 'That means no
contact at all – physical, verbal, electronic, or getting someone
to pass them a message.'*

*Carl Beasley, Portreach Council's director of children's
services, said: 'We have worked closely with the police, and will
continue to do so, in conducting enquiries that led to the arrest*

and subsequent charging of Brian Lawson for offences relating to minors.

'We would like to praise the prompt action of both the teaching staff and police in taking action and dealing with this quickly once aware of the concerns.'

Detective Inspector Leonard Pagett from Portreach Constabulary's Public Protection Department said: 'Specialist officers from our Child Abuse Investigation Unit have visited several families as part of our enquiries. Police are working closely with the County Council to identify, contact and speak with anyone who may have further information.

'Detectives are responding swiftly and sensitively to ensure families are supported while the court case continues.

'At this delicate early stage of the legal process, it's important for people to avoid jumping to inaccurate assumptions about this situation. We know there will be concern in the community, but please work with us by contacting police to discuss any information or queries you may have directly.'

Colin Williams, headteacher of Ashridge Falls Senior School, said: 'It is upsetting to inform parents that a member of teaching staff has been charged with offences relating to children.

'This is distressing for both parents and staff at the school, who are obviously shocked.

'We are working with the police to support this investigation, and I am reassured how quickly this has been dealt with so far.'

He added: 'I can understand that this situation will be of huge concern to parents and carers of pupils at the school, but I hope they can accept that, because the legal process is under way, we are unable to comment further at this time.

'I would, however, ask that parents and students refrain from speculation about the case, as such talk can be misguided and could even affect the legal process.

'*The safety and protection of children is our first priority and all staff are subject to enhanced CRB checks before they are cleared to work.*'

Lawson has been suspended by the school pending the outcome of the trial.

CHAPTER THIRTY-TWO

Sunday

KELLY

Fiona turns off the engine. It's strange to be back home. Feels like weeks since I was last here. I can hardly believe the regatta was only yesterday. I get out of the car, stretch and gaze around a street that seems all at once strange and familiar. The ground-floor curtains to the house opposite suddenly close, which is a little strange, seeing as it's bright daylight outside. Maybe they're having an afternoon nap. I turn back to see my next-door neighbour, Margo, look up from tending her front garden, her grey hair dishevelled and the knees of her trousers grass-stained. I manage to smile and give her a short wave. I should ask her about her husband Bob's broken wrist. She's always been a lovely neighbour, but I don't have the energy for a conversation right now.

'Shame on you,' she says, gathering her gardening tools and heading back towards her front door.

My mouth falls open, and I glance back to see if the boys heard what she said, but they're only just getting out of the car. Fiona, on the other hand, looks as outraged as I feel.

'What the hell?' she mouths at me.

I now see that a few other neighbours across the street have come out of their houses. They're chatting to one another, and not so subtly looking in my direction. This is ridiculous! Do they really believe I held Sophie prisoner in my attic? I'm a widowed mother of two who's known most of them for over a decade. I can't let the boys see that anything's wrong, so I usher them towards the house.

As we step in through the back door, the boys race off to their bedrooms, happy to be back. By contrast, I feel odd being back inside my home. Like I'm an intruder. My mind is racing. *Correction*, it's whirling and spinning, especially after what's just happened outside. Not to mention that I've just discovered Sophie's husband is a teacher at Ashridge Academy.

'What an old witch,' Fiona hisses. 'I thought Margo was supposed to be nice! Want me to have a word with her? Set her straight?'

'No, leave it. Let them all gossip. They'll soon get it out of their system. Unless…' I can't even complete my sentence.

'Unless *what*?'

'Unless I…'

'*What?* You'll be cleared of all this nonsense, Kels. And then your horrible neighbours will have to apologise for being total you-know-whats.'

'I hope you're right.'

'There's no "hoping I'm right" about it. The whole thing is preposterous.'

My belly feels like it's filled with rocks. Everything seems so hopeless and awful right now. And the worst thing is that I've felt like this before. Years ago, when I couldn't go anywhere without being stared at or bad-mouthed. When I was the subject of vile gossip. But I can't bring that up now. Not with Fiona, of all people.

'Thanks, Fi. I don't know what I'd have done without you this weekend. You should go, though.' I try and fail to sound brighter. I don't want to be a burden. 'You've done so much already, looking after the boys and picking me up from the station. I'm taking up too much of your time.'

'Don't be silly, Kelly. I'm more than happy to stay for a while. For as long as you need me to.'

'Thanks, hon.' I can't deny that it's nice to have a bit of moral support; someone to talk to rather than facing everything on my own. 'Do you want a cuppa?'

'Yes, but I'll make it. Why don't you go and have a shower and get changed? You must be feeling grotty after your night away.'

'You read my mind. I've actually been yearning for a long soak in a bubble bath, but I'll have one later. I'd like a cup of tea first.' I sit at the table while Fi busies herself making us tea. 'So what do think about Sophie's husband being a teacher at Ryan and Sonny's school? It's a bit of a weird coincidence, don't you think?'

'Hmm, maybe.'

'Why *maybe*?'

Fiona shakes the tea canister. 'You've run out of teabags.'

'New packet in the larder.' I stand up to fetch it, but she waves at me to sit back down.

'I guess he has to work somewhere. Ashridge Falls isn't exactly a huge place.'

'Yes, but if he's a teacher at school called Mr Jeffries, why did he say his name was Jones when he came round here looking for Sophie?'

'That's a good point.'

'I'll buy into the fact that he's a local teacher. But why did he feel the need to give me a false name? Unless he's up to something shady.' I lean my elbows on the table and rest my chin in my hands. 'This whole thing is so strange. I mean, first Sophie shows up here looking for somewhere to hide from him – her supposed abusive husband. And then she pretends that I've been holding her here against her will. It doesn't make any sense. I feel like my head's going to explode.'

'And you didn't accidentally lock her in the attic?' Fiona asks.

I give her a look. 'No, I didn't accidentally lock her in the attic. Why would I have done that? The door doesn't even have a lock. Anyway, she's claiming I tied her to a chair. And that's not something you can do accidentally.'

'Just asking. Trying to help you get to the bottom of what's going on.' Fiona brings our drinks over and sits next to me. 'Do you know which neighbour helped her "escape"?'

I shake my head. 'No. Not sure I even want to know. I'm certainly not going to ask. It's bad enough having all the neighbours gossiping about me, without having to confront them face to face. Although after the way Margo was behaving out there, it sounds like it could have been *her*. Sophie must have filled her head with all kinds of lies. I'm seriously considering moving house.'

'You can't let them drive you away.'

I sigh and lean back in my chair. 'You're right. I love this house. I could never move. But you know what I mean. It's not going to be particularly nice, having to face that lot out there every day.'

Fi blows on her tea and takes a sip. 'So what happens now?'

'I have to go to court the week after next.'

'Does that mean you'll need a lawyer? I could ask Nathan if he knows anyone good. I'm sure he does.'

'Actually, I quite liked the duty solicitor. They assigned him to me at the police station and he was quite straight talking and easy to get along with.'

'Yes, but is he any good? What's his name?'

'Saul Barker.'

Fiona gets out her phone.

'What are you doing?'

'What do you think? I'm googling him.' She taps and scrolls for a few seconds. 'Here he is. Ooh, I can see why you want to keep him. He's gorgeous.'

I shake my head and tut. 'Not interested.'

Fiona points at me. 'You've gone red. You think he's hot.'

'So childish.' I smile to let her know I'm not too annoyed.

She smiles back. 'I'm just trying to cheer you up a bit; lighten the mood. But I know it's not the time. I don't know what's wrong with me at the moment. My judgement's off.'

'It's the perfect time. Otherwise I'd just curl up in a heap and cry.' My voice cracks and I clear my throat to try to disguise it. But I'm too late, because Fiona throws her arms around me and squeezes.

'It'll be fine, Kel. I won't let anything bad happen to my best friend.'

'Distract me,' I say, pulling away from her warm hug and patting my cheeks to try to get my emotions under control.

'With what?'

'Anything. What's going on with you at the moment? I've been so self-obsessed that I've been ignoring all my friends lately. Tia wanted to talk to me about something and I just haven't had the time. So, is everything good with you and Nathan?'

Fiona shrugs and nods.

'Is that a yes? Or a not sure?'

'Things are the same as always.'

'He must be chuffed with his win yesterday.'

'Yeah. He really is.'

I get the feeling that Fiona doesn't want to talk about Nathan. I get that a lot since Michael died. My friends are wary of talking about their partners in case they upset me or something. Just because I lost my husband, doesn't mean I don't want to talk about my friends' relationships. But I won't push it for now. Hopefully if there was a real problem, Fiona would confide in me. 'And work?' I add. 'How's Salinger's?'

She doesn't answer straight away.

'Fi?'

'Are you sure you want to know?'

'What do you mean? Is there something up?'

'Don't worry, it's fine. I won't bore you with it now.'

'Fiona, tell me.'

She stares down at her mug and I notice a tear drip into her tea.

'Fi, what's wrong?'

'I'm sorry, I'm sorry.' She wipes her eyes. 'I shouldn't be burdening you with my crap when you've got so much more to deal with.'

'Psht.' I wave away her worries about me. This isn't like Fi. She never has emotional outbursts. She's usually the calmest, most self-controlled person I know.

'Kelly, I've done something stupid.'

'Haven't we all, love,' I quip, trying to put her at ease.

'This is *really* stupid though. And now I think I'm going to lose everything because of it.'

'You mean Salinger's?'

'I mean *everything*.'

'Nathan?'

'He won't forgive me. He's got such high expectations, Kelly. You don't know what he's like. He thinks I'm this perfect wife. He thinks I'm so successful and in control, but I'm not. It's all falling apart.'

I can't imagine what Fiona can have done that could be so awful. I bet it's not as bad as she thinks it is. She puts such pressure on herself. She always has. 'Just tell me, Fi. You know that if I can help in any way, I will.'

She sniffs. 'I know.'

I go over to the dresser and fetch her a tissue.

'Thanks.' She wipes her eyes and nose.

'So?'

'Earlier this week I had a visit from a couple of tax inspectors. They're doing an audit of my business.'

I relax a little at discovering her worries are business related. Not that I think it isn't important, but compared to her marriage or her health, hopefully this is more easily fixable. 'Try not to worry. I'm sure tax audits are quite common, aren't they?'

'I don't know. But… well… I think someone reported me.'

'They reported you to the tax office?'

She nods earnestly, her eyes still red.

'Why would anyone do that?'

'Lots of reasons. People don't like me, Kel.'

'Don't be ridiculous, of course they like you.'

'They don't. They think I'm a cold, snooty bitch. But it's only because of what happened. I just can't seem to connect with people.'

'You mean since…?' I don't finish my sentence; we both know what I'm talking about.

She shrugs and nods. 'But anyway, this is nothing to do with that. I'm rambling about stuff that isn't relevant. Basically, someone reported me. I think it could've been Molly, or maybe even Paul Barton—'

'Really?' I curl my lip. I'm not keen on our childhood dentist either. Even less so nowadays.

'Yeah, and he was all over you at my birthday night out.'

'Ew, don't remind me. He visited the school this week and told Sonny to say hello to "his beautiful mother".'

'He visited the *school*?!' Fiona's eyes widen.

'Only as part of a dental-hygiene thing. Nothing sinister. Barton's a prat, but I don't think he'd do something as awful as reporting you. Surely not. You think it could be him because he wants your premises?'

She nods and then shrugs. 'Maybe. But even though the thought of someone reporting me is horrible, that's not actually why I'm so upset.'

'So what is it?'

'I've done something stupid…'

I wait for her to go on, but she's obviously having a hard time getting it off her chest. 'You don't have to tell me if you don't want to.'

'No, it's, well it's embarrassing and humiliating, and I feel awful admitting it.'

'No judgement here.' I hold up my hands.

'Okay, so…' Fiona carries on staring at her mug of tea. 'I used money from the business to buy personal things like clothes, jewellery and home stuff. Things that I wouldn't have otherwise been able to afford.'

'I don't understand, Fi. What's wrong with that? It's money you earned, right?'

'Yes, but the things I bought weren't strictly things that related to work, I just paid for them as if they were.'

I still don't understand what the problem is.

She looks up at me and lowers her voice. 'I treated them like business expenses when they weren't. What I did is illegal. I could go to prison.'

'Oh.' I'm not sure what to say to her. Aside from the fact that I'm in shock we could *both* end up behind bars for completely different reasons. How did our lives start falling apart so quickly? Now I'm really beginning to worry for my friend. 'Well, I'm sure if you put the money back into the business it'll be okay.'

'I've spent thousands over the past few years. Too much to pay back.'

'*Really?* Look, Fi, I'm sorry if I'm way off the mark, but I thought you and Nathan were well-off. Like, multi-millionaire well-off.'

'We are. But I haven't exactly been straight with Nathan. In fact, he's the main reason I've been doing it in the first place.'

My blank expression must show that I'm not following.

'Nathan thinks I'm some mega-successful interior designer. He thinks I'm this incredible businesswoman. And, yes, I do okay. Salinger's is holding its own. But I don't earn as much as he thinks I do. Not enough to afford the clothes I wear and the car I drive. Not enough to buy him his expensive presents and go halves on the luxury holidays. So, when I'm running low on personal funds, I put things through the business.'

'But surely Nathan wouldn't expect you to match him in terms of earnings?'

'Kelly, Nathan expects a lot from me. Our relationship's always been built on the fact that we're each self-sufficient. We don't rely on one another. He's always liked that about me.'

'Well, that's fine. But he can't expect you to be perfect all the time. You should tell him what's been happening. He might be shocked at first, but he loves you, so he'll bail you out of this. He's your husband, Fi. I bet he'd hate to think of you going through this stress on your own.'

At my advice, Fiona nods. 'You're right… I'll tell him and I'm sure he'll help me straighten this whole thing out.' She bites her lip and blinks, trying to smile.

'Of course he will. Are you sure you're okay now, Fi?'

'Yeah, I'm fine. Thanks, Kelly. I'm sorry to have dumped this on you when your own situation is so crappy.'

'What are we both like?'

She gives me a small smile.

After more hugs and apologies on both sides, Fiona finally leaves. I look around the kitchen and wonder if these are going to be my last few days as a free woman. If this whole Sophie thing is going to ruin my life.

I check the kitchen clock and see that it'll be supper time soon. No time for that long, soaky bath I was dreaming about. Instead, I check on the kids before taking a brief shower and changing into fresh clothes, which definitely makes me feel less icky.

Back downstairs, I examine the contents of the fridge, but there's nothing much inspiring in there. Maybe I should order that pizza we were going to have yesterday. Yes. That sounds good. A family evening of pizza and a movie. The boys would love that on a Sunday night.

My phone pings. I take it out of my bag and see the battery's almost dead, so I plug it into the charger and check my messages.

The latest one is from a mobile number I don't recognise. As I read it, I feel a nervous surge of hope:

> *I can get the charges against you dropped. Meet me at Ashridge Falls Boathouse at 11.30 p.m. tonight.*

That's odd. Why would whoever it is want to meet me there? And 11.30 p.m. seems like a crazy hour to meet up. I text back:

Who is this?

I wait for a minute or so but, frustratingly, there's no reply. Could it be from Saul Barker? I haven't added his number to my phone yet, so I suppose it's possible… maybe he's found out that Sophie's lying. But I can't imagine that he'd choose such a strange venue so late at night. I root around in my bag until I locate his business card. I compare the number on the card to the number on my phone. They don't match, but maybe Saul has more than one phone. Or maybe it's from Ash. But I don't think so; surely he would call round or have me come into the station. It doesn't seem like the kind of message either Ash or Saul would send.

And then I realise that I'm being dense. This text has to be from Sophie. But if it is, then what's she playing at? And why the sudden change of heart?

CHAPTER THIRTY-THREE

FIONA

Sipping my warm G & T, I stare around my office, running my fingers across the marble desk. I pick up the hammered-brass pen pot and lay it down again, let my gaze drift over the art-deco black-framed windows and the carefully chosen artwork on the walls. This beautiful room that used to feel like a sanctuary is tainted. It doesn't even feel like mine anymore. What the hell am I even doing, skulking here, alone on a Sunday afternoon? Aside from the fact that I've never bought alcohol to drink on my own before – I've always been a social drinker rather than a solo drinker, but right now drinking feels like the only thing that will do. The only way to dull the fear.

After I left Kelly's place, I couldn't face going home to Nathan, so I came here instead. The tax inspectors won't return until tomorrow, so this could be the only chance I get to enjoy sitting in my office in peace. It's only a matter of time before HMRC discover what I've done. I don't know what will be scarier – going to jail or facing Nathan when he finds out. And I don't even want to think about what those threatening texts mean, or who they're from. I decide that, for now at least, I'm going to ignore them. At this moment in time, I have far more pressing things to worry about.

Faced with the realisation that my carefully ordered life could collapse at any moment, I have to face the fact that the only reason

I got into this tax mess is because I've been trying to live up to the impossible standards Nathan sets for me.

A few years ago I wore a dress from a cheap high-street store. It was a lovely dress – nothing wrong with it at all. Nathan asked me where I bought it, and when I told him he replied that if I wanted clients to think my business was cheap and classless, then 'by all means carry on dressing like a pleb'. His words, although delivered in a jokey tone and with a smile, chilled me, because I saw in his eyes that he would never accept anything less than perfect.

I drain my drink and pour another slug of gin and a slosh of tonic into the glass. It doesn't go down as easily without ice and lemon, but it'll do okay. The effect will be the same.

I know my husband can seem unreasonable at times, but it's only because I've never pulled him up on it. I never pushed back. The thing is, we enjoy the same things – glamour, beauty, perfection, control. I've let myself follow his unwritten set of rules. Rules that keep everything from descending into chaos. Only the chaos has managed to creep in anyway.

If only I had someone I could talk to about it. Someone other than Nathan who might help give me some clarity. Who could help guide me back to that place of lightness where we both started out. Before it all became too restrictive and dark. My parents are nice enough people but they're next to useless when it comes to talking about the big stuff. For a moment, I allow my mind to dip into the past. When I got into all that trouble at school, they were barely there for me. My mum, well, she just cried a lot, and my dad didn't say a whole lot of anything. It was all simply an unfortunate incident that was swept under the carpet.

I tried to talk to Kelly about it earlier, but I realised it wasn't the time. No matter how strongly Kelly assured me that she wanted to know, that it would help take her mind off her own troubles if I talked about mine, she doesn't need that kind of extra stress at the moment. Not with what she's going through. So I lied, assuring her that I would tell Nathan about my financial problems. She seemed satisfied that I was telling the truth. Happy that she had helped me to resolve my issue. But if Kelly knew what Nathan is really like, then she would know that there's no way I could ever tell him the truth.

My only other friend is Tia. And she's got her hands full with her kids. Anyway, who am I kidding, the two of us aren't nearly as close as we used to be. If I'm honest, I wasn't happy that she started going out with Ed after the two of us finished. I didn't think it was a very considerate thing for her to do to a friend. It violated our girl code. And, quite truthfully, Tia's a bit of a princess. She doesn't know how lucky she is to have Ed – he does everything for her, worships the ground she walks on, but all I've heard her do is moan about how he works such long hours.

I realise again that I might be just a teensy bit jealous of Tia, and that makes me uncomfortable. I knew back then that Ed wasn't the right man for me, but that doesn't stop me dreaming about what might have been. Conjuring up the fantasy that *I'm* the one he loves. That Rosie and Leo are my children. That I'm living this carefree, uncomplicated life with a kind and caring man like Ed. The idea of being in that type of pressure-free relationship sends me almost light-headed with longing.

Giving a deep sigh, I lean back in my chair. I've always been the strong friend – the one without any problems. I've never been one to moan or complain. I would hate to be seen as needy. So what should I do? I can't bear the idea of therapy. Of opening up my life to a complete stranger. I know a lot of people swear by it, but I'm scared of the types of questions they might ask. Of the feelings and emotions they might dredge up.

My whole body tenses as my phone vibrates with a text, the warm glow from my G & T already fading as I realise it must be Nathan wondering when I'm coming home. *Shit, I shouldn't be drinking.* If I arrive home half-cut, there's no telling what he'll do.

My skin prickles with dread and my brain switches to full alert. He probably thinks I'm still with Kelly. If I tell him where I really am, he'll be annoyed that I've gone to the office on a Sunday. We always said that Sunday would be the one day where we didn't work. Where we devoted time to one another. But the thought of going home makes me literally want to vomit. That can't be good. Maybe I should ignore the text. Turn off my phone and pretend it ran out of battery…

Reluctantly, I steel myself to look at the screen.

It's a text from an unknown number. I exhale and relax. *Thank you, God.* I realise that I've had a narrow escape this time. It wasn't a message from my husband, but this has been a wake-up call – he could call or text at any moment, and then it will be too late. I should get myself back home before Nathan starts to worry. Before he starts to feel annoyed that I've stayed out too long.

And then I realise that it's the same unknown number as before. It's from the same person who sent me those threatening texts. As I read it, my pulse begins to race as I understand that this person is behind all of it.

Hello, Fiona. I can make Mr Taxman disappear. Meet me tonight.

CHAPTER THIRTY-FOUR

TIA

I pick my way along the edge of the lake, the beam from my torch bobbing up and down, illuminating the path ahead. Am I crazy for coming down here alone at night to meet goodness knows who? What possible other choice do I have? It's either come here and meet the person who's been making my life a misery or stay home and risk them sending those awful images to everyone I know, including my husband.

The lake itself is black and still, the indigo sky studded with stars and a grey sliver of moon. Luckily, Ed isn't working tonight, but I had to lie to him, telling him I was going to Kelly's. Hopefully, after tonight, I'll never have to lie to him again. But maybe that's wishful thinking on my part. This isn't going to be a straightforward meeting, or why would they have gone to the bother of the photos in the first place?

As I walk, instead of fear, a gritty anger begins to flash through my veins, hot and furious. How dare this person screw with my life like this? How dare they try to intimidate and scare me? What could I have possibly done that's so bad? If I find out it's Fiona, I'll… I'll… Well, let's just say she won't get away with it. And if it's not Fiona, then I'm going to demand a bloody good explanation. I push away the thought that there's the tiniest chance the photographs could be real. That the man in the photo is the person

I'm going to be meeting tonight. That I could be putting myself in serious danger…

Should I have brought a weapon with me? But what would I bring? A knife? Maybe. But what if the person I'm meeting is physically stronger than me? Which, let's face it, is more than likely. They'd be able to overpower me and take the knife. The only thing that might have been useful is some kind of pepper spray. Why didn't I bring something like that? Probably because it's Sunday, the shops are all shut, and the text didn't give me any time to prepare. The texter must have arranged it like that on purpose.

I have to stop psyching myself out. Instead, I need to go back to channelling that anger. I can't go in there acting like a frightened little mouse. But as I draw closer to the boathouse, my legs turn soft and my fingers tingle – nerves are getting the better of me. Up ahead, the wooden building is still adorned with bunting from yesterday's regatta. It flaps forlornly in the weak breeze. The whole place looks abandoned. I glance around to check if anyone's near, but I can't see a soul. As I approach the wooden door, I slow down and try to make as little sound as possible. My heart thuds in my ears.

I wonder whether to try the front entrance that leads to the bar and function room, or to go round to the back gate where the spare boats and sailing gear are stored. I'm closer to the front, so I try that first. The door to the function room is usually padlocked when it's not in use, but tonight the latch is open. I push at the wood and the door swings wide. It's even darker inside the building. If it wasn't for the fact that the door was unlocked, I'd assume there was no one here. But I already know there's someone inside, waiting for me.

'Hello?' I cry out tentatively, cringing at the weakness of my voice, the dryness of my mouth. There's a muffled sound like someone in pain. I swing the torch beam up from the floor and gasp at what I see straight ahead.

In the middle of the vast black space, a dark-haired woman sits on a chair. She's been tied up and gagged. She screws up her face, her eyes closing, as the light from my torch blinds her. I lower the beam a little and she opens her eyes. I suddenly realise I know who it is. It's...

'Fiona?'

I walk towards her. 'Fi? Shit, *shit*. Don't worry, I'll get you out of here.'

Her eyes widen, and too late I realise she was trying to warn me.

A figure looms out of the darkness, cutting off my path. I cry out in shock and take a step back, still disoriented and confused by seeing Fiona tied up in here.

'Hello, Tia... Mrs *Perry*.'

It's a dark-haired man and he's carrying a lantern, illuminating the space around us. I recognise him, but it still takes me a second or two to place him.

'Mr Jeffries?'

He smiles and I realise that my senses were correct earlier – he *is* creepy.

'What on earth's going on?' I lower my torch, wondering if I could use it as a weapon. 'Why is Fiona here?' Could I bash him over the head with it? 'Was it you who sent me those pictures?' My voice tails off when I notice what he's carrying in his other hand – a large hunting knife with serrated edges. I swallow down fear and bile, my grip loosening on the torch as my palms begin to sweat. The torch clatters to the wooden floor.

Mr Jeffries raises the lantern in the direction of Fiona. 'Sit down, Tia.'

'What? I...' Hesitantly taking my eyes off him, I turn my head to look, and see an empty chair next to Fiona. Presumably it's been placed there for *me*. At the edge of the pool of light, I see another empty chair. My mind is racing now. I'm thinking that if Mr Jeffries sent me a set of fake pictures, did he also send some to

Fiona? And that third chair…? Is there another woman out there who's going to walk through the door, hoping to bargain her way out of her own personal nightmare?

'Did you hear what I said?' Mr Jeffries has injected some steel into his voice. 'Sit. Down.'

But I realise that if I sit down and allow him to tie me up, then I'm relinquishing everything. At least right now, while I'm free, I could try to make a break for it. I could run out of here and scream for help. Hope that someone hears.

'No you don't.' Mr Jeffries senses my hesitation, because in one swift movement he drops the lantern on the ground, grabs my arm and holds the knife up to my throat.

I gasp and try to lean away from the blade, but he's too strong. It's no good; I waited a second too long. Behind me, I hear the sound of the door closing. *Is someone else here?* Soft footsteps come up behind me.

'I told you to sit down, Tia,' Mr Jeffries says through clenched teeth. He looks grotesque in the lantern light. Shadows flicker across his face as he looms even closer, the tang of beer on his breath.

'You'd better do what he says.' A young woman's voice from behind. She walks around me, hovering just outside the pool of lamplight so I can't quite make out her features.

I shift my gaze back to Mr Jeffries. 'Why did you send me those photos? They're fake, right?' I still haven't moved towards the chair. I need to ask my questions before they gag me. 'Just tell me why you did it? What do you want? Money?'

Mr Jeffries sneers. 'Stop asking stupid questions and sit the fuck down.' He presses the blade to my neck, and I flinch at the pressure of cold steel against my skin. I can't feel if he's drawn blood. Would it hurt, or would my adrenalin mask the pain? I don't have the nerve to test his patience further, so I shuffle forward in the direction of the chair, catching Fiona's eye. I can't tell if she's scared or – knowing Fiona – angry. Possibly she's both.

This all feels so surreal. If only I hadn't received that text before I confided in Ed. I was all set to tell him, and if I had, I wouldn't have needed to come here. I would have called Mr Jeffries' bluff. Too late for regrets now. I'll have to make the best of it. Work out a way to get out of this nightmare.

Presumably these two want something from us. So as long as we give it to them, they'll let us go. At least I hope that's how it's going to work, because I don't even want to let my mind formulate an alternative scenario.

Mr Jeffries moves with me, the knife now millimetres from my throat. I reach the chair and he puts a hand on my shoulder, forcing me down into it. While he stands above me, the woman crouches down and shoves my legs apart, binding my ankles to the chair legs. She then moves behind me and pulls my arms around the back of the chair, tying them together. It's only been a few seconds and my limbs are already protesting. Next, she wedges a strip of material in my mouth and ties the two ends into a knot at the back of my head, catching a lock of hair in the process, which pulls painfully at my scalp.

This has all happened so quickly. How the hell did I let myself be captured like this? I can't believe I came here so willingly. Why is Rosie's teacher part of this? Does he have me mixed up with someone else? Did I do something wrong? But if it's something to do with school, then why does he also have Fiona? Unless it's related to that night out we had for Fiona's birthday. After all, that's when those photos were supposedly taken.

I'm just going to have to hope that whoever walks in here next is way smarter or stronger than me and Fiona. That they can somehow overpower these two psychos and get us out of here. If they can't, I have a horrible feeling that things aren't going to end well. Because Mr Jeffries doesn't seem like the reasonable type. I think he might be planning to hurt us. Maybe even kill us.

I struggle uselessly against my bonds and try to call out, but it's hopeless; all I can manage is a weak grunt. An image of Rosie and Leo jumps into my head. What will they do without me? *I don't want to die. Please, God, don't let me die.*

CHAPTER THIRTY-FIVE

KELLY

I close the front door and step outside into the warm night air. It's quiet out here, the excitement of yesterday's regatta now a fading memory. Most people are probably already tucked up in bed or preparing for the week ahead. It's the final week of the school term, so it'll be a busy one. I should be at home myself, catching up on the sleep I missed out on last night. I can't imagine that anything productive will come of a clandestine late-night meeting with an anonymous texter. But I have to give it a try.

After the weekend I've had, going out right now is the last thing I feel like doing. But if there's the remotest chance of getting these charges dropped and putting this whole episode behind me, then I have to do it, for me as well as for the boys. With their father gone, they can't also have a mother in prison. Who would look after them? Friends? Extended family? No, they need their mum.

I make my way towards the lake, to the boathouse to be more precise – a strange place for a meeting, but at least it'll be quiet there, away from prying eyes. If it is Sophie who's called this meeting then maybe I'll get a chance to ask her why she lied the way she did. Perhaps she had no choice. Maybe her husband coerced her into making the whole thing up. He could have done it to squash any rumours that he was abusing her. Put the blame on someone else. Make me look like the bad guy instead of him.

But what reason would I have to hold an innocent woman captive? Whichever way I look at it, the whole thing still makes no sense.

I rang Fiona to ask if she would babysit the kids while I'm out, but her mobile went straight to voicemail. I thought about calling Nathan to ask him to pass on the message, but I didn't want to impose; not after they helped out last night. And Tia's got her hands full with her own family. In the end, I asked my friend Marian, who sometimes volunteers at the shop. She was more than happy to do it, even though I said I might be quite late back. I could probably have left the boys on their own, but I wouldn't have been able to relax if they were home by themselves. Not after everything that's been going on.

I check my watch and see that it's already eleven thirty, so I pick up my pace and veer off the path, taking a shortcut, picking my way down the grassy bank. It's dark down here; I should've brought a torch. The darkness intensifies as I approach the hulking black shape of the boathouse. I thought security lighting would have flashed on, but as I walk along the path everything remains quiet and dark.

I reach into my bag for my phone and take a moment to turn on its torch. That's better. At least I can see what I'm doing now. The metal latch on the wooden door is unlocked so I push it open and hold my phone out in front of me to see inside. There's a strange mumbling sound, and a scrape of wood. Someone's already here, and they're not far away.

I'm suddenly gripped with fear. Why did I agree to meet at night in such a remote location? I should turn around and go back home, but the need to clear my name propels me forward into the dark interior. 'Hello?' I inch forward and peer ahead as far as the phone's torch will allow. 'Sophie? Is that you?' I turn around to see if I can locate a light switch on the wall, but I can't see one. I doubt we're supposed to be in here; that must be why the lights are off.

I turn at the sound of footsteps coming towards me from the left of the room. A lantern swings into view, and I see that the person carrying it is indeed Sophie. Not surprising, really, as this whole nightmarish situation is her fault.

'You came,' Sophie says, setting the lantern on the floor.

'Of course I came. I want to know what on earth is going on. Why did you lie to the police about me? Why did you...?' The words die on my lips. A man has joined Sophie. It's Greg, her husband – if indeed he is her actual husband. Sonny and Ryan seemed to think he's also Rosie's teacher. What did they say his name was? 'Mr Jeffries.' I say his name aloud. 'Greg.'

'Hello,' he says in a pinched tone.

I suddenly feel weirdly protective towards Sophie. She could be acting out of fear of this man. I look at her and try to convey with my eyes that I'm on her side. 'Sophie, are you okay? Are you being forced to do all this? Has he been abusing you?'

Greg gives a contemptuous laugh. 'I am still here, you know. I can hear you.'

I ignore him. 'Is he really your husband? Or, I don't know, are you part of a trafficking ring?' My theory may sound far-fetched, but this whole situation is off-the-scale weird.

Sophie doesn't reply. I can't decipher anything from her blank expression.

Greg laughs again. This time it's a proper belly laugh. 'You hear that, *Sophie*? Apparently I'm running a trafficking ring.' He turns back to me. 'Who's the one with the knife?'

I'm confused by his words until he jerks his head in the direction of Sophie's hand. Sure enough, she's holding the biggest, sharpest-looking knife I've ever seen.

My hands start to shake uncontrollably at the sight of it. What's she planning to do? Why would Sophie need a knife? I shove my phone into my pocket and take a step back.

'You need to sit down over there with your friends.' She gestures to her left.

Friends? I don't know what she's talking about.

Greg picks up the lantern and walks across the room. I press my hand to my chest as the light picks out two seated figures. They've been tied to their chairs and gagged. How did I only just notice them? And then my skin goes cold when I see who they are.

Sophie strides across the room and holds her knife to Fiona's throat. My friend's eyes widen in fear.

'What are you doing?' I cry. 'Don't hurt her.'

'I need you to sit in the third chair, Kelly.'

'Why?'

'Do you want me to hurt your friend?'

'Of course not!'

'Then sit down.'

On wobbly legs, I cross the room and do as she asks, sitting on the chair as though in a dream. A nightmare. Why the hell are Fiona and Tia here too? It doesn't make any sense. And Sophie… she seems nothing like the scared, frail girl who was hiding in my house. Right now she's strong-voiced, assertive, tough.

As Greg ties my wrists and ankles to the chair, I manage to spit out a couple of questions. 'Why are we all here? What have we done to deserve this? We don't even know you!'

Greg viciously pulls the zip tie tight against my wrists, making me cry out in pain. 'Really? Are you sure about that, Kelly?'

CHAPTER THIRTY-SIX

***History teacher facing child sex offence
allegations killed himself***

**Married father of two, Brian Lawson (41) has committed
suicide just three weeks before he was due in court.**

*Lawson was charged with committing sexual offences against
three girls under 16. One of these offences is alleged to have taken
place in July of this year. The other two incidents are alleged to
have happened last year.*

*Lawson's wife found him dead in a vehicle in his garage at
his home in Ashridge Falls on Monday night. The post-mortem
concluded that Lawson died from a combination of carbon
monoxide poisoning and sleeping tablets. Police say there were
no suspicious circumstances. An inquest into his death will be
held in January.*

*Lawson, who was from Portreach, taught history at Ashridge
Falls for 18 years. In a statement, the school said: 'We value
and promote the safety and wellbeing of all our pupils and take
these allegations very seriously. We will be working alongside
partners such as Portreach Council to look into the allegations
independently.'*

*The council said: 'We support schools in having effective
safeguarding procedures in place, which can be followed in the
event that any allegations are received.'*

Portreach Police said the three victims in the investigation have been updated and offered support by specially trained officers.

'Portreach Police takes all reports of sexual assault seriously and urges victims to come forward to report it, regardless of when it happened, safe in the knowledge that they will be treated with respect and dignity and that their allegation will be fully investigated,' said a police official.

'In circumstances such as these, where an alleged or suspected perpetrator is deceased, specially trained officers will continue to investigate a victim's account as far as is possible. Victims will also have access to support from a range of partner agencies.'

A family member of one of the victims commented: 'We know what's happened. He obviously couldn't face jail and he's taken the cowardly way out.'

Lawson was also blasted online for taking his own life.

CHAPTER THIRTY-SEVEN

Monday

FIONA

I've been tied up here for what must be over an hour now so it has to be after midnight. Aside from the fact that my wrists and ankles are burning where they've zip-tied me, it's been torture seeing my two friends walk into the same trap I did, knowing there was nothing I could do to warn them. That all I could do was watch in mute horror as he tied them up. And now we're all being held in this deserted wooden boathouse with no hope of anyone else coming along for hours. Will we even be alive by then? I'm not sure. Our two captors don't seem to be entirely sane.

I've been trying to work out how I fit into the equation. Greg and Sophie must be behind the tax audit. They must have reported me anonymously. But *why*? I don't even know them. And Kelly has just said she doesn't either. I'm assuming she never met either of them until Sophie showed up at her house with her bullshit story about needing help. The only person who seems to be connected is Tia, because Greg is Rosie's school teacher. Have Kelly and I been caught in the crossfire because of something Tia said or did?

My thoughts fizzle away as Greg comes and stands in front of us, Sophie by his side, that unfeasibly large knife still in her hand.

Greg's eyes harden as he begins to talk, and I see that his main focus is *me*; unless I'm imagining it.

'You might know me as Greg Jones or Greg Jeffries, but my real name is Greg Lawson.'

Hearing the name Lawson, my whole body tenses and the room starts to close in. *Lawson?* It can't be just a coincidence.

'Sophie's name used to be Natalie Lawson. But we were forced to change our names... because of the scandal. Because our mum wanted to give us all a fresh start. Sophie's my younger sister.' Greg gives me a penetrating stare. 'I see you recognise the name, Fiona. But in case your memories are a little hazy, let me fill you in.'

I'm finding it hard to breathe with this gag in my mouth. I can't seem to pull enough oxygen into my lungs. And it's too hot, too close. If this revelation is to do with what I think it is, then – aside from Greg and Sophie's psychotic behaviour – I really, truly don't want to be here. That episode from my past is something I've pushed to the darkest recesses of my mind, and whenever one of its slimy tentacles threatens to escape, I instantly squash it back down. So please, God, don't let it out of its box. Not now. Not ever. But as this man continues to talk, the past is racing towards me and I know that it's all about to be laid bare.

After her initial confidence, Sophie's eyes are mainly downcast now that Greg is talking. Only occasionally does she look up at any of us. In contrast, Greg's gaze glides across the three of us, his blue eyes glittering in the lamplight. 'In case any of you don't remember, seventeen years ago the three of you ruined my father's life. Brian Lawson was a well-respected teacher at your school, and he lost his job, his career, everything, after the three of you falsely accused him of sexual misconduct.'

I squeeze my eyes shut, as though that will block out Greg's voice. But his words come like lacerations, opening up the skin to make fresh wounds. He doesn't stop. It's all pouring out now in a torrent of bitterness and hatred.

'We were a normal, happy family. Me, Natalie, Mum and Dad. And then it all changed. Dad's name was splashed across the papers. He was beaten up in town. My sister and I were bullied at school. My mum's life was made a living hell. They accused her of being part of it. But you know all this, don't you? Because it's your doing.'

I shouldn't be shocked by his anger, but I am. I'm appalled by such naked, cold rage. He hates me. He hates us all. I vaguely remember that Mr Lawson had two children. But they were much younger than us, so we didn't know them. I didn't let myself think about what happened to them afterwards. I didn't let myself think about any of it.

Greg starts pacing, absorbed in his own story. 'And then, as if that wasn't bad enough, Dad was suspended from school. Of course, everyone assumed that he'd done it. That he'd be found guilty in court, lose his job and go to prison. It's supposed to be innocent until proven guilty, but that's never the case. It's trial by mob rule.'

I wonder what Kelly and Tia are thinking right now. I can see why Greg and Sophie gagged us all. He wants to have a captive audience. He wants us to listen without the right to reply. And what about Sophie? She's being very quiet. Is she as angry as her brother? Or is she just going along with him? From watching them both, it seems quite obvious that he's the one behind it all. She's barely glanced up while he's been spewing out all his pent-up emotions.

'But Dad couldn't cope with it all. With the accusations, the lies. He knew his career was over. Even our mother began to doubt his innocence. He thought he was going to lose his wife, his family, everything. He couldn't cope with the shame. He shut himself in his car and took his own life.'

Greg's breathing has grown heavy with emotion. But still Sophie stands there, head bowed, clutching the knife. 'So, after years of doing nothing, of letting you three get away with your teenage games, we decided that it was time to make you pay. To make you suffer just a little of what we suffered. We started with a few rumours. As a teacher, it was easy for me to arrange for some of the pupils to overhear a bit of gossip. Things like, "Rosie's mum is a murderer", and "Sonny's mum kissed a teacher". Nowhere near as bad as a sexual assault rumour, but enough to cast doubt on your characters. To give you a small taste of what it was like for us back then. And then we ramped it up a gear…

'We wanted you all to feel the despair and fear that my dad felt when he was wrongly accused. To ruin your lives the way you ruined my family. To make you suffer the way he suffered. Back then, you all thought you were so special. So popular and untouchable. You thought it would be funny to accuse an innocent teacher of sexual misconduct. Everyone knew you were making it all up, but it was too late for my dad. The damage had already been done. Once he was under suspicion for something like that, the school had to let him go. The other parents wouldn't have stood for him staying on.

'Fiona…' He fixes me with a stare that makes me squirm in my seat. It's only now I realise how much he looks like his father. 'We thought we'd tip off the tax office about you. Let them do a little in-depth investigation into your business. We know how you like everything in your life to be shiny and perfect, so it seemed like a good way to ruin your week.'

I should be shocked by what he's telling me, but the tax audit feels about a million miles away right now. Like it's happening to someone else; not to me. All that anguish and agonising over my business seems trivial now that I'm here, facing Brian Lawson's children, of all people.

'And Tia…' Greg switches his gaze to her, and I wonder what it is that this man has been putting her through. 'Those photographs were fun, don't you think? Sophie and I enjoyed Fiona's birthday party. To be honest, we went into that club with a plan to spike *Fiona's* drink, not yours. But we couldn't get near her, so we adapted our plan. Tia, you seemed to be having the most fun that night. You were certainly downing the shots. You made it so easy for Sophie.'

I think back to the night of my birthday, and I remember being annoyed by Tia's attention-seeking behaviour. Dancing and flirting, acting like it was her party. I didn't realise she'd had her drink spiked.

Greg continues. 'I bumped into you outside the club, just as the effects of the drug were starting to take hold, making you woozy enough not to recognise me. I kissed you. And I have to say, Tia, it was pretty sloppy. I didn't enjoy it at all. But at least Sophie was able to get a few good photos. The other images had to be photoshopped, but I think we did a pretty convincing job.'

I glance sideways at Tia to see her straining at her ties, angry tears running down her face. My heart goes out to her. She obviously had it so much worse than I did. A tax audit is nothing compared to whatever it was they put her through. I realise I'm lucky they didn't succeed in spiking my drink.

'Don't worry, Tia. You and I didn't actually do anything together – I'm not that desperate. Although I wouldn't put it past you to pretend that we did. That seems to be a thing with you girls – making stuff up. Crying wolf.'

My skin crawls at this, so I can only imagine how Tia must be feeling. I look across at her and try to convey my support, but she's shaking with rage as she glares at Greg.

'And finally... Kelly. Well, you've probably guessed what your personal hell was. My sister here is a good little actress, don't you think? She certainly fooled you. And now you're facing a prison sentence for holding her against her will. And when it comes out that she's Brian Lawson's daughter, the case against you will be even stronger.

'We've got it all worked out. How the three of you lured us here tonight because we discovered you lied about our father. I'm going to remove your gags in a minute and each of you is going to confess what you did back then. I'm going to record you and take your confessions to the police, to the papers and to the school. They're going to clear our father's name. He might not be alive to see it, but we'll make sure everyone else knows he was an innocent man.'

CHAPTER THIRTY-EIGHT

FIONA

Sophie walks over and uses the knife to slice off my gag. I swallow and gulp down air as she does the same to my friends. I try to catch her eye, but she still won't look at any of us. Kelly and I are quiet for the moment while we catch our breath, but Tia immediately lets out a torrent of abuse.

'What the fuck, Greg? You're Rosie's teacher! You've had access to my child! How is that possible? Are you even *qualified* or did you lie to the school to get the job? And spiking my drink! How do I know you didn't take me home? That you didn't take advantage of me? It's your word against mine!'

'Yes, Tia,' Greg replies. 'Funny how that works, isn't it?'

'You're a fucking nutter. Just like your dad.'

Greg strides over and slaps Tia's cheek, hard. She gasps, but the fury still shimmers in her eyes.

Greg turns to me as Sophie joins him once again. 'Got anything to add, Fiona?' he asks.

'I'm sorry,' I say, my voice weak and wavering, 'but you're wrong.'

'About what?' He seems bored by the question.

'About your dad.'

'It's only us here now,' he says. 'You don't have to lie any more. That's what this whole evening is about.' He waves his arms around. 'Being honest. Owning up. Confessing to your teenage misdemeanours.'

'But I didn't lie.' No matter how angry I might make him, I can't let him carry on believing his dad was a saint.

Greg's mouth tightens. 'This is getting tedious.'

'Your dad, I liked him. I thought he was good-looking and cool and a great teacher.'

'I know you did,' Greg says. 'That's what I'm talking about. You flaunted yourself at him, didn't you? And he rejected you, so you got your own back by making stuff up.'

'That's not what happened.' My mind reaches down for the memories I've suppressed for so long. I pull them out tentacle by slimy tentacle and force myself to face it all again. To make this man understand who his father really was.

'School had already finished for the day. But I went back to the classroom – I'd forgotten my history book. When I got there, Mr Lawson was still at his desk. We talked about the upcoming weekend. He wasn't like most teachers; he was easy to talk to. I told him there was a party going on, but I didn't know if I wanted to go to it or not. He said if he was my age, he'd go to all the parties because all he had time for these days was household chores and marking homework. We laughed.'

I'm back there in that room, the sunlight slanting through the high sash windows, falling in wide stripes across his desk.

'He… stood up and he kissed me. And for a split second I kissed him back. But it felt wrong. It felt gross. He smelled… grown-up. Nothing like the boys I'd kissed before. I tried to pull away from him, thinking we'd both be mortified, and he would apologise, and we'd never talk about it again. But instead, he started groping me and saying all this awful stuff. He wouldn't let go of me. He said he knew I fancied him. He said that he wanted to do all this stuff to me, which I'm not going to repeat here. And his hands were everywhere, and it was horrible. So I kneed him in the groin, and I ran.'

'Liar!' Greg cries.

Sophie is staring at me wide-eyed. I try to hold her gaze for a good long time. Try to get her to understand that I'm telling the truth.

'I'd never been so scared in my whole life,' I stutter. 'I felt physically sick. And terrified. I thought it was all my fault. It was only years later that I realised it wasn't anything I did. That Mr Lawson was in a position of trust. And even if I had wanted to kiss him, that he was still in the wrong. I was a child, a pupil at the school. I was under their care. Even if I hadn't been a child, the minute I pulled away, he should have let me go. Not forced me to carry on. Not put his hands on me. What he did was wrong.'

'Dad wouldn't have done that,' Sophie mutters, but she doesn't sound too sure of herself any more.

'Sophie, I'm sorry, but he *did*.'

'Fiona's telling the truth,' Kelly says. 'I know it must be a horrible thing to hear. Impossible to believe, especially if he was a good father. But you were children back then. Innocent. You're not responsible for what he did. You don't have to do this out of some sense of loyalty. I'm sorry for what you both went through, but you have no idea what it was like for Fi. She was a mess back then. She was so traumatised by your dad. And it wasn't just her. You must have known that other girls came forward after Fiona reported him.'

'All liars.' Greg glares at Kelly. 'Attention-seekers.'

'Fiona was our best friend,' Tia says. 'We were with her right after it happened. We saw how upset she was. We saw what she went through. You didn't see the effects of his behaviour. You didn't see how her personality changed. How she became nervous around boys. How she became more serious and stopped wanting to go out.'

I'm shaking now; my whole body trembling inside and out. I hadn't realised that my friends had noticed such a difference in me after that day. How they'd almost lived it with me. How they really tried to support me back then. I don't think I ever gave them enough credit for that.

'I didn't want your dad to die,' I stammer, 'but I've always told the truth. He shouldn't have come on to me like that. He shouldn't have touched me. And like Kelly said, it wasn't just me – he did the same to at least two other girls. If I hadn't reported him, he might have gone on to do it to even more.'

'Shut up!' Greg snaps. 'Just, all of you, shut the fuck up. I should've known you wouldn't admit the truth. That you'd all have your stories straight. Like when you lied to the police back then.'

'Actually,' Kelly says, 'Fiona didn't want to tell *anyone*. Straight after we got the truth out of her, she said she regretted telling us and she begged us to keep it quiet, but Tia and I persuaded her to report him because it was the right thing to do.'

'Why would we have made something like that up?' Tia says. 'It makes no sense. Before that happened we thought your dad was a great teacher. We liked him. All the kids did. And a lot of them were horrible to Fi afterwards. To all of us. Even some of the parents.'

Kelly clears her throat. 'We've told you the truth, now please just let us go. If you wanted revenge, you've got it. You've made our lives a living hell these past few days. We're good people. We did nothing wrong. Untie us now, drop the charges, and we'll say no more about it. We give you our word we won't go to the police.'

'Just, all of you, be quiet. I can't think.' Greg holds his head and walks away for a moment, out of the lantern's pool of light and into the dark shadows of the room.

While he mutters to himself, Sophie stands rooted to the spot as though she's paralysed. I can't tell whether she believes *us* or her brother. I think maybe she's torn. Maybe we're making her realise that her father wasn't the man she thought he was. Or maybe that's wishful thinking on my part.

Kelly tries talking to Sophie again. 'I know it must have been awful for you hearing that stuff about your dad back then. And then him committing suicide. It's a terrible thing you went through. But taking it out on Fiona and the rest of us isn't the answer. She's as much a victim as you.'

Sophie scowls at Kelly. It may be my imagination but I'm sure her cheeks flush, as though she's embarrassed. As though she knows she's in the wrong.

'Talk to your brother,' Kelly pleads. 'Listen to me, Sophie—'

'*Listen to me, Sophie*,' Greg mimics, stepping back into the light. 'As if she's going to be fooled by your pathetic lies. I should have known you wouldn't do the decent thing and admit to what you did.'

But Kelly isn't giving up. 'Sophie, your brother's angry. He's lashing out at us. But don't let him drag you down. Don't let him ruin your life. I thought we were becoming friends before, back at the house. If you won't let us go for *me*, then do it for Ryan and Sonny. They really bonded with you. Do you want them to grow up without their mum as well as their dad? Do you really want that for them? Could you live with yourself knowing you destroyed their childhood?'

'Boo fucking hoo,' Greg sneers. 'What about *our* childhood? Mine and Sophie's? Who's responsible for destroying that? Oh... yeah... it was *you*.' He stares at us each in turn before grabbing his sister's arm and pulling her towards him.

I wince as I see Greg's rough treatment of Sophie. 'Does he hurt you, Sophie?' I call out. 'Did he force you to do all this?'

'Shut up, bitch.' Greg's face is a mask of frustration and in that instant, I get a clear-as-day flashback of his father looking at me in the same way. The exact same expression when I wouldn't go along with what he wanted. It knocks the air from my body, and I feel as though I'm shrinking into myself.

Sophie follows her brother out of our view, and I can hear them having a whispered, heated discussion in the corner.

'Can you believe this?' Tia hisses, looking from me to Kelly. 'They're both insane. What they've put us through is—'

'Shh, hang on a minute, Tee,' Kelly replies. 'We need to hear what they're saying.'

Greg and Sophie are arguing. She's telling him that maybe they got it wrong. That they should listen to our side of the story. That deep down she always suspected their dad might not have been completely innocent.

But Greg isn't budging. 'How can you even think that?' he hisses. 'They need to admit that they lied. We need to see this through. You're just losing your nerve, that's all.'

'You're being stubborn, Greg. You should open your mind to the possibility that we've got it wrong.'

Kelly and Tia exchange anxious yet hopeful glances. I try to reciprocate, but I can't make my face work. I'm still in shock at the similarity between Greg and his father. It's like déjà vu. And I can hardly make sense of who is who.

'I'm not arguing with you, Sophie. We're doing this.'

'No.' Her voice rings out loud and firm.

'What do you mean, *no*?'

'I mean, I think we should let them go. I've had enough of this. It's *enough*, Greg. We need to stop before it goes too far.'

'Give me the knife, Sophie.'

'Why?'

'Just…'

There's a scuffling sound.

'I don't want to hurt you,' Greg growls. 'Just let go of it!'

There's another scuffling sound and they come into view, both of them gripping the knife handle, but Greg looks far stronger than Sophie. I'm jolted back to the present day, and I'm worried for her safety. The knife is perilously close to her face.

'Let go of the knife, Sophie!' Kelly cries. 'You'll get hurt! Leave her alone, Greg!' Kelly turns to me, her eyes wide. 'I can't look.'

As Greg wrestles the knife from his sister, she jerks backwards and falls. There's a thunk as Sophie hits her head on the corner of the bar. She goes down onto the floor with another dull thud.

I can't help crying out, wondering if she's okay. Realising self-ishly that she was our only hope of getting out of here unharmed.

Greg falls to his knees to check on her. 'Sophie! Soph!'

She's making moaning sounds, so at least she's alive. But she must be badly concussed. 'Call an ambulance!' Kelly shouts. 'Greg, that's your sister. What have you done? You need to call for help.'

'I told you to shut up!' He gets to his feet but he's out of breath and his eyes are glazed. He seems disoriented, slightly manic. He brandishes the knife and I notice blood dripping from his hand. He must have cut himself in the tussle. 'It's her own fault. She wouldn't listen.'

'Greg,' I say, trying to stay calm, 'you're bleeding. You need to bandage that cut. I know where there's a first aid kit. If you untie me I can—'

'Shut... the fuck... up,' he pants. 'This is your fault. First you drove my father to his death, and now my sister's on the floor unconscious. You made her believe your lies, but I'm not taken in by any of you. You've made some sort of pact, and you don't care whose lives you destroy to save your skins.'

'Just take a breath,' Kelly says, 'and think about what you're saying.'

'Don't patronise me, you hippy bitch.'

'I... I'm not. I'm just saying—'

'Shut up, shut up, shut up! I should have left you all gagged.'

I cringe back in my chair. Black spots float before my eyes. This man isn't in control of his thoughts. I'm sure he's going to do something stupid and I'm bracing myself for whatever it is. If only Sophie would wake up. She could at least continue trying to talk some sense into her brother.

Greg comes closer, leering at us, blood from his hand dripping scarlet spots onto the floor. 'I want to bring misery to your families the way you brought misery to mine after you killed my father. My sister's been sucked in by your lies but I'm not quite as gullible.' He makes a twisting motion with the knife. 'I'm going to kill each of you slowly, one at a time.' He locks eyes with me, and my heart goes cold. 'Starting with you, Fiona.'

I lean back as far as the zip ties will allow me. Kelly and Tia are yelling at him to leave me alone. To not do anything stupid. To not do something he'll regret. But Greg's eyes are wild, and I can tell that he's in no state to listen to reason. Blood whooshes in my ears.

In the few seconds I might have left, I think about my life. My *real* life, not the life I show everybody else. About how everything changed when Brian Lawson assaulted me. How I never trusted men after that day. How my relationship with Ed never even got off the starting blocks because I wouldn't let him in emotionally. How he tried so hard, but I was as cold as the lake in January. And then Nathan came into my life and managed to get past my defences. He was relentless in his pursuit of me.

But I screwed up. I let the wrong man in. Nathan isn't any better than Brian Lawson. How come I'm only seeing this now? Now that I'm only moments away from death?

CHAPTER THIRTY-NINE

KELLY

Tia and I are pleading with Greg not to hurt Fiona. I realise that he's never going to accept the truth. That he's been on this journey of bitterness and revenge for so long that it's impossible for him to admit he could be wrong. He has his father up on a pedestal, and he won't let mere truth get in the way of that.

'Okay, Greg!' I cry. 'Okay, you win. We'll admit it that we lied. You're right.'

Tia's looking at me like I've lost the plot, but I glare at her, trying to make her understand what I'm doing.

Finally the penny drops, and she nods at me. 'Greg, Kelly's right. Don't hurt us. We'll do what you want. We'll go to the police. We'll admit it, okay?'

Greg turns away from Fiona and looks from me to Tia and back again, his eyes suddenly sharp. I need to make him see that we're serious. It's the only way we'll leave here alive.

'Okay?' I nod, trying to get him to agree. 'Is that okay? We'll do it. You win. We'll tell the police and the school that Fiona made it up. That we all made it up.'

He steps away from Fiona and walks towards me, jabbing the knife in my direction. 'Don't think I don't know what you're doing. You think I'm some deranged lunatic without a brain. You're just saying this so I won't kill you and your friends!' He takes a breath and crouches down in front of me. 'You think I'm blinded by revenge. But you're wrong. I just want the truth. I just want…' his voice fills with emotion and he has to clear his throat. 'I just want my dad…' He squares his shoulders. 'I want my dad's name to be cleared.' He sniffs and stands once more.

'And you can have that, Greg. We'll clear your dad's name. Why does it matter whether I'm saying it because I believe it or not? The end result will be the same – your dad's name will be cleared.'

'No it won't,' he sneers. 'No it won't. And do you know why it won't? Because you're a lying bitch, just like your friends. Just like my feckless sister who promised to help me, and then betrayed me at the last minute.'

Next to me, Tia is shifting and writhing in her seat, straining to get free. But all three of us are trussed up good and tight. There's no way we'll get out of this without help. I need to *do* something. To cause a distraction. To yell for help. But I'm paralysed by fear. If I scream, there's no knowing what Greg will do with that knife. And the chances of anyone being able to hear us in here are slim to none. But then I think about my poor boys and what their lives will be like growing up without either of their parents. And I realise I can't allow that to happen. I can't give up. Not without a fight. Instinct takes over and I begin to yell at the top of my lungs: 'Help! Someone, HELP! HELP US!'

'Shut up!' Greg snarls.

Tia and Fiona join in, screaming and yelling for help that we know won't come. But Greg has already locked eyes with me. He takes two swift steps in my direction, his arm raised, the knife blade catching the lamplight as it swoops down towards my chest. I close my eyes, waiting for it to pierce my skin. Tensed for the pain. Tia and Fiona are now screaming at him to stop, but there's no sound coming out of my mouth any more. It's like I'm floating above my own body.

As the blade comes for me, there's a scraping sound and a cry. My eyes fly open to see that Tia has jerked her chair sideways into me, falling against my arm and pushing my chair several inches to the left. I register a searing pain and wonder what it could be, before realising with a jolt of shock that Greg has *stabbed* me.

But Tia's actions knocked out Greg's aim. The knife went into my shoulder instead of my chest. If it wasn't for her, I'd probably be dead right now.

I'm panting and trying not to freak out about the fact that I've been injured. 'Tee, are you okay?' I gasp. She's slipped off me and fallen sideways onto the floor, still tied to the chair. Greg jumps back, startled, the knife still in his hand, only now its blade is dripping with blood.

My blood.

He growls and kicks viciously at Tia's legs. 'Stupid bitch. What did you think you were doing?'

She winces and gasps. 'Trying to stop you, you fucking psycho! I'm not just gonna sit here quietly while you try to kill my best friend.'

'Greg, stop it, *please*,' Fiona begs. 'Kelly, are you okay? He's hurt you!'

'I'm okay,' I say, even though I'm far from okay. I don't even want to think about the wound in my shoulder. How deep it is. How serious it is. Because we're all still tied up and at this man's mercy. Despite Tia's well-timed manoeuvre, our nightmare is far from over. And Greg is now even more furious than before. I'm pretty sure he's about to try again. And this time he won't miss.

A shape catches my eye as it moves out of the darkness, and I hardly dare breathe. It's Sophie! She's alive. Our eyes meet and in this fleeting moment I try to convey all my fears and all my truths to her. I silently plead with my eyes before planting my gaze firmly back on Greg, willing him not to notice his sister. But he's seen my eyes dart away from the space behind him, where Sophie is creeping forwards. And we all see the whiskey bottle she took from the bar, now raised high above her head.

Is she going to be too late?

As Greg turns, she smashes it down on the side of his head and makes a grab for the knife at the same time. He lunges for her and I can't stop myself from screaming. But I'm mistaken; it wasn't him lunging for her, he's flailing forwards against his sister. The bottle did its work. Greg collapses to the floor unconscious, the knife clattering down at his side, and the room falls silent.

Sophie stands there above her brother, panting and crying. And then her knees give way and she sinks to the floor.

'I'm sorry,' she says. 'I'm so sorry.'

I can't tell if she's talking to us or to Greg. 'Sophie, are you all right? You were unconscious. Do you need medical help?'

'Never mind her,' Tia snaps from the floor. 'What about you, Kels? Are you okay? That bastard got you.'

'It's just my shoulder, I think.' My vision blurs and I feel like I'm about to vomit. I close my eyes and try to breathe.

'Kelly!' Fiona cries.

'Sophie, untie us,' Tia orders. 'Kelly needs an ambulance.'

I open my eyes again. 'Is he… alive?' I stare down at Greg's immobile body.

He groans in response and I flinch.

'You better tie him up,' Tia says. 'Because if he wakes up now, you just know he's gonna be mad. Even madder than before.'

Sophie wobbles to her feet and sways there for a moment. She looks unsure of what to do.

'Sophie…' I try to sound as calm and gentle as possible. 'Can you come over here and cut us loose. Tia and Fiona can help you tie him up and get us some medical attention. You're probably concussed.'

Sophie does as I ask, first reaching down to pick up the knife. She comes towards me and I tense up, fearful for a moment that she might want to hurt me. But she wipes the blade on her jeans before slicing into the zip ties, carefully edging the tip of the blade inside the plastic on my wrists. I swear under my breath as the zip tie breaks and my body jolts, inducing a white-hot pain in my shoulder.

'Sorry.' Sophie winces at my expression.

'It's fine,' I gasp. 'Tia, are you okay? You went down quite hard.'

'Yeah, just a bit bruised I think.' She scowls up at Sophie. 'Glad you finally saw sense.'

Sophie cuts the ties on my ankles next. 'I think I always knew my dad was guilty.'

'So then why the hell did you go along with your brother?' Tia cries. 'If you knew he was guilty…'

'Because… I don't know. Greg's the only family I've got left. He loves me. He looks after me. Practically raised me after it happened. My mum shut down after Dad killed himself. I got the feeling she didn't love Greg and me quite as much afterwards. It was like she saw us in a different light. We had his genes. We were tainted.'

'I'm sure that's not true.' I know there's nothing that could make me love my boys any less.

'I wanted to believe that my dad didn't do it. Greg was so convincing. So *sure*. I just couldn't go against him. But then, meeting *you*, Kelly…' She looks up at me. 'You took me into your home without even knowing me! You were so kind. No one's ever been that kind to me before.'

I'm finally free and I stretch my legs out, wanting to rub at the sore spots on my ankles where the ties dug in, but I'm too scared of moving in case I make my shoulder worse. So I stay seated for now while Sophie sets to work freeing Tia.

Tia scowls. 'If you thought Kelly was kind, why did you turn her over to the police with those false accusations?'

'I told you why – Greg said I had to. He said it didn't matter how nice Kelly seemed. He said all that mattered was getting justice for my dad.' Sophie stops and takes a breath, wiping at her face. I realise she's crying. 'He was so angry. He told me that we couldn't let any of you get away with it. I'm sorry, but he's not an easy person to say no to.' She's sobbing and shaking now as she turns to Fiona. 'I loved my dad, but I'm gutted that he did this. I'm so, so sorry for what he did to you, Fiona. For how he made you feel.'

'Thank you,' Fiona replies, but she looks dazed and exhausted.

'I just was so confused about everything. I sensed Dad was guilty, but I didn't want to admit it. Because if I did, then what did that make *me*?'

Greg moans again. Once Tia is free she snatches up the packet of zip ties from the floor and sets to work securing Greg's wrists together, and then his ankles. I don't know how she can bear to touch him. The man is a monster.

Tia steps away and reaches for her phone, which is in her bag on the floor. She swipes at it a few times and puts it to her ear while Sophie takes the knife and releases Fiona.

When Sophie's done, she sits on the floor hugging her knees to her chest. I want to comfort her, but I can't move. I'm feeling woozy again, and my shoulder throbs like it's on fire. I focus on Sophie to try to take my mind off the pain. 'You should have come to speak to us years ago. We would never have blamed you. I feel bad that you've held onto all this pain for so many years.'

'I'm sorry, Kelly.' She sniffs. 'I wish we could go back to being friends. I wish I hadn't let Greg talk me into any of this. It was all so crazy. You know I'll go to the police and tell them everything. They'll drop the charges. You can all go back to your lives. I promise.'

'Thank you. And you know… we *can* still be friends, Sophie.'

She gives me a sceptical look. But I mean what I say. I liked Sophie from the moment I met her. She felt like a lost soul when she showed up in my garden, and I wasn't too far off the mark. Maybe I can help her find a new purpose in life. I slump down in my chair and close my eyes.

Fiona is crouched in front of me, asking if I'm okay, telling me to stay awake, that help will be here soon. But everything seems to be fading. The last thing I hear is Tia on the phone, her voice frantic, panicked:

'Ash? Yeah it's me. There's been a situation. You need to come to the boathouse. It's urgent. Get an ambulance here. Soon as possible... Yeah I'm fine, I'm fine. It's not me. It's Kelly.'

CHAPTER FORTY

Seven months later

TIA

I kiss Ed and run from the front door to the car, my head bowed against icy needles of rain. She only lives a few minutes' walk away, but I don't want to get drenched and have to sit in damp clothes all evening. I'll drive there and leave the car overnight so I can have a few drinks. It is a celebration after all.

I slide into the car, my hair already dripping with rain, and start up the engine. I'm looking forward to tonight. We've all been so busy over Christmas that we barely had time to get together. We're due a well-deserved catch up. And now the fallout from the Greg-and-Sophie nightmare is behind us, maybe we can concentrate on having a laugh for a change.

Both Lawsons are fully recovered physically and are serving time in prison. Greg will be lucky to get out in the next decade, and Sophie is serving two years. Fiona's visited her a couple of times and Kelly tries to visit at least once a month. They're more generous towards her than I would be. If I never see either of the Lawsons again it'll be too soon.

Kelly's stab wound wasn't life-threatening. But it scared us all. Made us realise how close we'd come to not making it out of that boathouse. Made us realise that we'd all been given a second chance at life.

I drive carefully down the rain-drenched street. The last thing I need is a car accident. Luckily, the roads are empty. Who else would be crazy enough to go out on a Monday evening in February in this weather?

After that terrible night, I had no choice but to tell Ed about everything that had happened in the run up to it, including receiving those photographs. He was furious with Greg and Sophie. Devastated that they'd spiked my drink and put me in such a compromising and distressing position. But after everything had sunk in and he knew that I was safe, he was also a little upset that I hadn't confided in him in the first place. That I hadn't shared my fears with him, my own husband.

Ed was hurt that I'd thought he might not believe me. He asked me to think how I would feel if the situation was reversed. I agreed that I'd been wrong not to trust him, but hindsight is a wonderful thing. We gradually found our way back to one another. Stronger than before. But also more considerate. More careful of one another's feelings.

I realise I've already arrived at Kelly's, and it's another mad dash through the rain to her house. Luckily, I don't have to wait too long before the door opens, and Fiona stands before me with a glass of wine in her hand.

'Tee, come in.'

'Congratulations!' I step inside and we kiss one another on the cheek.

'Thank you.' She breathes in and smiles at the same time, letting out a happy sigh. I take in her stick-thin figure and gaunt face. Fi's lost weight these past few months – she needs to pile on a few more pounds, if you ask me. But she says she has no idea why because she's never eaten so much junk food in her life.

I can attest to that; I nearly fell off my chair when I saw her – Miss Calorie-Counting Salad Junkie – eat a cheeseburger last month. Right now she takes a huge slug of wine. 'Kelly's in the kitchen getting the casserole out of the oven. Do you want red or white?'

'Red please.' I manage to find a space to hang my coat up in the hall and follow Fiona into the kitchen. 'Hey, Kels, that smells great.'

Kelly's crouched in front of the oven. She turns around as I walk in, her cheeks pink from the heat. 'Tia, hi! Sit down, I'll dish this up in a sec.'

'Where are the boys?'

'Upstairs. I told them I'm having a girls' night. No boys allowed.'

'No you didn't.'

'No, you're right, I didn't.' She laughs.

'I'll go up and say hi in a bit.'

'Great, they'd love to see you.'

Lately, Kelly has been staying home a lot more and volunteering a lot less. She told us that she thought her volunteer work might have been a way to escape her real life, to not have to deal with Michael's death and with her grief. Now that she's eased off on the hours at work, she's been able to spend a lot more quality time with Ryan and Sonny. They all seem to be doing better. Especially Ryan, who's so much happier both at home and at school, where he's reconnected with his friends. There's also another reason why Kelly hasn't been working quite such long hours these days.

'How's that delicious man of yours?' I ask with a teasing grin.

Using a pair of oven gloves that look like they were made in the seventies, Kelly carries the chipped blue casserole dish over and sets it down in the middle of the table. 'He's fine thanks, Tia.' She pulls a face at me and sticks her tongue out, her cheeks turning an even deeper shade of pink.

Kelly's been seeing Saul Barker, the defence solicitor who was working on her case. He asked her out on a date the week after all the charges were dropped and, after quite a bit of dithering, she finally said yes. Saul is divorced with two teenagers, so he and Kelly have a lot in common. She insists it's not that serious, but I think it is. I think she's just saying that to protect herself.

Kelly dishes up the food while Fiona pours me a glass of red and tops up Kelly's glass.

'So, Happy D-Day, Fiona,' Kelly says, holding her glass up.

'Happy D-Day, Fi,' I echo.

'Thanks, girls.' Fiona smiles. We knock our glasses together and each take a drink.

'How does it feel to be a single woman again?' I ask.

'Bloody brilliant.' Fiona grins. 'I feel like I can actually breathe now that I have the decree absolute in my possession.'

'No more Nasty Nathan,' I reply.

'Too right,' she says. 'You're looking at a divorced woman.'

'And a gorgeous one at that,' Kelly says.

The day after our traumatic experience in the boathouse, Fiona told Nathan she was leaving him. He didn't take it well. He begged her, yelled at her, pleaded and sulked. Tried every trick in the book to make her stay. But when he threatened her with violence, I got Ash to put the frighteners on him, threatening Nathan with a long prison sentence if he so much as looked at Fiona in the wrong way. That seemed to do the trick. But the bastard got his revenge by only agreeing to the divorce if she admitted to adultery, and then screwing her out of every penny.

And Fiona could have done with every penny. She confessed to us that she'd been taking money out of the business to pay for her own designer clothes and jewellery – not because she wanted that stuff for herself, but because she was trying to live up to the impossible standards that Nathan set for her. She'd been writing the purchases off as business expenses. So, when Greg and Sophie sent the tax inspectors round, Fiona was terrified that the truth would come out. But, thankfully, the auditors never discovered her deception.

Fiona admitted everything to us. Being more financially stable than me, Kelly is helping her to pay back the money to the business and in the meantime Fiona has moved into Kelly's place. It suits them both really well for the moment. Kelly and I are glad to be supporting Fiona financially and emotionally. She's never been one to ask for help before, so it's nice to be able to do something for her for a change. Especially after hearing how rough she had it with Nathan for so many years.

Aside from her short interlude with Ed, Fiona has never had a good romantic relationship in her life, not since Brian Lawson's assault on her when she was fifteen. Now she's started counselling sessions and it's really helping, although she's adamant she wants to remain single for the rest of her life. She says that once she's got her business back on track and has her own place to live, she's going to try to adopt a child. That she's realised a family is the thing she's yearning for. Her own family were never particularly warm-hearted towards her, so she deserves that at least.

I put my fork down for a moment and reach for a slice of bread. 'I know it's a great day for you, Fi, getting your divorce through and everything, but aren't you just the teensiest bit pissed off that Nathan's got the house and the money? Didn't you at least want to put up a bit of a fight to get some of it? You're more than entitled, after what he put you through.'

Fiona puts her glass down. 'I know he got all the money, but I actually don't care. If he thinks he's got one over on me, it'll keep him off my back. Make him feel like he's scored a win. After being in that suffocating house for so many years, I just want my freedom. To do what I want, when I want. To wear what I want. Eat what I want. Not feel scared in my own home. To have all *that*... well... it feels like I've won the lottery.'

I shake my head. 'I'm so sorry you had to put up with that shit for so long. I wish I'd known sooner.'

'I didn't want anyone to know,' she replies. 'I think I was in denial. I felt this... well, it was a kind of *shame*. I didn't want anyone to know because I couldn't handle people's pity or judgement. I didn't want to admit that my marriage was a failure. I know it sounds ridiculous.'

'Not at all,' Kelly says. 'It's too easy for other people to point fingers and judge. To say you should've done this or that. But the truth is that unless you've lived that person's life, you have no idea what you would do or how you would react in their shoes. It's arrogant to think otherwise.'

'Thanks, Kels. I really thought I loved him. Maybe I even did at one time, because it wasn't like he was *always* so controlling. When we first met, he made me feel amazing, like I was this superwoman who could do anything. He said he admired me. That he'd never met anyone like me.' She gives a short bitter laugh. 'What a mug I was to fall for his bullshit. What he really meant was that he'd never met anyone so easy to manipulate.

'When I was with him, that situation became my normality. I accepted that that was my life. I didn't dare let myself think about leaving. And in the rare moments that I did, I couldn't see a way out that didn't end in violence.' Fiona blinks and takes a deep breath. 'But, anyway...' She waves her hand as though banishing him from the room. 'Enough about him. Tonight isn't about the crappy past; it's about new beginnings.'

I raise my glass. 'To new beginnings.'

'New beginnings,' Kelly echoes.

Fiona, Kelly and I clink glasses and I count myself lucky to have the best friends anyone could ask for. Okay, so it hasn't always been the easiest of friendships, but who said anything good came easy?

A LETTER FROM SHALINI

Thank you so much for reading my tenth psychological thriller, *One of Us Is Lying*. I can't believe I've written ten already; it doesn't seem possible! I do hope you enjoyed it.

If you'd like to keep up to date with all my latest releases, just sign up at the following link and I'll let you know when I have a new novel coming out. Your email address will never be shared and you can unsubscribe at any time.

www.bookouture.com/shalini-boland

I love getting feedback on my books, so if you have a few moments, I'd be really grateful if you'd be kind enough to post a review online or tell your friends about it. A good review absolutely makes my day!

When I'm not writing or spending time with my family, I adore chatting to readers, so please feel free to get in touch via my *Facebook page*, through *Twitter*, *Goodreads* or my *website*.

Thanks so much,
Shalini Boland x

ShaliniBolandAuthor

@ShaliniBoland

4727364.Shalini_Boland

shaliniboland.co.uk

ACKNOWLEDGEMENTS

Without the encouragement of my wonderful mum, I would never have become a writer. She used to be a primary school teacher and instilled a love of books and poetry in me from a very early age. She read every one of my novels and was always so proud and supportive. When I started writing this book, she was diagnosed with stage three ovarian cancer. We all tried to stay positive, but sadly she didn't make it, and passed away peacefully on December 29th, 2019. I'm so sad she never got to read my latest novel, but I feel blessed to have had her in my life for so many years, even if it doesn't feel like nearly long enough. Sleep well, Mum. Love you to the moon and back, xxx.

Thank you to Ruth Tross for being such an incredible editor and for looking after my books – and me! It's been an absolute pleasure to work with you and I truly appreciate all your kind and supportive emails over the past few months.

Thanks also to my lovely editor Natasha Harding who's been cheering me on from the sidelines this time, due to the arrival of her second beautiful little boy!

An immense thank you to the talented team at Bookouture, especially Oliver Rhodes, Jenny Geras, Alexandra Holmes, Hannah Bond, Peta Nightingale, Kim Nash, Noelle Holten, Natalie Butlin, Alex Crow and Jules Macadam. You are the dream team.

Thanks to my brilliant copy editor Fraser Crichton for your edits, honest comments and suggestions. And thank you once again to the fabulous Lauren Finger for another excellent proofread.

Thank you to author and police officer Sammy H.K. Smith for advising on the police procedure, especially as you've had your hands full with your work, kids and a house move! As always, any mistakes and embellishments in procedure are my own.

I feel very lucky to have such loyal and thorough beta readers. Thank you Terry Harden and Julie Carey. I always value your feedback, opinions and friendship.

Thanks to Arran Dutton at Audio Factory and to the supremely talented Katie Villa for your stunning narration of my novels. You always manage to bring the books to life.

A huge thank you to all my lovely readers and to the book bloggers out there who take the time to read, review or recommend my books. It means more than you could ever know.

Finally, I want to thank Pete Boland who has managed to keep everything going over the past few months, and who invented the invaluable 'room of tranquillity' for me!! (AKA a quiet room to read or write with a cosy fire, scented candles, a cup of tea and no interruptions.)

Made in the USA
Monee, IL
20 November 2020

48711134R10156